# DARK HEART SURRENDER

## LEE MONROE

Hodder
Children's
Books

A division of Hachette Children's Books

A Catalogue record for this book is available from the British Library

ISBN 978 1 444 90870 1

Typeset in Berkeley Book by Avon DataSet Ltd,
Bidford on Avon, Warwickshire

Printed and bound by CPI Group (UK) Ltd, Croydon, CR0 4YY

The paper and board used in this paperback by Hodder Children's Books
are natural recyclable products made from wood grown in
sustainable forests. The manufacturing processes conform to the
environmental regulations of the country of origin.

Hodder Children's Books
a division of Hachette Children's Books
338 Euston Road, London NW1 3BH
An Hachette UK company
www.hachette.co.uk

YA

*For Naomi, my excellent editor and dear friend*

# PROLOGUE

The corridors were deserted as I crept along them, my heart in my mouth. The place was eerie at night; all those abandoned classrooms, the sound of a loud clock ticking like a bomb coming from one of them.

'Ashley!' I called, my voice echoing. 'Ashley!'

A sound made me turn to look back down the corridor, but there appeared to be nothing. Nobody. I took a step backwards.

'Is anyone here?' I waited, my hands curled up in my pockets. I wanted to get out of here, but I couldn't leave until I'd found Ashley at least. Something was wrong.

And then, as if in slow motion, a silhouette began to appear around the corner. Not human. Bigger than a dog, but elegant, with a sharply pointed head and a gazelle-like body.

I blinked. I couldn't be seeing this. An animal inside the college.

I couldn't make out any features; the creature, whatever it was, was still a silhouette against the moonlit window at the far end of the corridor. I swallowed.

'What . . . ?'

The animal's finely pointed ears pricked up and I glimpsed its imperious snout and then, against the dim light, the almost amber colour of its coat.

The animal seemed to be changing before my eyes, the body shrinking and altering its position. I peered, in spite of my fear, and saw it stand upright.

It was not an animal. It was a human. I felt as though I was going to black out.

'Who is it?' My voice was reedy, scared.

'Don't be frightened,' a familiar, almost mocking voice told me. 'I'm glad you came.'

'Where's Ashley?' I said more forcefully. 'What have you done?'

He laughed. 'Ashley,' he repeated. 'I had almost forgotten about her.'

'I don't know who you really are –' I tried to stop the shaking come through into my voice '– but I'll just forget about everything . . . if you tell me where she is.'

'It's not that simple, Jane.' He took a step closer to me.

'What do you want from me?' I crossed my arms protectively over my chest. 'It's like you've singled me out.'

'Perceptive.' He moved even closer and I saw the vivid contrast of his hair against his flawless skin. 'But it isn't exactly you we want . . .'

'Then who?' I played innocent; I knew exactly who he wanted.

'He's big enough to take care of himself,' he said. 'And he has known this time would come.'

And then he was standing right next to me, so close I could feel his breath on my face. His eyes, glinting and sharp, made my skin tingle. It wasn't the first time this boy had had this effect on me. He reached out then and touched my hair, so softly, tenderly, that I relaxed my arms a little.

'I don't want your help.' He took a strand of my hair, twisting it gently in his fingers. 'I've only ever wanted one thing from you.'

'What?' I breathed.

Didn't I already know what he was going to say? Hadn't I known all along the price I had to pay?

Positioning himself so that he was looking right into my eyes, he waited a few seconds so that I could take in his full mouth, the cool blue of his stare.

'You, Jane,' he said. 'I want you.'

# CHAPTER ONE

'What are you doing?' I asked my sister, who had my entire collection of cheap jewellery laid out on my bed.

She scrambled over to the mirror on my bedside table holding an earring against her ear and pushed up her long blonde hair, looking at her reflection from every angle.

'Dot.' I put down the magazine I was reading, and frowned at her. 'Got a date or something?'

'Ugh, no.' She screwed up her nose. 'I was just seeing how I'm going to look.'

'How you're going to look when?'

'When you and Luca get married,' she said airily. 'And I'm your chief bridesmaid.'

'My only bridesmaid, you mean.' I shook my head. 'What am I saying? Luca and I are not getting married. We're far too young for all that.'

Dot turned to face me; she had a humouring look in her eye.

'Not right now, maybe. But Luca hasn't moved in with us because the two of you are "seeing how it goes", has he?'

I laughed. 'I guess. But we don't need to get *married*.'

'Oh.' Her face crumpled a little. 'Ever?'

'I don't know!' I smiled. 'You'll get to be a bridesmaid one day, babe. I'd place a bet on it. Ambitious bridesmaids always get their way.'

'So.' Dot plumped herself down next to me. 'You are happy, aren't you?'

'Of course,' I said. 'Really happy. I didn't think I could ever be this happy.'

I still hadn't totally absorbed the fact that Luca and I were finally together, and nobody, nothing, was trying to pull us apart. As I felt Dot lean in to me, pick up Mum's magazine and absorb herself in the Stylehunter section, I thought of how much she didn't know. The only one who knew the truth was my mother. And she was the only one who understood. Luca wasn't like anyone I had ever met – quite literally, because he was only half human. Yet the two of us were soulmates. A notion I would have found ridiculous before I met him, but now . . . The boy who came into my life in my dreams

6

turned out to be real. It's like the stuff of romantic comedies, except that Luca is also half wolf. He comes from a world called Nissilum. One vast world populated by all kinds of supernatural creatures. The kinds you only read about in books – or so I thought. Vampires, witches, angels. All stripped of evil intent, with rules and a strict moral code. Luca had broken the rules to be with me. The ultimate romantic gesture.

I sighed out loud and Dot looked up.

'What?' she asked.

'Nothing.' I ruffled her hair. 'I was just thinking how incredibly lucky I am.'

'Hmm.' Dot hesitated. 'Does Luca have any family?' she said after a bit. 'I mean, he never talks about his family. Nor does Mum or Dad – or you. Are they all dead or something? Did they die in a horrible car accident?'

'Nothing like that,' I told her, picking my words carefully. 'They just live a long way away . . . and he doesn't really get on with them.'

'That's sad,' she murmured. 'I can't imagine never seeing you again. It would be so awful. Wouldn't you miss me, too?'

I looked down at her. 'I certainly would. But you and I – we're never going to fall out.'

'I bet Luca thought that once,' she said thoughtfully. 'I

bet he never imagined it either. He must have *really* fallen out with his family. Big time.'

'Something like that,' I said, biting my lip, wondering how she got to be so grown up all of a sudden.

Apart from Dot's sudden spurt of emotional intelligence, I was taken aback by how her words made me feel a sudden fear. The family bond is strong, and the bond between a girlfriend and a boyfriend is rarely that unbreakable. Luca and I had only just begun a normal relationship and, ahead of us, there was acres of time. Time for us to fall out of love, and for Luca to realize he had made a terrible mistake.

Suddenly the world, and my happiness, seemed just a little bit fragile.

# CHAPTER TWO

The old man looked up from his newspaper and gave the boy a bemused, dry look.

'You're late,' he said, but without judgement, as though he were just stating a fact.

'I got caught . . .' Luca shrugged off his cagoule, spattering old Pete's newspaper with drops of rainwater. His clothes underneath weren't much better, his T-shirt sticking to his stomach. He peeled it away, grimacing. 'I've never seen rain like that.' He looked up at Pete, who was now regarding him sympathetically.

'Out back,' he gestured with his thumb. 'Clean shirt and overalls, hanging up. Leave your wet clothes next to the boiler and they'll be dry in a couple of hours.' He sniffed, dropping his eyes back to his paper.

'Thanks.' Luca walked carefully out to the storeroom; he needed to get out of his jeans.

Inside Pete's tidy storeroom, rain thumping on the corrugated roof, the boy took a moment to inhale the smell of hardware: tools, pots of paint, the lattice of pigeonholes carefully labelled with essentials for the trade – nails, two dozen different sizes of hammers and screwdrivers. Luca loved the smell of all this . . . practicality. Though he was beginning to shiver from the damp, he smiled to himself. A surge of well-being came over him. He opened the cupboard by the door, where Pete's spare overalls hung from one hook and a clean denim shirt from the other.

'OK out there, boy?' Pete cleared his throat, scraping his stool back. 'We got work this afternoon, out by the old army training ground. Demolition job.'

Luca heard Pete moving around the workshop and, registering what the old man had just told him, his good mood evaporated.

The army training ground. A place he had no wish to return to. It was there, nearly two years ago now, that Raphael, heir to Nissilum's Celestial family, had held Jane and her family hostage, intent on revenge for his father Gabriel's death. Raphael, half mad with anger and grief, had blamed Jane and her mother – Gabriel's long-forgotten love – for his father's fate. Luca and his younger sister Dalya had arrived just in time to stop Raphael. It had been a day like today, pelting rain, the whole place damp, dark and deserted. A lot had happened since then . . . Luca and Jane had been apart for a long time, while Luca tried hard to be an obedient son, wanting to please his family by marrying into his breed. He hadn't gone through with it; he had never stopped loving the beautiful mortal girl and now they were together, living with her family here on Mortal Earth. It was what they had both wanted, never to be apart. But Mortal Earth held dangers of its own . . . Today's casual news from Pete was a salutary reminder of that.

Luca took a couple of deep breaths, closing his eyes, not just at the horrific memory but at the thought of what he had nearly lost for ever.

Jane.

'Luca.' Pete stuck his head round the door. 'Rain's easing off now. What's keeping you?'

Luca shook his head, reviving a smile for the old man. 'Sorry, Pete. We're leaving now?'

'Good a time as any.' Pete narrowed his eyes for a second, as though detecting a false bravado in Luca's tone. He was a shrewd old guy, Luca had already recognized that. He'd given Luca the job in his small independent construction company on a good word from Jane's father Jack, but it hadn't been long before he'd picked up on the

11

aura around the boy. As though he had smelled the wolf on him. Luca knew that there were mortals who had an extra sense in that way – who could detect a supernatural presence. He just hadn't expected this gruff and practical old man to be one of them. Pete had questioned Luca for a long time on his background and, though Luca had worked out a story ahead of time with Jane and her mother, he was unprepared for the level of interrogation on his first day in Pete's yard.

'Pale, aren't you, kid?' Pete had leaned in closely, his eyes sweeping over Luca's delicate cheekbones, his jawline, his extraordinary green eyes, dark-lashed, gleaming. 'Celtic?'

Luca had just nodded, not knowing what Celtic meant, but realizing it was better to comply with the old guy's assumption.

'You used to heavy work, then? A lot of physical stuff going on here. Lifting, shifting, carrying . . . Not a job for a faint heart or a weak constitution.'

'No, sir.' Luca had pulled up his shoulders, setting his jaw. 'I did a lot of that stuff for my dad. He had a similar set-up to you. I've been helping him out since I was a kid. I'm strong – I don't look it, but I am.'

Pete had nodded, the beginnings of a smile appearing on his face. 'Sure, sure. I believe you, son. It's what Jack told me too.' He'd looked down at his hands. 'But, if you don't mind me saying, you look the serious type . . . sensitive. I got to be sure you won't break down crying once the wrecking ball comes out.' He'd glanced up, almost fondly, at Luca. It was then that Luca knew instinctively that the old man would be on his side . . . if he ever needed him to be.

'Well, come on,' Pete said now. He reached over, pulling the overalls straight on Luca, brushing at something on the collar in a paternal way. 'We have to pick up a few things for the job.' He wrinkled his nose. 'It won't be the most pleasant of jobs – creepy old place. Full of ghosts, bad energy . . .'

Luca swallowed, forcing himself to look unaffected, casual. 'The sooner we get there, the sooner it's over, I guess.'

'Exactly.' Pete lightly punched the boy's shoulder. 'That's the attitude I like. I'll meet you out front in two minutes.'

# CHAPTER THREE

'See, this is exactly why I would like a lock on my room.'
I put down my bag, glaring at Dot. 'Did I give you
permission to borrow my favourite T-shirt?'

Dot opened her blue eyes wide. 'I didn't know. I'm
sorry.' She swivelled her head to appeal to my mother,
who watched the two of us wearily.

'No harm done, hey?' She ruffled Dot's hair before
smiling at me. 'We'll wash it and then you can have
it back.'

'Not the point,' I snapped, wondering why I was such
a grouch today. I'd overslept and missed half of the first
Art class of the new term. 'I need some privacy.'

'Well, we don't have locks except for the bathroom.
You know that.'

'Tell her to keep out of my things then.' I cast another
glower at Dot.

'What's the matter with you lately? It isn't like you to get so wound up over stuff like this.' Mum looked concerned, sighing. 'This must be the terrible teens at last.'

'Mum!' I wrinkled my nose. 'You make me sound like a little kid.'

'Then don't act like one,' Dot supplied chirpily, though backing towards the door. For a moment I felt furious, but then I took in Dot nervously hopping from foot to foot and I smiled.

'Yeah, yeah,' I said softly to my mother. 'I suppose it's college. I can't seem to catch up. I'm panicking, I guess.'

Mum looked stern. 'I knew it would be too much, Luca living here.'

'No. It's not Luca . . .' I hesitated. 'Well, yes, it is Luca. But it has to be this way . . . I can't, I couldn't—'

'I know.' With a sigh, Mum pulled out a chair from the table and sat opposite me. 'And I'm not suggesting that Luca goes back home.' She lowered her voice, both of us aware that neither Dot nor Dad knew the whole truth. 'But this is your future. You need to focus on your studies for the next eighteen months. Luca will have to take a back seat.'

I nodded. 'You're right. But he's given up a lot for me.

I can't just ignore him after all that sacrifice.'

'Luca is going to be busy himself, earning some money.' Mum drew up her shoulders. 'Old Pete will keep him occupied, believe me.'

'I know. I'm probably worrying too much.' *About everything*, I added to myself. Luca and I had been so happy to be together again after all that had happened in Nissilum. There had been a time – an eternity it had seemed then – that I thought I had lost him for ever. I guessed I had Soren to thank for changing things. Soren had come in and out of my life so dramatically. For a while I had even felt that I had more of a bond with him than— I shut my eyes, forcing that thought out. It felt disloyal. But I missed Soren. He had seemed to understand me, like Luca did. But half vampire, half angel, Soren's future lay back in Nissilum, where he now shared equal status with Raphael, heir to the Celestial dynasty. Half-brothers who had no affection for each other. But they had to make it work.

'Jane.' My mother's voice cut through my thoughts. 'You've gone into one of your daydreams again. What are you thinking about?'

'Nothing.' I hadn't told Mum half of what had gone on back in Nissilum. She herself had been embroiled in a fatal love triangle there. It meant she knew things not many mothers would understand. But it was a past she wanted to leave behind. I smiled at her, changing the subject to something more mundane.

'They've asked me to chair the student council at college.' I shrugged. 'For some reason they think I am a calm, reliable person with principles.'

'All true.' Her mother smiled. 'Kind of. You don't want the responsibility?'

I fiddled with one of Dot's pens lying on the table. 'Not really. I mean, it's flattering, but it's just an extra layer of work and more of my time. And I can't turn it down because that would look bad and . . .' I let go of the pen and pushed my head into my hands. 'I don't know why I am getting so stressed out. All this, it's kind of unprecedented, you know, me being thought of as a normal human being.'

We looked at each other, the irony of the situation registering. I was far from a normal human being. Not with all that had happened over the past year or so. But I was also no longer the loner, the freak I had been for so long. I had friends now, and social invitations I mostly turned down. I was popular.

'Anyway.' I took a deep breath and glanced up at the clock. 'I'm going to have a bath and an early night. I don't think Luca is back till late.'

Reaching the foot of the stairs I looked back at the kitchen where Mum was still seated at the table, watching me with a look of pride tinged with worry.

'Don't worry, Mum,' I called out to her. 'I'll make it all work.'

She smiled. 'It's the real world, darling. Good old-fashioned everyday responsibility. You'll get used to it.'

I pushed open the door to the converted attic room that was now Luca's domain. He was sitting on the bed, prising off his boots. At the sound of me coming in, he looked up, a broad smile breaking through the exhaustion I saw in his face.

'Hey,' he said softly, 'did I wake you up coming in?'

I moved closer, perching next to him. Even after everything we'd been through I still felt a kind of shyness sometimes whenever I was near him. I pulled at my oversized T-shirt, trying to cover my knees.

'I couldn't sleep anyway.' Almost on cue I yawned deeply and Luca laughed.

'I'm sorry.' He stopped trying to get his remaining boot off and sat back, putting one strong but slender arm around me. I shivered – not cold, but tingling at his touch. 'How was your day?' he said, studying my face.

'It was tough. I have so much catching up to do – and suddenly all this stuff is expected of me.'

'Stuff?' Luca stroked my shoulder. 'What kind of stuff?'

'Well, along with all the studying I have to cram in, it seems to be the general consensus that I would make a good figurehead for the student council.' I shook my head, a half-smile on my face. 'They're mistaking my stunned silence as composure, or maturity, or something.'

'But that's great.' Luca squeezed me. 'And you're all of those things. Composed, mature – and principled.' He tucked a lock of hair behind my ear. 'It's about time you started seeing that too.'

'Really?' I felt myself squirming with a kind of pleased, but still disbelieving, feeling. 'I don't know. I just want to get on with my life quietly.'

'Nonsense.' Luca's eyes gleamed proudly. 'Since when have you ever been such a mouse?'

'But I always thought that's what I was.' I shook my head. 'The one in the corner, watching everyone else. Never the centre of anything.'

'Which is precisely what is so great about you – your modesty.' Luca bent down and finally finished removing his boot and his voice was muffled when he added, 'And what I love about you.'

Looking down at his tousled brown mop of hair as he bent over, I resisted the urge to say something soppy in reply.

'You should have seen me earlier. Mature and composed is not how my mum would describe it,' I said quickly instead.

Luca sat back up. 'So I get to miss out on your tantrums.' He wrinkled his nose. 'Not fair.'

'I wouldn't call them tantrums exactly,' I said indignantly. 'It's not easy dealing with little sisters.' As soon as the words had left my mouth I regretted it, seeing the faint flicker of sadness in Luca's eyes as he must have been thinking about his own little sister, Dalya. 'Sorry, that was insensitive.'

Luca drew me to him, his soft lips brushing my cheek. 'It's fine. You shouldn't be treading on eggshells around me.' He paused. 'I think that's the expression anyway.'

'I'm impressed.' I picked at a thread in the seam of his jeans. 'Soon you'll be fluent in Mortalese.'

'Sounds like some kind of deadly disease.' Luca pulled me even closer, his chin resting on my head, and I inhaled his familiar scent. College, studies, extracurricular commitments all faded away in this moment. I thought of the conversation with my mother earlier and wondered how I could have got myself so wound up. Luca was here at last and we were finally together. Nothing was going to stand in their way any longer. All the trauma and the heartache of the last year was over.

Everything was going to be OK. It had to be.

'So how's it going at Pete's? What's he got you working on?'

Luca's hesitation was just a split second too long and a small crease appeared in his forehead as he frowned.

'What?' I eyed him. 'Is it the work? I'm sure there's something else you can do if the construction is too boring—'

'It isn't that,' Luca replied carefully. 'It's just we . . . well, we went over to the army training ground today. A property developer has bought up the land and everything needs clearing out.' He trailed off, avoiding her gaze.

'Oh. Right.' I knew that my shoulders visibly slumped. 'Sorry, I mean. How awful. That place . . .' I swallowed, remembering that terrible night. 'So creepy.'

'It doesn't get any less creepy in the daylight either.' Luca bit his lip. 'All those weird metal tools, like instruments of torture, rusting away.'

'I remember when I first went there.' I forced myself to remember being in the car with Evan, who turned out to be Raphael, and the aura of the place. Deadly, full of watching eyes somehow. 'It seemed so full of ghosts.'

21

'It is.' Luca said obliquely. 'That's exactly what it is.'

My eyes widened. 'Are you serious?'

Luca's intake of breath was sharp. 'I can smell the dead.'

'What?' My own breath practically froze in my throat. But as I stared at Luca's profile, I saw the faint quiver of his cheekbone and I pushed him hard, watching as he collapsed into laughter.

'Don't ever do that again!' I said breathlessly, trying not to laugh along with him. '"I can smell the dead"!'

'I'm sorry.' Luca's eyes were a little damp from laughing and I realized how great it was to see him like this. My outrage – what there had been of it – dissolved as I couldn't help grinning at the sight of him.

'Seriously though.' I arranged myself crosslegged on the bed. 'It can't have been great.'

'Horrible – and I wasn't entirely joking about the feeling I get from there. Of course I can't smell the dead. But I could sense danger.'

I nodded. 'Me too. There's something . . . some bad spirits around that area – like something awful happened there once.'

We looked at each other, gravely now, and for the hundredth time I felt that bond charging between us. An understanding.

'But you don't have to worry about that,' he said, tracing a finger up the bare part of my leg before putting his palm over my knee protectively. 'I won't let anything bad happen to you. Not again. I promise.'

'Thank you.' I picked up his hand and threaded my fingers through his. It felt good to know Luca wanted to protect me from all the bad things that could happen now.

But we both knew he couldn't. Nobody could.

# Chapter Four

Clearing out the first of the damp Nissen huts was difficult and exhausting. Luca worked hard to get as much done as quickly as possible and to hide his nausea from Pete.

Everything other than the dirt-caked floor was rusted. Metal contraptions resembling torture instruments lay abandoned or hung creaking from two poles – or beams – from the roof. The wind caused the metal to creak and whistle. Luca avoided looking too closely at anything. He rubbed his face, which was reacting to some kind of dust, grime or rust allergy. His eyes smarted. His head felt heavy and light simultaneously.

After he had shifted most of the more manageable rusting rubble to the sides of the hut, he kicked at a larger machine of some kind on the ground unnecessarily, simply out of discontent.

'Making progress?' Pete's gruff voice came from behind him. Turning he saw the old man at the door, his eyes sweeping the contents of the hut.

'Think so.' Luca pulled himself up straight. 'But we need another pair of hands.'

Pete moved from the door, keeping his eyes on the boy. 'Should be fine if we keep at it. You struggling?'

'No!' Luca's response came out more emphatically than he had intended. 'I mean, it's just it will take us twice as long.'

'Doesn't bother me. We have the time. The developers are paying by the day. 'Pete chuckled but he took in the look of anxiety on Luca's face. 'If you're not up to it, son, there are plenty of kids who'll take over the task.' He kept his eyes on Luca's, testing him.

'Fine. That's fine.' Luca turned away, swallowing back the bile in his throat.

Pete perched on the broad handle of the machine. He crossed his arms over his chest and looked around him, chewing slowly on his top lip. Self-conscious, Luca remained standing, exposed somehow.

'No need to be afraid, boy,' Pete said then, quietly. 'Rumour is things have gone on here. Tales of mad dogs, wild animals at night.' He scratched his head. 'And there was one time, a year or two ago, it's said there was a confrontation of some kind.'

Luca's heart picked up a pace, though he kept his voice steady when he replied. 'Yeah, I heard something.'

'But the people around here . . .' Pete waved his hand about dismissively. 'They like to exaggerate. See, nothing much of anything goes on up in this mountain district. But in this kind of place, I guess it's associated with conflict. A place where the military practise battle. A place of danger. People like to imagine that conflict still goes on here, long after the military have left – that there are evil forces at work.'

'Do you believe them?' Luca finally turned to look at the guy. 'I mean, do you believe there are evil forces here?'

Pete scratched his chin thoughtfully. 'I believe there are things out there that we may not be able to see, or understand, that don't amount to much good. That doesn't mean that this place is a hotbed of evil.' He paused. 'I do think there are some pretty fierce wild animals out here. Wild dogs, wolves maybe.'

Luca knew his blood vessels were expanding. For a frantic second he thought he might be turning, but there was no full moon tonight. He was anxious. He felt somehow threatened. Some basic, primal instinct was closing in on him. He concentrated on regulating his breathing. Slowly it returned to normal.

'I'm not afraid of wild animals,' he told Pete. As he spoke he finally made eye contact with the old man. 'In fact, human beings scare me more.'

There was a split second of confusion on Pete's face before he smiled broadly at the boy. 'I think you're wise,' he told him. 'Scariest of them all, I reckon.'

Luca and Pete shared a relaxed moment, one of understanding, before Pete got to his feet. 'It's getting dark again,' he said, dusting off his trousers. 'I think we should knock off for the day, start again bright and early tomorrow.'

'Sure.' Luca smiled, relieved. He watched as Pete walked over to the hut's entrance, then turned to find his jacket. He'd taken it off pretty early on and spotted it hanging on a nail on the wall near the back of the hut. As he crossed to get it, he tripped for the twentieth time that day on some piece of debris on the floor. His foot had encountered something hard and a twinge of pain shot through it. Wincing, he looked down at the offending article, but as he did so something else caught his eye. Jewellery. A chain, delicate, feminine, lay glinting slightly where his foot was. He bent to pick it up and felt another rush of bile coming up from his stomach.

The necklace was sticky with blood. Fresh blood.

# CHAPTER FIVE

I stared up at the college noticeboard, plastered with flyers on extracurricular classes, sports, stuff for sale, the date for the next student council meeting.

It was a pivotal moment. I was either in or I was out. Years of feeling like the outsider made me want, instinctively, to turn away. Student council wasn't for me. I am not that kind of girl.

Except something had changed. Actually not just one thing. But a whole lot of things. And now, well, maybe I *was* that kind of girl.

'Jane?' The college principal was at my shoulder. I could smell her perfume, something mid-range expensive, strong and floral. I turned slightly, giving her a half-smile.

'Hi, Mrs Connelly.' She smiled back, her eyes flicking back to the noticeboard, settling, I knew without looking, on the notice about the student council meeting.

'So,' she said quietly, 'have you had any thoughts about taking up leadership?'

I shrugged, feeling the heat on my cheeks. 'I don't know. I have so much on. And, really, I'm not sure I have the right kind of personality.'

'I disagree.' Her tone was mild, yet firm at the same time. 'You have a kind of strength, a healthy disregard for what others think of you. You're sensible. And I have noticed your maturity, your focus, your . . .' She paused, taking in my startled expression. 'You aren't convinced?'

'I don't know.' I shook my head. 'I think you're projecting a little too much—'

'Projecting? Now there's a word.' She grinned. 'See, I told you. You're a little more mature than most girls your age. You seem to have a wisdom beyond your years. I don't know where it comes from. But I can see it. I have watched you these past months.'

I cringed, recalling Mrs Connelly's 'spontaneous' visits to classes over the last couple of terms. Standing at the back of the room, observing. I'd had no idea she was scouting the joint for a political prodigy. Then again, I was a little wrapped up in other things at the time. A certain Soren Balzac, for one. He and I had sparred often during his tutorials. I suppose to the outsider it might have looked like I was more questioning than the rest of the class.

But maybe it didn't matter what had motivated my assertiveness with Soren. It just meant I wouldn't let things drop. I always wanted answers.

'OK,' I said, after what seemed like a very long pause. 'What would it involve exactly?'

'Well, a big part of the role is to be a kind of counsellor to the other students. Someone they can come to with their issues about life at college. Not personal problems as such, though perhaps any difficulties they have with their studies because of obstacles outside of here. But mostly, things they would like to see improved. It is your role to be a representative of the students' needs.' She sighed. 'Some of them will be petty – or things we can't change. Some of them will be valid and I will need to know about them.'

'Isn't that the job of a teacher, a . . .' I stopped. I was going to say 'grown-up', but Mrs C seemed to have intuited my thoughts anyway.

'It's the job of an adult, yes,' she told me, looking intently into my eyes. 'Which is what you are, isn't it?'

'Well, not quite. I mean, I'm not eighteen yet,' I began a little pathetically. What was my point? Isn't this what I wanted? To be seen as an adult? I smiled then, not needing to look at Mrs Connelly to know what her response would be. 'OK. I'll give it a go. Maybe a trial run for a few months.'

'Of course,' she said quickly, as though she was worried I would change my mind. 'Why don't you start today?'

'Today?' I looked at my watch. It was four p.m. I had no more classes. I had been hoping to get home to Luca.

'If you don't mind,' she said briskly. 'We have a new student. She started last week. Her name is Polly Ellis and she needs a mentor.' Mrs C bent a little, lowering her voice. 'Her family have been through a hard time in the last few years and Polly lacks confidence. But she is very bright, if a little surly. She needs to be encouraged, brought out of her shell.'

*She sounds like who I used to be*, I thought, not sure I wanted to meet with my former self.

'She reminds me a little of you,' Mrs C said lightly, echoing my thoughts, her lips twitching slightly. 'I don't know why exactly.'

'OK, so,' I shifted awkwardly on my feet, 'where is she, this Polly?'

The girl sitting in front of me twisted a strand of long red, poker straight hair in her fingers. It was coarse-textured like she'd used hair straighteners on it. I could see the slight kink of curls at her crown. I resisted the urge to tell

31

her she should keep it natural. With her perfect, creamy-white skin, a little freckled over her small nose, and her pale-blue eyes – masked as they were by thick black eye-liner – she looked like a pre-Raphaelite painting. The Lady of Shalott. Except for the grungy leather jacket and the tight tartan dress, the black tights and the creepers, that is.

'You done staring at me?' she said in a monotone. She stuck the strand of hair in her mouth and sucked on it in a pointed kind of way. If she'd given me the finger she couldn't have made it more obvious what she thought of me.

'Sorry,' I said, trying to put some authority into my voice. 'I was just thinking that you looked like a painting.'

Her little nose wrinkled up, but she looked interested. 'A painting?'

'Yes. Like a Rossetti . . .' I drifted off, seeing the obliviousness in her eyes. 'It doesn't matter. I guess I am just trying to say you're – striking.'

'Yeah?' She shifted in her seat. 'Thanks.'

'So,' I leaned forward, cupping one knee with my hands, 'you've just moved to the area?'

'No.'

'Oh. Only you've just started here. I thought maybe—'

'Yeah, well,' Polly looked down at her hands. 'I kind

of . . . well, my parents kind of . . . well, they're not too keen on schools.'

'Oh.' I shrugged. 'You've been home-schooled?'

'No.' Her tone, again, was flat. 'Not really. I had what you might call a sporadic education.' Her words dared me and I was intrigued.

'Not so sporadic surely,' I said, 'with vocabulary like that?'

'Good one,' she said, and for the first time she smiled. She really was beautiful, I realized. Pearly-white teeth, rose-coloured lips. She looked young, too, all of a sudden. More vulnerable . . . more human.

'So,' I hugged my knee tighter, wondering if I was up to this challenge. 'You're obviously clever. And you've decided to come to school to do your A levels. Work towards a future?'

I couldn't believe I was talking like this. Like a teacher. Or my mum or something.

Polly shrugged. 'I don't know. I guess I hate my parents and coming here means I get away from them.'

I tried not to smile. 'You hate your parents? Why?'

'They're stupid. And they're afraid.' She sat back, again daring me.

'Afraid of what?'

'Of me.' Her smile was quite cat-like. Powerful. She

was unnerving me. There was a pause while I struggled to respond, but Polly broke the silence. 'And my brother. They're afraid of both of us.'

I remained speechless. Polly was holding court here. Totally in control. I began to doubt Mrs Connelly's faith in me. I hadn't a clue how to talk to this girl.

'Your brother?' I prompted, cocking my head, aiming for reassuring.

'My brother, Ade.' All of a sudden Polly was warming up. Her whole demeanour was softer. She sat forward. 'He's older than me. He's training as an electrician. But that's just to get some money in the bank. He doesn't care about it. He's been doing a few jobs, you know, on the quiet. One day very soon he'll have enough saved up to leave home for good. Somewhere a long way from here. He's going to take me with him.' Her eyes gleamed.

'I don't understand,' I said. 'I thought you wanted to be here in college?'

'For now, yeah. But as soon as Ade gets his new place I'm out of here.' She sniffed, pulling the lapels of her leather jacket close, over her chest. 'This is just an amusing way to pass the time.'

'Polly.' I hesitated. I wanted to strike a balance between friendly and serious. 'If you stay at college you'll get qualifications and then you can create your own future.

You won't need your brother to do that for you. And you'll make friends here. You'll have a life outside your home. It might make—'

'You think,' Polly leaned forward, her expression hard again, 'you think I care about that.' She pursed her lips, studying my reaction. 'I have Ade to look after me. Why would I need a degree? Or friends?'

This girl was odd. Weird. Intense. And there was something about her I recognized. I couldn't put my finger on it. I had never seen her before, yet she looked familiar.

'Well,' I persevered, 'until then, until you move away with Ade, I'm here to help you. Anything you need advice on. Come to me.' I smiled somewhat falsely.

'There is something.' Polly ran her zip up and down her jacket without taking her eyes off me. 'I'm a little worried about Ade. I think he needs to get out more.' She smiled a sugary smile. 'You seem cool. And you're only a little younger than him. Ade's kind of shy around girls. Would you mind if I set you two up on a date?'

I resisted telling her that if her brother was as strange as her I would pass, thank you. Instead I pretended to look flattered, even managed to blush a little.

'I don't think my boyfriend would like that,' I told her, but smiling. 'Maybe I'll ask one of my friends.' I thought of the twins, Ashley and Emma, an idea forming in my head. 'I tell you what. If I can find your brother a date, will you promise to give college a proper shot, for a term at least?'

Polly flared her nostrils, clearly disliking the switch of power here, but she seemed to be thinking about it.

'Well,' I said subtly glancing at my watch. It was nearly five-thirty and I'd had enough of Wednesday Addams for one day. 'What do you say?'

Polly shrugged. 'OK. But you set the date up first, yeah?'

'Sure.' I picked up my satchel. 'I'll try. Got a photo of your brother handy?'

She raised a finely plucked eyebrow before digging her hand into her bag and drawing out her phone. I watched as she scrolled through photos.

'Here.' She held out her phone and I took it from her. My eyes widened. Ade was like a Titian god. Short auburn hair, and eyes like his sister's, though sharper and more flinty. He was squinting into the sun, giving him a cruel expression. Arrogant. His skin was tawny, lightly freckled like Polly's, and his shoulders were bare, showing the tops of taut muscled arms. Ade was kind of devastating.

I swallowed, finally looking back up at Polly.

'He's . . .'

'Beautiful,' she replied, snatching back the phone and pressing a button so that the picture disappeared. 'Shame you don't want him.'

Ignoring that, I reached over the desk for a pen and scribbled down some digits on a piece of paper, which I held out to her.

'My number. Text me that picture and I'll see what I can do.'

'I've picked out the classes I want to take,' Polly said calmly, taking my number and plumbing it into her phone. 'But if it's boring here, or if anyone gets on my case, I'm going. I don't need qualifications to do what I want to do.' Giving me a cryptic look she waltzed past me and out of the room.

# CHAPTER SIX

Luca was getting used to Anna Jonas's cooking. He was bemused by the frozen peas and the oven chips: grainy and synthetic in texture but curiously pleasant once they were doused in the bright-red tangy sauce she put on the table at every meal.

But this evening even a king's banquet would have left him cold. He couldn't get the sight of that delicate necklace, sticky with blood, out of his mind.

'You're very quiet, Luca,' said Anna, flicking a look at Jane, who seemed similarly distracted. 'Bad day at the office?'

Luca was bewildered by her words. He turned to Jane.

'It's an expression that middle-aged people use,' she said, rolling her eyes at her mother. She took Luca's hand under the table and squeezed it. In return he pressed his thigh against hers.

'Are you OK?' she whispered.

Luca mustered a weak smile. He realized that the whole family was looking at him in concern now.

'I'm just tired. I think I underestimated how exhausting clearance work can be.' He smiled. 'Or how draining.'

'You're out at the old army training ground aren't you?' Jack Jonas dropped his serviette on his empty plate. 'A lot of grisly equipment out there. Place has been deserted for a decade at least.'

'It's haunted, that place,' Dot put in matter-of-factly. As usual the last to finish her meal, she speared a chip with her fork, dipping it daintily in tomato sauce. 'That's what Danny in my class said anyhow. His dad was in the army.'

'It's not haunted,' Anna said sharply, rising from the table. 'That's silly nonsense.' Neither Dot nor my father had any memory of the danger we had been in at the training ground all that time ago. The time Evan – or Raphael as he really was – had tried to kill the Jonas family to avenge his father's death. There was a pointed silence, though Dot was oblivious.

'His dad said they used to think they saw these weird foxes, only they were bigger, like giant foxes, and they had weird-coloured eyes and sometimes they turned human, or something . . .' Dot trailed off a little doubtfully.

39

But Luca felt a stir of recognition. He had heard of this creature in Nissilum mythology. A large and malevolent animal, half fox, half human. Like a werewolf, its metamorphosis from fox to human was dependent on environment. Not on the full moon, but on temperature. This fox thrived on heat. As the climate grew warmer it kept its human form. In the dead of night, when the temperature dropped, it was an animal once more. Vicious, hungry, and craving not just human blood, but the human soul too. Ulfred, Luca's father, used to speak of these creatures' particular rivalry with werewolves. Their sense of superiority. They considered themselves more agile, more intelligent, less vulnerable to human weakness. The species had a bent to evil that could not be diluted. There were none on Nissilum. They didn't pass the test, as it were.

'Giant foxes?' Beside him Jane snorted, though she was still holding on to his hand. 'Whoever heard of giant evil foxes?'

Luca kept his grip on her hand steady, careful not to betray his creeping sense of unease. The necklace in blood. And now Dot's innocent reminder of what still lurked out there.

'Want to go and hang out in the attic?' Jane asked, startling him as she cut in to his thoughts.

'Yes, you two go on up,' said Anna, swiping Dot's plate off the table and putting it into the dishwasher.

'Thank you for the delicious meal,' said Luca. Out of sheer habit he gave a small deferential bow towards Anna. He was aware that this was a source of amusement to the family, but years of ingrained etiquette back on Nissilum made it feel odd not to show respect towards his elders.

'Come on, Prince Charming,' said Jane, pushing him gently towards the door. 'We need to have some alone time.'

Jane was waiting for him when he got back from his shower. She sat crosslegged on the bed, her dark hair falling about her shoulders as she bent over a textbook. He smiled at her childish socks, red with white stars. Jane had changed a little physically since he'd first met her. She'd been beautiful then, with a delicate, sensitive kind of beauty, her grey eyes, large and sad, her body changing into a woman's, giving her a kind of endearing awkwardness. But now, now she had a different kind of allure. More assured. Graceful in the way she moved. Her shoulders were a little broader and there was a curve to her hips where she had once been skinny. He took a moment to take her in. And to feel how lucky he was to have got her back. And then, underneath this feeling, there was a sense of fear. That she would be taken away from him, or outgrow him. He had been at pains to let her know that her going to college made him proud, but in truth he felt twinges of jealousy when she glossed over certain details of her day. When she mentioned names that he hadn't heard before. He wondered whether he should stop working for Pete and join her there. His own education had fallen by the wayside. But he had to repay her parents for taking him in and, besides, he wanted to provide for Jane, sooner rather than later.

She looked up, finally detecting his presence.

'Hey,' she said, pushing her hair behind her ears. 'How long have you been standing there?'

'Not long.' He smiled, tightening the towel around his waist. 'What's that you're reading?'

'Oh, just some notes I made today.' She leaned back against the pillows. 'My first day as student counsellor. Mrs Connelly wants me to mentor this new girl. So I met her after my classes. Really strange kid.'

Luca flopped down on the bed beside her, adjusting his towel again.

'Don't bother on my account,' Jane said as she reached out and touched his damp skin. 'Nice abs, by the way.'

Luca laughed, blushing a little. 'Don't change the subject, Jonas,' he told her in a mock-stern manner, and hiding the desire he had felt when she'd touched him.

She sighed. 'OK. Well, this girl, Polly, sits in front of me. So defensive and angry. She obviously thought I was a dork, at first anyway. And it turns out she couldn't care less about studying. I have a feeling her family are travellers or something. At any rate she despises them. Can't wait to leave home. Coming to college is her solution. That and running away with her older brother.' Jane paused. 'She tried to set me up with him too.'

Luca tensed instinctively. 'She what?'

'Don't worry,' Jane nestled her head in the crook of his neck. 'I told her I had a boyfriend.' She laughed lightly. 'As if I could be interested when I have you.'

'I'm almost reassured,' said Luca dryly. Again he hid his true feelings. The thought of another guy hitting on Jane made him uncharacteristically tense, jealous all of a sudden. He was determined never to reveal this to her. In his mind, jealousy was a coarse and pointless emotion.

Jane ran her fingers down his bare arm, causing his nerve endings to flutter. A feeling of total peace came over him for the first time that day. As her fingers arrived at his hand he grabbed them, then gently lifted her hand and kissed it.

She stroked his hair. 'You've had a tiring day. And I'm droning on about some angry teenager. I'm sorry.'

Luca shook his head. He really didn't want to tell Jane about his day. Particularly not about the necklace he'd found. There was probably an innocent explanation for that, he tried to tell himself. It wasn't necessary to drag her in to it.

'I like hearing you talk,' he said instead. 'It has this incredible calming effect on me.' He glanced up at her, narrowing his eyes comically. 'Except for the bits about other guys taking you out. That tends to do the opposite.'

'Good. I'm glad you're not sick of me already.' She leaned in closer to him. 'But seriously, I want to know about your work with Pete. It must be awful being back there.'

'Yeah. It's . . . well, it's not so bad,' he said. 'I mean, it's so cold and damp and abandoned, and the work is tough.' He bit his lip. Omitting the most important detail of the day was harder than he'd thought.

'What is it?' Jane pulled away from him, her eyes sweeping his face. 'There's something you're not telling me, I know it.'

He returned her gaze, on the brink of denial, but something about her anxious expression told him that honesty was the best policy.

'I found something,' he said then. 'In one of the

huts, on the floor. Lying there like it had been wrenched from its owner.'

'What?' Jane drew her hands up to her neck, afraid.

'A silver chain – a necklace.' He let out a breath.

'Is that all?' She visibly slumped in relief. 'I thought you were going to say you'd found a severed head or someone's arm—'

'It was lying in fresh blood,' Luca continued, cutting through her. 'The necklace was lying in blood.'

# CHAPTER SEVEN

I upturned my backpack, knowing my bike lock was in there somewhere. Heat spread through my face, coming up from my neck, as I rifled through the various bits of rubbish lying on the corridor floor. At last I saw the lock, half trapped in my purse. I grabbed it and quickly gathered up my things and stuffed them back in my backpack.

'Hey,' said a gruff voice behind me as I got to my feet. 'You got my brother a date yet?'

I turned, flushed, and forced myself to smile at Polly, even though I was irritated. It was nine a.m. and mornings were never my strong suit.

'Hey.' I slung my backpack over my shoulder. 'Good to see you here.'

'Well?' she persisted.

'Well, not yet,' I said, flustered. 'But today. Today I'm having lunch with a couple of people.' I glanced anxiously out of the door, spotting my unlocked bike resting against the wall.

'Huh,' said Polly, watching me. 'Not quite so interested in me today?'

I frowned. 'Of course I am. It's just I need to lock up my bike.' I gestured outside. 'Sorry, I'm a bit distracted.'

She nodded, smiling a little unpleasantly. She looked different today. She'd let her hair dry naturally and it hung in thick red curls down to her waist. Her dress was black and short and tight, and her legs were bare and startlingly white. On her feet she wore green Doc Marten boots. It was a difficult look to pull off for most people, but she looked stunning.

And she knew it. Several male students passed us, their eyes drawn appreciatively to Polly. The girls looked her up and down with suspicious, narrowed eyes.

If she realized they were looking at her, Polly didn't show it. Instead she stepped a little closer to me, her pretty nose wrinkling at the tip, her pale-blue eyes holding me there.

'What's your story,' she said in a breathy half-whisper, 'Jane Jonas?'

I couldn't remember telling her my surname. I guessed she must have asked Mrs Connelly, or another student. It didn't matter, except for the way she was scrutinizing me now, which was making me uncomfortable.

'What do you mean?' I said, as lightly as I could.

She smiled again like a sleepy cat. 'Oh, don't mind me,' she said. 'I like to freak people out a little. It amuses me.'

'I'm not freaked out.' I widened my eyes, just to reinforce the message that she was failing in her mission. 'Does that disappoint you?'

She shrugged. 'I can see the panic in your eyes.'

I swallowed, a familiar feeling coming back to me. Intimidation. I hadn't felt that since I was face to face with Sarah Forrest, the school bully who had tormented me three years earlier. She had made it her personal mission to give me a nervous breakdown – and very nearly succeeded. I'd been taken out of school and Mum had taught me at home. I took a deep breath, determined not to go back there.

'OK, Polly,' I told her breezily. 'I have things to do today. If there is nothing I can help you with then I'll see you later.' I checked my watch. 'I'll come and find you at about three p.m. I might have a date for your brother by then.'

At once her face lit up. 'Cool,' she said. 'But just one thing . . .'

I shrugged good-naturedly. 'OK. What's that?'

'She'd better be beautiful. And no one fat or stupid.

My brother doesn't go out with fat ugly chicks with nothing in their heads. He might be shy but he's got very specific tastes.' She looked me up and down. 'You understand me?'

I gaped at her, on the verge of saying I was not a dating service, and her brother could find his own perfect girlfriend; but something about her expression made any response freeze in my throat. Her eyes seemed to change shape in front of me, lifting either side to become more almond-shaped, narrower – and the pale-blue of her irises seemed almost opaque.

'I . . .' I began, trying to take control of the situation, but I got no further. It seemed futile to defy this girl.

'So we're clear,' she said, enunciating each word as though I was hard of hearing. 'You'll find my brother the perfect match.'

*Match?* An odd way to describe a girlfriend, at least coming from a teenager it was. It sounded so clinical, official.

'I'll do my best,' I said at last, dragging my eyes away from hers. 'But I'm busy today. It might not be possi—'

'Great.' Her lips twisted into a friendly smile. 'I'll be outside, where you have your bike, at four.'

It was an order. This girl felt she could order me around.

A surge of students entered through the door, pushing past where we stood, one of them knocking Polly's bag off her shoulder roughly.

'Watch it,' she snarled, causing the offender – a boy I recognized from my History classes – to jerk away from her.

'Fine, dude,' he said, giving her the same interested look I'd noticed practically everyone else giving her. 'It was an accident, OK?'

Polly simply stared at him imperiously as he shuffled off to catch up with his friends, throwing a final look back at her and muttering something under his breath.

'Idiot,' said Polly, taking a pack of cigarettes out of her pocket. I refrained from telling her smoking wasn't allowed inside. She already knew it. And she would have enjoyed letting me know she didn't give a damn. Taking a cigarette out and putting it in her mouth. She started to turn back to the exit, giving me a last smirk before she did so.

'Later, alligator,' she said. 'Have a great day.'

As I watched her disappear outside, I puffed out my cheeks. I was tired and the last thing I wanted to do was match-make. I hadn't slept at all the night before after Luca's news. He'd tried to backtrack a little, claiming there must be an innocent explanation to what he'd found in the training ground; it had been dragged in there from somewhere else, or someone had lost it and it had been found by a wild dog or a cat or something and brought, like an offering, into the hut. But that didn't seem right to me. The training ground was miles from anywhere. And why was the chain covered in blood? Luca had been freaked out, I could see that. But I guessed he didn't want me to worry, too. Not after everything . . .

I reached my locker and stuffed my backpack inside, taking out my phone and my purse and putting them in my hoodie pocket. My mind was whirring overtime. I had to focus. Leave all that creepy stuff behind. I'd just have to put the necklace out of my mind. For the next few hours at least.

Emma and Ashley were sipping their hot chocolate when I arrived in the canteen at twelve-thirty.

'Well, hello, Mrs Luca,' said Ashley, shuffling along the bench to make room for me. 'We thought you'd dropped us. Now that you've got a live-in boyfriend and all.'

I'd told A&E as much as they needed to know about Luca. That he was my childhood sweetheart who'd moved away, but that first love never dies and we couldn't stay apart, blah blah blah. Fortunately, being hopeless, unquestioning romantics, the twins bought the whole story. Which obviously saved me a whole lot of awkward explanations about parallel worlds and werewolves. Thinking about it now, I nearly laughed out loud. They'd freak if they knew.

I gave Ashley a half-hearted eye roll instead. 'Hardly,' I said. 'What with my parents and my little sister watching our every move.'

'Still, you must be happy, right?' Emma leaned forward, desperate to hear my tales of cohabiting bliss. 'You finally got your boy back.'

I allowed myself and them a small satisfied smile. 'I did.'

'And?' Ashley raised an eyebrow. 'Is it amazing?' She cocked her head and lowered her voice. 'Or disappointing?'

'No!' I tossed my hair, which irritated me as that's something I swore I would never do. 'It's great.'

'Ashley's just jealous.' Emma gestured at her sister. 'She wants a boyfriend.'

I nodded slowly at Ashley, drawing in my breath. 'Well, as it happens, I might just have a guy for you.'

'Huh?' Ashley coughed up some hot chocolate.

'Eww, Ash.' Emma made a face. 'Gross.'

'Who? Is he a friend of Luca's? Is he smouldering and gorgeous? What's his body like?'

'Come on, Ashley,' I said laughing. 'Don't you want

to ask a few questions first?'

'You!' Ashley wasn't doing a great job of hiding her delight. 'Come on then, spill.'

'Well.' I took a breath. 'You know Mrs C wants me to head up the student council this year?

'Yeah—' 'No—' said the twins in unison. 'Whatever. That's great.'

'Right.' I grinned. 'Well, my first duty is to mentor a new student. This girl, Polly, she started here a few days ago— '

'Hey, is that the ginger girl?' Ashley asked. 'The ginger Goth?'

'Well, I guess you could describe her as that. She's really nice,' I carried on, hoping I sounded like I meant it. 'And she has a brother.'

Ashley's smile faded, understanding. 'OK.' She glanced quickly at Emma.

'Ash doesn't do gingers,' said Emma brightly. 'He's got to be a ginger. I mean, that runs in families, right?'

'Yes, he has red hair,' I said carefully. 'More auburn than red really.' I paused taking in the obvious disappointment on Ashley's face. 'You want to see a photo?'

The twins gave each other a meaningful telekinetic twin look before turning their attention back to me.

'I suppose,' Ashley shrugged.

I dug in my pocket for my phone, located Ade's photo and passed it over to the girls.

I watched as their eyes widened and Ashley's expression went from crestfallen to gobsmacked in the space of three seconds.

'Wow,' she breathed. 'I never thought a ginger guy could be so hot.'

'Yeah . . . I mean . . . He's actually really . . . hot,' echoed Emma, craning over Ashley's shoulder to look more closely.

'See?' I summoned a smile, though inside I was wondering what I had got Ashley into. I didn't know Ade. All I had to go on was Polly's description. And that wasn't exactly reassuring. That and the obvious intensity of her relationship with her brother. I felt a moment's guilt. Ashley was a sweet, straightforward girl. She didn't need some weirdo and his sister in her life.

'So, he wants a date?' Ashley prompted, finally handing back the phone. 'With me?'

'He wants a date with a beautiful, bright girl with the body of a supermodel,' I told her. 'Which would be you, Ashley, yes.'

'He's way out of my league,' she said, holding out her hand. 'I need another look.'

Grinning, I gave her back my phone, and watched as

the twins dissolved into quiet shrieks over Ade's picture. I hadn't quite thought through the reality of the situation, which could well be that Ade would eat someone like Ashley for breakfast. I didn't believe Polly's story for a minute. Any relation of hers had to have the arrogant gene. And there was no denying he was hot. But for now I was enjoying thinking about someone else's romantic future for a change.

'So,' I said, once the giggling had died down, 'I can tell Polly you're up for a date?'

'Only if Emma can come too,' said Ashley seriously. 'We go everywhere together.'

'But this is a date, Ash.' I smiled in a compensatory way at Emma. 'I don't think that would be his idea of a double date. I don't think it's anybody's idea of a double date.'

'She's right, Ash.' Emma nudged her sister. 'You should go alone.'

Ashley looked stricken and, underneath the make-up, she looked very young all of a sudden.

I sighed, knowing what was coming. Might as well pre-empt the inevitable.

'You want Luca and me to come with?' I suggested reluctantly. 'Like a proper double date?'

'Would you?' She reached her hand over the table. 'It's just, he's a stranger and . . .'

55

'Of course,' I said firmly. It was a good idea. I didn't trust Polly, why would I trust her brother?

'Brilliant.' Ashley slid the phone over to me and grabbed hold of Emma's arm. 'I've got a date, Em!' she squealed. 'A proper date!'

My heart was already sinking. Now I had to break the news to Luca. I just had to hope that Ade was normal. Because if he had even the faintest whiff of bad-ass about him, then Luca would sniff it out in a heartbeat.

Sometimes heightened sensory perception wasn't all it was cracked up to be.

# CHAPTER EIGHT

Pete's tea took some getting used to. Luca blew on it, wrinkling his nose at the murky grey colour of the liquid inside the mug. He missed his mother's tea. He'd never tell Jane that, and truly it wasn't much of a sacrifice, but this synthetic perfumed concoction was not what he would define as a cup of tea.

He put the mug down and felt in his jacket pocket, drawing out the small plastic bag he had been hiding in there since the day before.

Pete was on his way to a supplier's and the place was empty. Much as he liked the old man, Luca enjoyed being alone at the yard. It was peaceful. Being surrounded by equipment, tools – practical stuff – calmed him. Aside from being with Jane, just sitting with the sound of Pete's ancient old clock for company was something Luca found he looked forward to these days.

Still holding the plastic bag in his hand, he took a breath, then carefully and efficiently opened it.

The blood had dried brown, no longer adhesive. As he touched the chain it crumbled off, speckling his leg with tiny flakes. He winced, a bad taste in his mouth again. The chain was delicate and so tainted by this dried blood. He stared at it, trying to form a picture in his head of the owner. It had to be a woman, or a girl. It looked like a celebration present, like the bracelet Ulfred and Henora had given Dalya when she'd reached her tenth year.

At the thought of his little sister Luca felt a wave of protectiveness. He closed his eyes for a second, determined not to become sentimental.

How had the necklace come to be in that stinking place?

Pete's cat, a stringy tabby, appeared, slinking through Luca's legs. Any minute now it would sense the animal in Luca and arch its back, hostile and threatened. But Luca was clearly losing his touch because the cat remained affectionate. Luca looked down to see two of the creature's paws resting on his boot, its face upturned, meowing in greeting.

Luca half smiled, unsure whether to be glad or slightly offended that he was no longer considered dangerous. He reached out a finger to stroke the cat's neck, both of them enjoying the comfort they offered each other.

Luca considered throwing the necklace in the trash and forgetting about it. There could be any number of explanations. It could be rat's blood, anything. But that didn't explain the bright sheen to the silver. It had to have been left there recently.

He heard the sound of the van pulling into the open yard out front, relieved that Pete was back. Quickly he dropped the necklace back in the plastic bag, stuffing it away in his pocket again.

The cat fled, knowing Pete had little patience or affection for it. Luca felt half sorry to see it go.

'Tea still hot?' Pete called, pushing open the door. 'I'm parched.'

'You were quick.' Luca stood up.

'Wrong day. Got five minutes down the road before I remembered.' The old man shook his head. 'Old age, you see, the memory starts letting you down.'

'I'll make more tea,' said Luca. He went through to the tiny kitchen and put the water on to boil. He inspected the array of tea on the shelf above the hob. There was nothing resembling the ground-up leaves that Henora prepared and kept in a stone jar in the kitchen back home.

Home. Luca took a deep breath. This was his home now. This was his life.

Pete had turned the radio on low and Luca heard the soft murmur of the announcer's voice, then some music; the kind that Pete liked: blues, quiet drums. Luca had grown to quite like it too.

'Getting thirsty out here,' Pete called dryly. 'What you doing, boy? Growing a tea plantation?'

Luca smiled to himself, adding milk to Pete's mug and leaving his own black. He carried the tea out and set it down on the table, sitting on a stool and cradling his mug between his hands.

'Has anyone been out there – to the training ground?' he asked, breaking the soothing silence.

Pete glanced up from some documents he was looking at.

'Only us.' He held eye contact with Luca. 'Why?'

Luca hesitated. 'I found something last time, on the ground.'

'I imagine so,' Pete raised an eyebrow. 'Plenty of rusting equipment—'

'No. It was jewellery. A chain . . . a necklace . . . a woman's chain.' Luca swallowed. 'It was lying in blood.'

Pete's eyebrows rose subtly, questioning. He didn't speak, waiting for Luca to go on.

'Fresh blood,' Luca finished. He picked up his mug and drank some tea.

Pete remained silent for a few seconds longer before finally drawing in a breath and twisting his mouth to come up with a proper response. 'Animal,' he said finally. 'Must have been a wild animal. A dog, or a fox, or something.' He sniffed, ready to drop the subject.

'A fox?' Luca's memory stirred. The conversation with the Jonases the night before came back to him. 'Of course. Yes, but . . .'

Pete smiled. 'But what?'

'I don't understand how the blood could be fresh. There must have been someone there – nearby . . . The blood was sticky. Blood dries quickly, Pete.'

'Well, it probably came from the animal. Cutting itself on some bit of sharp old metal in there. A nail . . . anything.' Pete sighed. 'Why would you think it was anything suspicious.'

*Because I am trained to think like that*, Luca thought. *I see danger everywhere*.

Instead he forced himself to look sheepish, embarrassed for overreacting.

'I don't know. I suppose it's that place.' He shook his head, picking up his mug again. 'It has that effect on me.'

'Well, don't let it. We have to get on with the job. We can't be reacting like babies every time we stumble across something we don't like the look of.' Pete shuffled the papers in front of him into a neater pile and put them into a plastic envelope. He grimaced down at his untouched tea. 'If I were you, I'd put more energy into making a proper cup of tea.' With a humorous nod at Luca he got up from the table, taking his mug with him. 'You'll get there,' he said over his shoulder.

Luca watched the old man disappear back out to his tiny office, then looked down at the black liquid left in his own mug. It had indeed been disgusting and left an unpleasant dry taste in his mouth. He pushed the mug away from him, putting his head in his hands. Pete's explanation was reasonable. But it didn't explain where the animal, or whatever it was, had found it, or why it had brought it into the hut from what must have been some distance away. No one lived for miles around the training ground; it was just a vast expanse of country lanes. Not the kind of place you went to for a walk, either. And though he knew it was stupid, Pete's mention of foxes had sent a chill through Luca. Could it just be a coincidence that Dot had talked about the mythical fox yesterday and brought the creature back into Luca's mind. No one he knew of had ever seen these creatures. But Ulfred had spoken of them in almost reverential tones, with a kind of respect for such a powerful animal. Luca trusted his father's wisdom and his instincts, even though he was a long way from all the beliefs and mythology of Nissilum.

Pete came back out of his office. He was putting his jacket on; buttoning it up to the neck, he checked his watch. 'I have to get home, son. My wife needs something doing at home – and the grandchildren are coming over later.' He smiled. 'They're practically all grown up now. But they still like to visit and get spoiled by my old lady.' He nodded at Luca. 'Let's call it a day. If the weather's not against us tomorrow, we'll be back at the grounds.'

Luca stood, relieved. Finishing early meant he'd be home before Jane. They'd get a decent evening together. 'If that's OK?' he said respectfully. 'You're sure you don't need me to do anything around here?'

'No, that's all right.' Pete yawned. 'You get on home to that beautiful girl of yours. Be back here in the morning.' He picked up a bag of tools, heading for the door. 'If you could just lock up after me?'

'Sure.' Luca slipped a hooded sweatshirt over his head.

'And listen.' Pete paused. 'Stop filling your mind with dark thoughts.' He stared at Luca, his eyes serious now. 'There is such a thing as a self-fulfilling prophecy you know.'

# CHAPTER NINE

'We don't have to stay long.' I bent to look in my dressing-table mirror, holding up earring options to my ear. Past my reflection I glanced at Luca, sitting on the end of my bed, doing up the sleeve buttons of his crisp white shirt. Abandoning both pairs of earrings, I adjusted my dress – a tightish, black, short shift I'd bought in the charity shop in Bale a few weeks earlier. I pulled my fingers through my hair and wondered if I ought to put on more make-up. I reached down and picked up my kohl pencil.

'You look lovely,' Luca said behind me. 'Simple. Beautiful.'

I turned to him, smiling. 'You wait till you see Ashley. She's so glamorous. I'm going to look like a regular plain Jane beside her.'

'Never.' His eyes travelled up and down my body and

we shared a moment of mutual desire. We'd been having a lot of those moments lately. It was getting almost awkward. I smoothed down my dress with my hands, not wanting to meet his eyes all of a sudden. We had never done more than touch and kiss each other, but it was getting harder to ignore the impulses that happened when we were alone. We both wanted it, but it couldn't happen. Not in this house. And there was a part of me that felt scared that if we finally did it, then some magic would disappear. Everything was so perfect between us. I didn't want anything to spoil that.

It was the end of a long week at college, and we should have been looking forward to the freedom of the weekend. No work for Luca, no studies for me. Instead we were heading out on a Friday night for a double date. Neither of us looking forward to it.

I slipped on some flat ballet pumps and settled myself next to Luca on the bed. Luca had refused to dress up too smartly but had compromised on a shirt, dark-blue jeans and his black-and-white trainers. To say he looked gorgeous in his white shirt was an understatement. I never got tired of looking at his beautiful, slender face or his graceful but strong hands. The past few weeks had seen his chest grow more muscular too. Not some cheesy six-pack, but broader, more like a man's.

'You look lovely too, you know,' I told him, slipping my arm through his and stroking his hand. 'In a manly kind of way, obviously.'

He put his arm around me and at his touch I felt all tension slip away.

'I don't want to go either,' I said softly, resting my head on his shoulder. 'But we should think of this as karma. Doing something selfless for somebody else. Maybe it means that we'll finally be left alone to do what we want.'

'You mean no pesky vampires, or meddling wolves getting in the way?' Luca said. 'I hope you're right, and that whatever "karma" is, it works.'

I forced myself to look at the clock on the wall above my door. 'We'd better get going.' I sighed. 'I said we'd meet them in the diner at eight.'

'So, this kid – he's the one that girl Polly tried to set you up with?'

'Her brother, yeah.' I looked sideways at him. 'He's probably a bit strange, like she is.'

'So you arranged a date with a friend of yours without knowing anything about this guy?' Luca frowned. 'I would never—'

'Yes, well,' I said, irritated. 'We'll be there, won't we? If there's anything funny about him, we'll be there to protect Ashley.' I knew he was right. I should never have given in to pressure from Polly. But then Luca didn't know Polly and how persuasive she was. Or rather, how intense and intimidating.

Luca could see I was riled and, typically, he wanted to correct that. He squeezed my hand. 'I'm sure it will be fine.' He let go and stood up, tucking in his shirt. 'I will want to stay till the end, though. I think we should see her home.'

'I don't think that's necessary,' I began. 'He'll be harmless.'

Luca gave me a long, careful look. 'I'll be the judge of that.' He was smiling but he meant it. I didn't know whether to find that reassuring or unnerving.

It seemed I could take the boy out of Nissilum, but maybe I couldn't take Nissilum out of the boy.


Through the windows of the diner I spotted Ashley waiting in a booth. She looked pretty, but nervous, fiddling with her clutch bag. I saw her take out her phone and place it in front of her on the table. Then she adjusted her top – a black off-the-shoulder slinky thing. Her blonde hair hung in loose ringlets in a side ponytail. She looked sexy, but vulnerable too.

I caught hold of Luca's hand. 'I hope he's nice,' I said. 'Ashley looks terrified.'

Luca peered through the window too and frowned. 'He's late. It doesn't bode well.'

But as he spoke, the sound of heavy footsteps made us both turn. A boy – tall and broad-shouldered – was heading straight for us. As the street light hit him, I saw his striking dark-red hair and marble-toned complexion.

He eyed us, a flicker of recognition in his expression.

'Jane and Luca?' he said, holding out his hand and taking mine. 'I'm sorry I'm late. I'm Ade.' He smiled, a devastating smile. Boyish, cheeky. Not a hint of anything dangerous about him. He glanced through the window and spotted Ashley. 'Oh dear.' He turned back to us. 'I'm already in trouble.'

'Let's go in,' said Luca firmly, apparently not yet taken in by Ade's friendliness. 'We don't want to keep a lady waiting, do we?'

I saw, just for a moment, Ade's friendly expression evaporate and the look he gave Luca was sharp and threatening. I wouldn't have been surprised to hear a low, defensive growl come out of his mouth. But, catching my eye, Ade smiled contritely.

'I walked from home,' he said. 'My car is being serviced and the buses around here, they're infrequent to say the least.'

I felt relieved. If he'd walked, then he wouldn't be

taking Ashley home. I was beginning to feel like a concerned parent, which I had to shake off before I spoiled the evening with my own nerves. I didn't know why I felt so responsible, or so anxious, or why Ade's physical presence made me a little jumpy.

If Ashley had looked nervous waiting, then at the sight of all three of us coming towards her, she looked positively scared. Her eyes were fixed on Ade.

'Ashley.' He bent to kiss her cheek. 'I'm so sorry I'm late.' He stood back to look at her. 'Wow. When Polly said you were attractive, I didn't realize she meant stunning.'

While Ashley blushed, shuffling down the banquette to make room for him, Luca and I exchanged a look. Luca's was full of mistrust. I frowned, trying to send him the psychic signal to keep his thoughts to himself, but he had already made up his mind about this stranger, that was obvious.

'So,' I asked, watching Ashley powder her face. 'What do you think?'

Ashley had seemed overawed for the last hour, watching Ade's every facial move, looking stunned. She'd hardly said a word, as Ade did all the talking. I had to admit he was impressive. Started training to be an electrician when he was sixteen, working hard and saving his money, he seemed to be the man of the household. He talked a lot about Polly fondly, explaining that her abrasive nature took a little getting used to, but that she was a sweetheart underneath. He hardly mentioned his parents. So when Ashley finally contributed to the conversation by asking about them, he seemed almost taken aback.

'Oh, we don't get along,' he said, looking awkward for the first time. 'My sister and I were adopted when we were very young, and everything was OK when we were little, but then my mum got ill and my dad spent most of his time looking after her. Polly and I were kind of left to our own devices.'

'Oh.' Ashley's eyes were practically brimming with tears. 'Is your mum OK? Is she still ill?'

Ade shrugged. 'She has a disease of the nervous system. It means she can't move around much by herself and now her brain is affected.'

'That's awful . . .'

'Poor woman . . .' Luca's and my words collided together.

'Yeah. It's hard for her.' Ade looked as though he would rather be talking about something else. 'It's hard for all of us.'

'What's your mum's name?' I asked. 'My parents might know her.'

'I doubt it,' he said quickly. 'The two of them have hardly been out of the house in ten years.'

'Still,' I persisted. 'My mum might know—'

'I don't think so,' Ade snapped. 'She's hardly the most sociable of women.'

There was an awful silence. I looked down at my menu. I had obviously hit a very raw nerve. The funny thing was, Ade seemed more irritated by his mother's illness than concerned or upset.

'Polly talks a lot about you,' Ade said to me then, amiably now.

'Oh?' I lifted my head. 'We kind of got off on the wrong foot.'

'She really likes you.' Ade smiled. 'Jane this, Jane that . . .'

I could feel Luca's eyes on me. I made a self-deprecating face.

'I hardly know her really. I'm just trying to help her find her way around college, you know, get back on track.'

Ade smiled. 'Personally I think she should stay the course and get her qualifications, but she seems intent on leaving home as soon as she can.'

'With you.' I studied him. 'Don't you two have some kind of plan?'

'Polly is a bit of a dreamer,' said Ade. 'She's had a tough time and she has this idea that she and I will be better off without Mum and Dad.' He looked sad, all of a sudden, and beneath his intense blue eyes there were shadows.

I glanced over at Ashley, who was listening intently. Ade had barely noticed her for the last twenty minutes. I wondered if Polly had been right about him needing a girlfriend. It didn't look like it to me.

Beside me Luca shifted in his seat. I knew without looking at him that he was uncomfortable.

'Ashley is a twin,' he said suddenly to Ade. 'Did you know that?'

'Really?' Ade turned to her, his expression working hard at being interested. 'So there are two of you beautiful creatures prowling the corridors of that college?'

Ashley giggled uncertainly. She felt out of her depth, I could see that. Ade's eyes flickered over her dismissively before returning to his menu.

'You and Polly,' Ashley went on. 'You look like twins. I mean – you look so alike.'

Ade stiffened slightly, still studying his menu. 'We're brother and sister,' he said after a pause. 'I've heard there can be a physical resemblance between siblings.'

The air was stiff with his sarcasm. Ashley's face dropped, confused, while Luca moved angrily next to me.

'Asshole,' he said, just loud enough for Ade to hear.

Ade looked up. 'What did you call me?' His eyes narrowed and his face grew taut, as though all the muscles stood to attention, and there was the faintest of tension tics in his neck. Pushing his hair back off his face, he did have an almost animal-like expression.

'I don't know who you think you are. If this is your idea of a joke – acting cool and actually downright rude – it isn't funny to treat people like that.' Luca's tone was quietly furious.

Ashley had gone pale. I smiled at her across the table. She shifted away from Ade, taking hold of her bag.

'I think I'll go now,' she said quietly, grappling for her coat, which had become squashed underneath her.

'You should stay,' said Luca, his eyes rooted on Ade. 'You haven't done anything wrong.'

Ade held up his hands. 'Look, I think we've all got off on the wrong foot here. I'm sorry. I've had a hard day. Just before I came out, my mother – well, she needed my help, and she and Polly had had some kind of row . . . My dad has the night off tonight. He has one night a week for himself. And my mum, she can be

73

difficult.' He turned to look at Ashley. 'I didn't meant to hurt your feelings.'

Ashley nodded, but resumed wrestling with her coat. 'That's fine. Still, I'd better go.' She managed a weak smile. 'And I'm sorry about your mum. It can't be very easy.'

'Ashley, don't go.' Ade touched her shoulder. 'I'm really sorry. I've been told I don't make a great first impression. Please,' he pleaded with her. 'I'd like you to stay if you can forgive me?'

Still flinty-eyed, Luca watched Ade's every move, but I felt myself softening towards the boy – he looked genuinely remorseful. Perhaps we had misjudged him. And it did explain Polly's aggression. I nudged Luca.

'Why don't we start again?' I said brightly. 'Let's order some pizza. I'm starving.'

Ashley looked uncertain, but stopped putting her coat on.

'Luca?' I stared at the side of his head.

He sighed, finally switching his gaze from Ade to me. 'OK, then.' He picked up a menu and looked quickly at the list. 'Margherita for me.'

I pushed away my plate. Turned out I hadn't really had much of an appetite, I'd only managed to eat a third of my pizza. Ashley had nibbled at the salad she'd ordered. Only the boys had eaten everything on their plates. Typical. Nothing seems to come between a boy and his appetite.

'So.' I turned to Ade. 'You're not taking Polly with you, when you leave home?'

He shook his head. 'It's better that she finishes her education. She'll understand that eventually.'

'Right now she seems pretty convinced she's going with you.' I felt a bit bad about this line of questioning. Some double date this had turned out to be. But maybe it was a good chance to get to know the mysterious Ade and, through him, his angry little sister Polly. I'd been watching him subtly as I ate, while he made small talk with Ashley, and she was right, the resemblance between them was striking. Polly's hair was a few shades lighter, but their features – delicate, sharply feline, and the piercing blue of their eyes – was almost identical. Even the number of freckles across their noses. They really could be twins.

Ade looked troubled. 'Like I said, Polly's not had an easy time. She's never got on with our parents; she relied on me for company, support, that kind of thing. For her, the fact that Mum and Dad were not our blood relatives, well, it was impossible for her to bond with them.' He lifted his chin, and his eyes drifted over to Luca beside me and they seemed to harden a little. I frowned.

'Go on. Polly's . . .'

'She's disturbed.' He tapped his head pointedly. 'You know, emotionally volatile.'

'Is she also disloyal?' Luca cut in icily. 'Like you are.'

Ade didn't react, his expression stayed impassive.

'I'd like to help Polly,' I said. 'Encourage her to stay at school. But it's hard. She doesn't like me much, that's obvious . . .' I stopped, realizing that six curious eyes were upon me.

'But she asked you to set Ade up on a date,' said Ashley. 'She must have trusted you.'

Luca reached over and put his hand over mine, and I caught Ade's expression grow hard as he watched.

'Oh, she really thinks you're something special,' Ade said cryptically. 'I told you that she talks about you a lot.' He smirked. 'Ad nauseum, in fact.' Only the new warmth in his tone told me he was joking.

'I think you're exaggerating,' I said uneasily.

He shook his head, chasing a solitary caper around his plate. 'Not at all. And now that I've met you I can see exactly what she means. You are something special.' He glanced over to Luca. 'I don't need to tell you that, though, do I, Luca?'

I knew it was taking every ounce of Luca's self-control not to rise to Ade's provocation. The only sign of his anger was his leg trembling beneath the table.

'What's the matter with you?' Ashley suddenly rose from her seat, putting both hands on the table in agitation. 'You arrive late, you're rude to me and to my friends, you're totally flirting with Jane, and now you're goading Luca into some kind of fight.' She glared at Ade. 'I'm sorry you're adopted and you don't like your parents, and I am truly sorry that your mother is so ill. But you're behaving like an asshole, Luca's right!'

Ade looked startled and a little impressed. His mouth hung open as he saw Ashley with new eyes. I couldn't help a small smile myself.

'You're right,' he said, and then he took her hand gently, coaxing her into sitting down again. 'I am an asshole. And you deserve better.' He shook his head. 'Polly is always saying I'm rubbish when it comes to socializing. I think she hoped I might have better manners tonight.' Still holding Ashley's hand, he cocked his head to the side. 'How about a picnic, just the two of us on Sunday? Do you think you could give me another chance?'

'I don't think so,' she said firmly. 'I already gave you a chance earlier and you've blown it. But I agree with you on one thing: I can *so* do better.'

She grabbed her bag and her coat and got up from the

table. I could see she was trembling. I was just about to reach over and slap Ade's face, when he rose from his seat, catching Ashley's bag, halting her in her tracks.

'Please,' he said, 'allow me to show you I am not all bad. One more chance? Ashley?'

Ashley looked back at him, her face twitching with indecision. Ade had turned up the charm to maximum and really looked like he meant every word. That, and the fact that I could tell she thought he was majorly hot, made her relent.

'OK.' Then she said, a little petulantly, 'But you'd better be on your best behaviour next time. I don't date assholes.'

'Noted.' He bowed his head sullenly and then something seemed to pass between them. I hoped it was mutual respect.

'We'll take you home, Ashley,' said Luca, getting to his feet.

'Yep.' I stood too, looking quickly at Ade. 'You two go to the car. I just want to talk to Ade about Polly.'

Luca frowned at me. 'OK. But don't be long.' He could hardly bring himself to look at Ade. 'We'll be outside. Right outside.'

'Sure.' I smiled reassuringly. 'I'll be two minutes.'

'Fine.'

Giving me a final worried look, Luca followed Ashley

to the door. I waited until they were both outside before I turned on Ade.

'What the hell was that?' I said, all my anger rising to the surface now the others had gone. 'I did Polly a favour. I didn't want to. But she seems to think you're just a shy loner who needs to meet the right girl.' I shook my head at him. 'How well do you and your sister really know each other, I wonder?'

Maybe it was because we were alone and Ade wasn't under such scrutiny, but the strutting alpha-male was gone. And in his place stood an awkward, hulking boy – albeit one with the looks of some kind of classical god. He shuffled his feet, taking in a deep breath, finally looking me in the eyes.

'She knows me better than I know myself,' he said, his voice gentle now, and serious. 'She knew I needed to find exactly the right girl. She knew that once I saw you I wouldn't be satisfied with someone like Ashley.' He rubbed at his head, as though trying to find the right words to continue. 'She's your friend and she's obviously pretty, in an insipid kind of way. But next to you . . . Well, it's as though the plain daisy had been planted near a rare, beautiful orchid.'

'Come on!' I said. 'You can't expect me to fall for that phoney rubbish.' I glared at him, sounding way more furious than I felt. It was something about his eyes. The ice had melted, so that they were limpid blue pools. They seemed to cast a spell. It was ridiculous. Completely ridiculous that I could fall for this.

'I don't expect anything of you, Jane,' he replied quietly. 'I know better than to assume anything with a girl like you. It's clear you are not conventional.' He turned to look out of the window where Ashley and Luca stood waiting. 'You and Ashley, you are different species.' He picked up his jacket, his demeanour humble.

'Just don't hurt Ashley,' I warned him. 'Leave her alone. Don't toy with her when you're not even interested in her.'

Ade buttoned his jacket, before his gaze met mine again.

'And what of your beau?' he asked me. 'Is it serious?'

'As serious as it gets,' I told him firmly, taking a step closer. 'See, you and Luca – well, it's kind of like a pond weed next to a magnificent oak tree.'

Grabbing my bag from where I'd been sitting, I cast him one last withering look and went to join my boyfriend and Ashley outside.

# CHAPTER TEN

Luca's hand gripped the steering wheel as we pulled away from the kerb outside Ashley's house.

'I'm sorry,' I said to his taut cheekbones as he stared straight ahead. 'That was a truly bad idea. The worst.'

He relaxed his grip a little. 'Not your fault. The guy's an idiot.'

I nodded. 'I warned him off Ashley. If he even tries to go near her he'll have me to answer to.'

Luca's face relaxed and I saw the twitch of a smile. 'That should do it,' he said dryly. 'He looks like the kind of psycho who'd be scared off by a girl.'

I whacked him.

'Steady,' he said, though he was half laughing now.

'I have to report back to Polly, I guess,' I said, sighing. 'How exactly am I going to tell her that I think her brother is an immature game-player and he'll date Ashley over my dead body?' I shook my head. 'She obviously thinks the sun shines out of his arse.'

Luca's expression darkened again. 'I have a feeling she'll find out who he is,' he said, glancing in the rear-view mirror.

'Really?' I stared at his profile. 'What do you mean?'

Luca drew in such a deep breath it silenced me.

'Luca?' I peered at him. 'What do you know?'

He continued staring ahead for a few seconds before finally turning to meet my eyes. 'He's . . . I . . .' He frowned, obviously regretting saying anything.

'What? He's what, Luca?'

'I don't know. I may be wrong. But I sensed something about him. Something wrong. Bad.' He closed his eyes. 'It is probably nothing. But I felt as though I recognized him.'

'You've seen him before? You mean on Nissilum?'

'Not exactly. No. I mean, I just felt he was bad news.' Luca spoke quickly, as though anxious to shut down the conversation. 'That's all.'

'Well, yeah. I'd say he's bad news. The way he acted . . . But let's just forget about him for now. I have to face Polly on Monday. Until then I kind of want to pretend Ade doesn't exist.'

'If only he didn't,' Luca muttered.

By the time we had pulled into my front yard the atmosphere in the car had turned weird. I was tired and I didn't want to talk about Ade any more. But Luca's instincts – well, they weren't usually wrong. He'd been right about Evan – or Raphael as he turned out to be; he'd known he was dangerous. And if he thought Ade was bad in some way, then Ade probably was bad.

'Let's reconvene at a later date,' I said solemnly, taking Luca's hand and squeezing it. 'I just want to go to sleep now.'

He responded, snaking his fingers through mine. 'Of course,' he said, holding my hand tight. 'It's just me and my ridiculous heightened sensitivity. It's a drag, I know.'

I laughed, not wanting to let go of him. 'As drags go, it's not so bad,' I said. 'It's an endearing drag, really.'

'It's just – well, I'm not sure you should hang out with his sister, either,' Luca said, not biting into the lighter atmosphere I was trying to create. 'They could both be bad news.'

'Luca,' I sighed, letting go of him and leaning back in my seat. 'Ade might be a touch . . . troubled, but I doubt that he and Polly are dangerous or anything. They've got this messed-up stuff going on at home. They hate their adoptive parents. Not exactly the perfect conditions for a secure state of being.' I looked at him staring intently at the floor between his legs. 'They're just . . . mortals, you know. Fallible human beings.'

'I know that.' Luca's tone was serious and he didn't look up. 'And if they really were just fallible human beings then you'd be right. There would be nothing to worry about. But I don't think—'

'Jane?' My mother stood in the back doorway, silhouetted against the light from inside. 'What are you two doing sitting out here in the dark?'

I glanced at Luca. 'To be continued,' I murmured, reaching for the door handle.

Luca put on a not very convincing smile. 'Let's just forget it.'

'Sure.' I managed a small smile. 'We'd better get in, or Mum will think we've had a row. I'm not sure I can pretend that everything's OK.'

'But it is OK,' Luca said, rubbing at his temple. 'This is not about us. It's about that . . . creep.'

I waved at my mother to signal that everything was fine and we'd be just there, then turned back to Luca.

'Why are you so caught up in Ade?' I studied his face. 'So he was a jerk. We'll never have to see him again.'

Luca opened his mouth, about to speak, but then closed it again and closed his eyes.

'Luca?' I took hold of his hand. 'What is it? What's the matter?'

'It's just . . . there's something about Ade that I recognize.'

'Don't tell me, he's an evil force from Nissilum in the body of a mortal?' I was joking, but a shiver ran through me as a memory of Evan resurfaced.

Luca intuited my thoughts, because he squeezed my hand back tightly and suddenly there was reassurance in his expression.

'Don't be silly,' he said softly. 'Nothing like that.'

'Well, what do you mean, then?'

'I just have a funny feeling about him. A familiar feeling.'

'Well, that's probably because he's a total messed-up creep. You've met a few of those over the years.' I stopped short of citing Luca's brother Lowe as an example. 'You're kind of on the lookout for trouble, don't you think?'

'Maybe.' He nodded. 'You're probably right.'

'Jane.' My mother was rapping on the car window. 'Are you two going to stay in here all night?' She peered in at us. 'What's going on?'

I pulled at the door handle. 'We're coming. Now.'

Mum stepped back as I opened the door and got out of the car.

'So how was the date?' She looked warily at me. 'You two had fun?'

'Great,' I said brightly. 'Just great.'

'Right. Well, I'm making some hot chocolate, if you want some.'

'Just what I feel like.' Luca tossed the keys over the bonnet of the car and I caught them, handing them over to Mum.

As she and I walked back into the house, I looked back over my shoulder at Luca, who hadn't moved. He wasn't looking at us; his gaze was directed back down the track, over the tall trees at the three-quarter moon that hung there, so peacefully in the sky. I frowned, remembering that the time of the full moon was nearly here. It was difficult for Luca, I knew that. Always having to think ahead to that time. Wary of the effect it had on him. Here on Mortal Earth it was more difficult to find a place to turn. A place where nobody would see. I felt a surge of love for him, for the sacrifices he had made to be with me. Not seeing his family, living with strangers, in a world that would never accept him as he truly was.

As for me, I didn't know what I would do without him now. It frightened me sometimes how easily I had adapted to having him here, day in day out. And it frightened me even more to think that he might be taken away from me.

Could there be something out there that would take him away from me?

# CHAPTER ELEVEN

'What do you mean, you need to go back?' Jane dropped her bag on the floor and sat down at the table.

Luca swallowed. 'It's Dalya's birthday.' He sighed. 'Her twelfth. That's a special anniversary on Nissilum. It is officially the transition from cub to—'

Jane's eyes widened. 'Oh. Well, of course. I didn't realize. Of course you must go.'

Luca felt terrible. It was true enough that the twelfth year had significance back home. But not quite as much as he was suggesting. His own twelfth year had been spent helping Ulfred clear the hay bales for harvest on the nearest farm. They had both been so exhausted by the end of the day that Luca's birthday slipped both of their minds. When they had arrived back home, Henora had left the remains of a nut cake for him, with a solitary candle burning in the centre. Luca had gone to bed without celebrating and without much caring about it either. It was an old tradition and not many families held to it any longer. Dalya would have a couple of her friends to lunch, and Henora would present her with a piece of jewellery, and that would be that. He missed Dalya, that was for sure. But it wasn't Dalya he was going back for.

'Maybe I could come too?' Jane said hopefully. Her eyes, flickering nervously, made his guilt worse.

'It's just family, really,' he said, looking down at his hands.

'OK.' Jane's tone was stiff, wounded. She scraped her chair back. 'How long for?'

'Not long.' He looked up, smiling. 'You'll hardly know I'm gone.'


It was dark outside his house. The dawn was attempting to break as Luca walked quietly through the gate and up to the back door. A couple of wild cats stood like sentries either side of it, their ears gleaming and curious. Luca nodded at them. Some unspoken greeting between animals. The wild cats had never evolved to anything more than wild cats, but like all cats they had that knowing, sharp intelligence, that extra sense.

Opening the door seemed to create a cacophony to

Luca's ears, though in fact it hardly made a sound. He was feeling extra sensitive. Nervous of seeing his family for the first time since he'd left.

He saw straight ahead of him that the light was on in the kitchen. Someone was already up.

'Who is it?' A young female voice, slightly shrill and wary. 'Lowe, are you up already?'

Luca peered around the kitchen door to see Dalya bent over a book at the table. She looked up, at first blinking in confusion, before her brain caught up with her eyes.

'Luca!' she gasped. 'You came!'

'Ssh.' Luca moved towards her, putting his arms around her and pressing his head to hers. 'You'll wake them.'

Dalya wriggled in his embrace. When she looked at him, her eyes were bright, glad to see him.

'You remembered!' She was pleased, two pink spots of pleasure on her cheeks. 'I didn't think you would . . .'

'Of course.' Luca let go of her and sat down next to her on the bench. 'But I also need to see Ulfred.'

'What's wrong? Is it Jane? Has something happened to her?' she said anxiously.

'Nothing's wrong. And Jane is fine. Really.' He ruffled her hair. 'I just need to ask Ulfred about something.'

'Oh.' Dalya closed her book. 'We miss you. Henora doesn't say it, but she is sad. I didn't think you were going to come back.'

'In truth, neither did I.' Luca shrugged. 'I realize I have disgraced this family.'

'Henora has softened towards you. At first she was furious, and would not have your name spoken, but now . . . well, she has begun to talk about you. Memories of when you were young. I think she regrets her harshness.'

'And Ulfred?'

'Ulfred has always understood. You know him. He is more forgiving than her. Henora says that you and he are like peas in a pod.' She shuddered a little. 'Which means that she and I are alike, no doubt.'

'Identical,' said Luca teasingly.

'I wouldn't mind her strength,' Dalya said sombrely, all of a sudden.

'Me neither.' Luca sighed.

'But you are strong. Strong enough to follow your heart.' Dalya yawned. 'They'll all be up soon. Are you going to sit here waiting for them?'

'No.' Luca looked alarmed. 'I . . . well, could you tell Ulfred that I will wait for him outside. I don't want to cause a fuss.'

'OK.' Dalya nodded. 'Will I see you again?'

'I hope so.' He took hold of her hand. 'Thank you, Dalya.'

The necklace was still there in its bag in his pocket. Such a tiny delicate chain, yet it might have been a lead weight the way he was so aware of it. Luca walked out into the middle of the field opposite the house and sat down in the long grass. It was hot and he lay back, waiting for his father – if his father were to come.

Eventually he heard the rustle of the grass and he sat up, seeing Ulfred advancing towards him. His face betrayed no emotion whatsoever. Luca began to think this might have been a bad idea.

'Luca.' Ulfred nodded at him. 'How are you, boy?'

'Good.' Luca got to his feet, unsure whether to shake his father's hand or embrace him. There was a formality between them that had never existed before.

Ulfred glanced back at the house. 'Henora is asleep,' he said. 'She has been having trouble . . . since you left.'

'I'm sorry.' Luca felt anxious. 'I'm sorry for the trouble I've caused.'

'Oh.' Ulfred waved a hand dismissively. 'She's highly strung – always has been, as you know.'

'I'm happy – with Jane.' Luca said, by way of

justification. 'Her family are good people.'

'I'm glad.' Ulfred's shoulders seemed to droop then. 'And you are making yourself useful?'

He meant, was Luca earning his keep. The stigma of his son doing nothing but be waited on by Anna Jonas would be too shameful to Ulfred, Luca knew that. He was quick to explain.

'I have a job, Ulfred. I pay for myself. And one day I will support Jane, too.'

'Good.' His father hesitated briefly, before asking, 'And how are you coping – when the full moon comes? Are you safe?'

Luca sighed. 'It isn't easy. But I have found a place. High up on the mountain, where nobody ventures. So far, Jane's family are oblivious to my need to turn. Except for Jane herself, that is. She doesn't find it easy either, but she knows I have no choice.' He smiled. 'It is worth the sacrifice, Father. Even though I wish things were straightforward. Where Jane lives, it is thankfully remote. If it were anywhere else . . .' He trailed off, meeting Ulfred's eyes.

'So . . .' The older man eyed him. 'Why have you returned?'

Luca felt again the necklace in his pocket. He hesitated before drawing it out. Saw Ulfred's gaze flicker over it.

'You've brought a gift?'

'Not a gift.' Luca looked down at the chain. 'I found it at this place where I have been working. A horrible, dank place with a bad aura to it.' He held it up in its plastic shroud, the blood visible on it. 'In itself it may be nothing, but I just have this bad feeling. And there was something Jane's sister talked of at the meal the evening I found it. Something that triggered a memory.' He paused. 'Something I heard you talk of years ago, when I was just a child. The creatures that were never allowed on Nissilum?'

'Oh.' Ulfred's expression was wry. 'Well, there were plenty that never came here . . .'

'A rare species,' Luca went on. 'Foxes of some kind.'

'Ah. The Vulpecula.' Ulfred shook his head. 'Deadly beyond redemption.'

'The Vulpecula. Yes, that's right.' Luca nodded. 'They take on human form?'

'Indeed.' Ulfred stroked his beard. 'They are not unlike the werewolves . . . Not unlike us in that, biologically speaking, they are essentially animal – in their case fox – but have human genes too. Unlike us, they are primarily in their animal form, but they can, and will, turn into human beings when the need suits them. They shapeshift. They do not turn by force of the moon. And

93

they can stay human for as long as it suits them to do so. But as humans they have all the wile and cunning of foxes themselves. That, and a quite mesmerizing presence.' He hesitated. 'But they are rare. In fact, I thought they were extinct. The Vulpecula have not been sighted or heard of for a long time – decades. The assumption has been that they had all but died out.'

'All but,' Luca said, swallowing. 'I am not so sure about that.'

'Luca?' Ulfred frowned. 'Son? You have seen the Vulpecula? On Mortal Earth?'

'I don't know.' Luca felt like backtracking. 'I hope I'm wrong . . .'

# CHAPTER TWELVE

'How's it going with Polly?' Mrs Connelly took off her glasses and studied me over her desk. 'She's settling in OK?'

I shrugged. 'I suppose so. I haven't seen too much of her.'

'Oh?' She frowned. 'I thought you were—'

'Well, I've been checking in on her,' I said, needlessly studying a fingernail. 'She seems to be fine on her own.'

Understatement. Every time I'd seen Polly she'd been surrounded by a throng of boys, coolly absorbing their desperate attempts to chat her up. Poised, perfectly in control. I had no idea how she was doing in her subjects. I didn't have the time, or the inclination, to nursemaid Polly.

'She's quite a vulnerable young woman,' Mrs C said thoughtfully. 'Looks and acts tougher than she is. I think she needs a little support.'

You support her then, I thought uncharitably.

'I guess I've been a little busy the last couple of weeks.' I tried and failed to suppress a yawn.

'Is everything all right?'

'Yes.' It was my turn to frown. 'Why wouldn't it be?'

'I hear you have your boyfriend living with you.' She raised an eyebrow. 'That must provide a little distraction. I imagine it's hard to concentrate on everything that's going on here. Your responsibilities . . .'

I hid annoyance. 'I'm not shirking my responsibilities,' I told her. 'I'm just getting my priorities in order.'

'Your priorities?' She inhaled disapprovingly. 'You don't get these kinds of opportunities very often, you know.'

'I know.' I clasped my hands together, trying to keep a lid on my feelings. 'But there's nothing to worry about. Luca doesn't interfere with my life at college. Or my studies.'

'Hmm.' She picked up a file lying in front of her on the desk, opened it and flicked through it. 'Your grades are high.' She looked up at me. 'Just be careful they stay that way.'

'OK.' I was confused now. If I didn't know better, I would think Mrs Connelly was threatening me. 'But like I said—'

'I've got things to do,' she said, getting to her feet. 'As I am sure you have.' She checked her watch. 'I strongly advise you reconnect with Polly. She needs a good role model to aspire to.' She smiled at last. 'Don't you think?'

I stared at her. 'I suppose.'

'Good.' She picked up my file and tucked it under her arm. 'I'll check in with you next week. See how you're getting on.'

The cafeteria was crowded. Over by the window I spotted the twins, heads bent together, talking seriously. I bit my lip, my gaze travelling further round the hall. In the opposite corner, a crowd of noisy boys were gathered round a lone female who sat coolly drinking a smoothie through a straw, her red hair held away from her face in a loose ponytail.

I sighed, moving to the queue for hot food and picking up a tray. Polly hardly looked like the kind of girl who wanted a 'role model to aspire to'. If I went over there, I'd get the familiar disdainful look I always got from her. Honestly, I had better things to do than babysit her.

I had my eye on the last baked potato, willing no one else to take it. Lately I felt starving all the time; I guessed it was everything that was going on, all that I had to think about. I picked up a bag of crisps from the rack and a strawberry smoothie, and pushed forward in the queue.

'I'll take the spud,' said the nerdy-looking student in front of me. His backpack butted into my chest and I rolled my eyes, inwardly cursing him. Normally I didn't care about stuff like this – but lately everything was getting on my nerves.

Once I had got all my lunch – reluctantly trading the potato for a portion of shepherd's pie – I did a quick recce of the hall again. To my right, Ashley and Emma were still deep in conversation and I wasn't sure I could face their chatter today anyway. Which left Polly and her admirers on the other side. I cast a glance over and saw that a few of the boys had left her table, leaving a seat free next to her. And she was looking straight at me.

'Hey.' I put down my food. 'Mind if I sit down?'

'Free country.' Polly gave me a twisted, obviously fake smile. 'I have a class to get to anyway.' She fiddled with her bag.

'OK.' I shrugged. 'I thought you might want to talk. I haven't had a chance to catch up with you since—'

'Since that distrastrous date you fixed up my brother with?' Polly dropped her bag and stared hard at me.

A forkful of shepherd's pie halted on its way to my mouth. 'I'm sorry?'

'Yeah . . . your boyfriend is obviously some kind of psycho. Ade was totally freaked out when he got back. Not to mention Barbie over there.' She flicked a look over at Ashley, who was getting up from the table with Emma. 'I mean, what were you thinking? Did you really expect my brother to hook up with . . . with *that*?'

I put down my fork. 'So what exactly did Ade tell you?'

'Just that you guys made him feel like an idiot. You and Luca, that is. The airhead just giggled like a moron.' Polly raised an eyebrow, brushing a strand of hair out of her face. 'I'm surprised at you, Jane, most of all. I mean, I thought you were a bit of a weirdo; I didn't think you were mean.'

'OK.' I took a breath to remain calm. 'That is totally unfair. For your information, Ade hardly spoke to Ashley all night. He practically ignored her, in fact. And he was rude and arrogant. And . . .' I stopped, for some reason I didn't want her to know the most heinous part of the evening – Ade coming on to me when the others were outside.

Polly stared at me for what seemed like hours before she spoke again. 'Don't tell me,' she whispered. 'Ade liked you.'

I felt my face getting hot, whether from anger or

embarrassment I couldn't be sure. 'I don't think "like" is the word,' I began.

'Fancied you then.' Polly shook her head. 'What's the matter, Jane? Are you some kind of virgin or something? You've gone all coy.'

'No.' The heat was getting worse. 'And we're getting off topic here. It doesn't matter whether Ade fancies me or not. He behaved like an asshole.'

'Good diversion.' She picked at a fingernail. 'You seemed awfully riled up back then.'

'That's because your brother told you a pack of lies,' I said firmly. 'It wasn't the way he described it at all. And him hitting on me when my boyfriend's back was turned – that was obnoxious.'

'Sure. I suppose he thought it was worth a try,' she went on. 'Given the signals you were giving him.'

'I . . .' My mouth fell open while my brain worked hard to think of a comeback.

Polly didn't wait for my answer, though. She got to her feet, swinging her bag over her shoulder. 'You can deny it all you want,' she said, 'but you've just confirmed exactly what Ade told me.' She smiled tightly, stepping over the bench. 'It's so obvious.'

I shut my mouth at last, too infuriated to respond to this bullshit.

'I'll say hello to my brother for you,' she said breezily over her shoulder, heading for the doorway. 'He's been asking about you a lot.'

I waited until she had disappeared before I let out the breath I had been holding in. Looking down at my cold food, I certainly didn't feel hungry any more. In fact I felt sick. Really sick at the thought of what Ade had reported back to Polly about that night. What a creep.

I picked up my fork again and stabbed at a dried-up piece of potato. A flash of Ade's cruel blue eyes taunting me. The eerie paleness of his skin came into my mind, much as I wanted to push it out again.

I had never given him any signal that I liked him, had I? The thought that I had given him that impression left me go cold. And angry too.

I loved Luca. He had been the only boy I wanted in the diner that night.

Hadn't he?

# CHAPTER THIRTEEN

'Son.' Ulfred sat with his hands clasped together, looking down at the ground. 'Why all these questions about the Vulpecula?' He looked up and sideways at Luca. 'You came all the way back here to—'

Luca shook his head. 'I don't know. I . . .' He realized it was futile to try and pretend he had just been wondering. Ulfred would never believe that. Luca had not been back to Nissilum since he had left.

His father was staring expectantly at him. 'Have you seen something, Luca?'

'Not exactly. More like got a sense. I met this kid. About my age. He had the strongest, most aggressive aura about him. It was intoxicating.' He stopped then, realizing that what he had just said hardly amounted to evidence of the Vulpecula on Mortal Earth.

Ulfred sighed. All at once he looked weighed down,

troubled. He picked up a twig lying on the ground and poked at the earth with it. Luca watched him, anxiously.

'Ulfred,' he said in a half-whisper. 'What is it?'

His father thought for a moment before answering. 'It's . . . well, I hope – I'm sure – that what you sensed amounts to nothing much. But the Vulpecula are not like us here on Nissilum.' He turned to Luca. 'They make the Borgias look like innocent lambs frolicking in the grass. Not even the Celestial Family felt magnanimous enough to give them a chance. Their legend is of such darkness, such pure evil. There is no scrap of goodness in those creatures.'

Luca stared, unblinking. 'I must have made a mistake,' he said quietly. 'I'm sure I did. I am so wary of darkness, of danger on Mortal Earth. Perhaps sometimes I imagine things that aren't there.'

'Perhaps.' His father nodded. 'I hope that's it.' He frowned again, deep creases in his forehead ageing him all of a sudden. 'My great father – your great great father – he fell victim to a member of the Vulpecula. The last – we thought the last – of them roaming Nissilum, looking for trouble.'

'Really?' Luca sat up. 'He *saw* one of them.'

'You could say that. He was hypnotized, more like. The Vulpecula's powers – well, they're subtle at first.' He sighed. 'So sharp. Sharper than the rest of us. Their reputation for cunning is not just a myth. Their mental stealth matches their physical agility. They put Haris under some kind of spell and, for a while, he almost became one of them.'

'You don't speak much of Haris.' Luca thought for a moment.

'He succumbed to a dark energy. He allowed himself to be killed.'

'By the Vulpecula?'

'We don't know. His bones were found in a remote region of the south. Miles from his home. It was the first time a wolf had not been strong enough to defeat death.'

'I didn't know.' Luca ran a hand through his hair. 'No one ever said.'

'My great mother ordered us never to speak of it. A bad omen for the Hunters, she said, "To give up like that".'

'But why? Why did he give up? What happened?'

Ulfred sighed deeply. 'He allowed himself to be seduced by the Vulpecula.'

'What do you mean?' Luca asked. 'A romantic seduction?'

'It's more complicated than that. He found himself helping them to gain status on Nissilum. They offered him and his family some kind of supreme protection. For all time. They "arranged" for the family land to be increased, way beyond legal perimeters, by terrifying the surrounding landowners into submission. Slowly, my great mother found that her old friends would not speak to her, avoided her. She was excluded from all social events. My father, he remembers being shunned by people he had known since birth.'

'So the whole family were ostracized?' Luca shook his head. 'That's awful.'

Ulfred nodded. 'My father left home, came all the way across country beyond the great barrier, to forge a new life for himself. I was not allowed to see my great parents for years. My father was so furious. My great mother was staunchly loyal to her husband, of course. She refused to facilitate a reunion, refused to beg Haris to stop.' He paused. 'Of course, he couldn't stop. He was under some kind of spell. She knew that. Though my father did not find out until Haris was dead.'

'I never knew any of this. But what happened to the Vupecula then? How did they come even to be on Nissilum?'

'In those days, visitors were allowed on Nissilum for short amounts of time. After a few months they needed to present the correct paperwork or be deported. The Vulpecula would never risk being exposed, so they all left.

And were never seen or heard from again on Nissilum.'

'Where did they go? Mortal Earth?' Luca swallowed, not really wanting to know the answer to his question.

Ulfred didn't answer for a long time. He simply stared ahead of him and then finally took a breath, saying, 'No one knows for sure.'

'But then they could be alive – on Mortal Earth?' Now it was Luca's turn to stare into the distance. It was a remote possibility and it seemed ridiculous. But if it was true, then he and Jane were in danger.

Suddenly he couldn't wait to get back to her. He got to his feet, putting one hand on his father's shoulder.

'I need to go,' Luca told him. 'I just—'

'Yes.' Ulfred closed his own hand over his son's. 'I understand. You must go.'

Luca had got a few steps away before he heard Ulfred call out to him.

'You will tell me, won't you, Luca? If you need help, at any time. You would always tell me?'

Luca felt a lump in his throat at his father's words.

'Of course,' he told him. 'Always.'

# CHAPTER FOURTEEN

I was still fuming as I cycled home. Polly's little theory was ridiculous. The memory of Ade's face that night, mocking and entitled – every time it came back to me, I felt my face setting in fury.

As if I would ever want someone like that!

I changed gear going up the steep hill, the final leg of the journey. I realized my heart was beating too fast and my body took over, draining my thoughts, and I felt strength sapping out of me as I slowed.

I stopped, taking a breath and dismounted, looking around me in the twilight. It was so quiet and peaceful, except for that feeling of dread that was creeping over me that made all my cognitive powers seem to run in slow motion.

In the undergrowth, in the banks either side of the road, night-time creatures rustled. I jerked out of my torpor to see a flash of amber-coloured fur darting through the bushes. My heart stopped beating for a moment, my eyes fixed on this creature, rippling stealthily up the bank.

'Who's there?' Still holding on to my bike's handlebars I craned forwards, but the animal, whatever it was, was fast moving out of sight. As it reached the top of the verge, at the point where the thick woods began, it turned, its eyes flashing in the darkness, looking straight at me.

I felt air rushing through my head, forcing out all thoughts, leaving just the impression of this silky-coated creature. For a moment I forgot where I was, where I was going, as a sound like tinkling bells cut through the vacuum.

The blare of a car horn blasting jolted me out of my thoughts. I turned, squinting at the glare from the headlights, as a figure got out of the driver's side and started talking to me.

'What's going on?' I heard, though I didn't know who had spoken, me or the person standing before me. 'Jane?' My eyes swam into focus and I recognized Luca anxiously watching me.

'Oh.' I looked down at my bike and then back up at him. 'I guess I just got tired. This hill, it's too steep.'

'And you have no lights.' Luca stepped forward and took the bike out of my hands. 'Not functioning lights, anyway.'

'I thought I'd make it back,' I rubbed at my head, 'before it got really dark.'

'Are you all right?' He put one hand out to touch me. 'You seem a little dazed.'

'I'm fine.' I finally managed a smile. 'How was work?'

Luca shrugged. 'Back at the old training ground tomorrow. I had some errands to run today.' His eyes flickered uneasily.

I moved to give him a hug. 'I'm shattered.' And it was true; I felt stupidly tired, as though someone or something had sucked all the energy out of me. I put my arm through Luca's. 'Can I have a lift?'

'There's no way you're riding that bike with no lights,' he said protectively. 'So get in the car.'

'Are you OK?' I said, resting my head on his shoulder. 'You look weird.'

'Weird?' He put his arm around me. 'No, well . . . I'll tell you about it later.'

There it was again, that uneasy feeling.

'Something's happening, isn't it? Something strange.'

Luca's silence wasn't reassuring. He kept his arm around me, gently guiding me back to the car. Once we were both inside he put the keys in the ignition, then hesitated.

'I went back to see my father,' he said.

'To Nissilum? I thought—'

'I wasn't going to go back – not for a while anyway. But I needed to talk to Ulfred. He's a wise man and he knows pretty much everything there is to know about the history of Nissilum.'

'What did you need to know?' I asked. 'You live here now, Luca. It's a little dull, I realize that, being so mortal and all, but—'

'I needed to ask him about the Vulpecula,' he interrupted me. 'They're an ancient breed of malevolent fox.'

I stared at him for a second before I started grinning. 'Are you serious?' But a sudden recollection of a dinner conversation we'd had struck me, wiping the grin off my face. 'I mean – they're real?'

'They were.' Luca leaned back in his seat. 'We thought they were extinct long ago. But now, well, we don't know. Ulfred told me a story about my great great father Haris that casts doubt on that theory. Apparently he made some kind of pact with the Vulpecula a long time ago and there were consequences – fatal consequences.'

'They killed him?'

'Nobody knows. He could have killed himself.'

I sighed. 'Not another one.'

'I don't know,' Luca said. 'It's all speculation really, but Ulfred certainly has a lot to say about the Vulpecula and their particular, deadly power. They use mental stealth, tricks of the mind, to trap their prey. They're vicious, but not until they have used all of their mind games to cause harm. They deal in trades. They were forbidden from gaining citizenship on Nissilum, and they wanted revenge for that ultimately. They tried to use my great great father to gain them that right.'

'How?'

'He had great influence with the Celestials apparently, so they used him and then cast a spurious spell on him. I suppose it was a kind of brainwashing. The desired result being that they would be installed on Nissilum as rightful citizens, despite the fact that they had no intention of abiding by its laws.'

'Well, it didn't work, did it?' I said, my heart in my mouth. 'If it had worked then Nissilum would be a very different place today.'

'It didn't work. But the Vulpecula didn't disappear as everyone thought or hoped. Or at least, I don't think they did.'

We looked at each other. We were both of thinking the

same thing. I remembered the flash of an animal I had seen only minutes before. It seemed ridiculous that these deadly foxes were here and—

'Hey.' A hand was rapping on the car window. Luca and I jerked, startled. Tentatively Luca wound it down and a head of tousled red curls appeared at eye level.

'Ade?' Luca was trying hard not to appear freaked out, which he was – we both were. 'What are you doing up here?'

'I came walking.' Ade's grin was broad and it seemed genuine enough. 'I think I got a little lost.' He looked over at me in the passenger seat and his expression was guileless, innocent almost. 'That'll teach me to be adventurous.'

I glanced at Luca. 'Well . . . we can give you a lift back home.'

'No,' Ade said too quickly, but then the smile returned to his face. 'I mean, I can walk back. It's not too late, and I can take care of myself.'

'OK then.' There was a few seconds of awkward silence, before I found myself speaking again. 'I live up that track. Would you like to come in for some tea or something?' I had no idea why I had suggested that; the words had come out of my mouth before I could stop them. Luca was frowning at me, I could see it out of the corner of my eye.

'I don't want to bother you,' Ade said. 'But I did want to apologize. To both of you, for my behaviour the other night.'

'It's not us you should be apologizing to,' said Luca in a low voice.

'Yes. I have tried calling Ashley several times. But she won't take my calls.' He shrugged. 'I guess I've blown it there.'

'Uh huh.' Luca's hands were gripping the steering wheel tightly.

I bit my lip. I knew I should be hostile too. Hadn't I been cursing Ade all the way home? But somehow my brain was erasing all my anger. And the way he was looking at me, so eager to be friends, no trace of arrogance . . . I was starting to feel sorry for him.

'I'll only stay a bit,' he told us. 'If your offer is still open.'

My mother was gazing at Ade as though he were the prodigal son. She seemed entranced by his Titian looks.

'Extraordinary colouring,' she cooed. 'People are so weird about red hair. I think it's beautiful.'

Luca and I exchanged a look. It was hard not to be amused by Mum's fawning. It was so unlike her. Even Dot was sitting with her chin in her hands, staring intently at the stranger in our kitchen.

'I'll shave it off one day,' he said, smiling at her. 'It's been more trouble than it's worth. People seem to think that it defines me somehow.'

'People are so ignorant.' She poured out some tea and handed Ade a mug. 'Did you get teased at school?'

Ade's face went blank for a moment. 'At school?'

'Yes. Kids are the worst.' She sat down. 'Jane knows all about that.'

'Mum!' I glared at her, before rapidly composing myself and turning to Ade. 'I had a bit of trouble at school. But then I was home—'

'What kind of trouble?' Ade's eyes seemed softer than usual, almost dewy with concern.

I shook my head, not wanting to pursue the subject, but again, finding myself talking.

'They didn't like me because they thought I was different. They don't like anyone different.'

'That's certainly true.' Ade drank some tea. 'I'm sorry you had a hard time.'

'It's over now.' I glanced sideways at Luca who looked unmoved. 'And now I am happy.' I put out my hand and took Luca's, but it felt limp.

'Yes,' my mother said briskly. 'All in the past.' I saw her eyes flick up to the clock on the wall. 'Would you like to stay for dinner, Ade? It's getting late; I'm sure you must be hungry. You boys always are.'

There was tension in the air. I saw Ade considering, hesitating, before clocking Luca's distinctly unfriendly expression.

'That's kind.' He stood up and drained the rest of his tea. 'But I have to be getting back. My grandparents always have food on the table at the same time.'

'You live with your grandparents?' Mum raised an eyebrow. 'I didn't realize . . .'

'No, just visiting, while my parents sort things out.' Ade's face darkened a little; all of a sudden he looked smaller, like a little boy. 'They're getting on a bit, my grandparents, and they don't like their routine disrupted.' He shrugged. 'I don't want to upset them.'

'That's considerate.' Mum looked approving. 'Your grandparents live in Bale? I'm sure Luca or Jack will give you a lift back.'

'That's kind, but I'll walk. I like walking.' Ade told her. 'Grandpa Pete will come and get me if I get lost.'

'Pete?' Luca leaned forward. 'Did you say Pete?'

'Yeah. Pete Henshaw?' Ade said. 'You know him?'

'I work for him.' Luca answered slowly. 'For his construction company.'

'Oh yeah. He mentioned that.' Ade grinned. 'Well, that

he had help. I used to help him. A couple of years back, before I decided on my vocation.'

'Right.' Luca's face had drained of colour. 'Well, he's a good man.'

'The best,' said Ade. 'He's practically the only person I really trust. He's been like a father to me.'

'Oh, that's nice,' Mum said soothingly, her heartstrings well and truly pulled. 'Everyone needs someone they trust completely.'

Luca and I looked at each other.

'Well, I'd better be going.' Ade went over to the sink and washed up his cup. Turning back to us he pushed his sleeves up his arms, drying his hands on a tea towel. There was a mark, just above his wrist, a wound of some kind, scarring now, but still faintly bloody.

'You cut yourself?' Luca asked, his voice all of a sudden like granite.

Ade looked blank for a few seconds before looking down at his arm. 'I did it the other day.' He tugged his sleeve back down over the cut. 'Thanks for the tea, Mrs Jonas. I hope I'll be seeing you around.' He didn't look at me or Luca and now seemed in a hurry to get out of the house. Before we knew it the back door was banging shut.

'Well, he seems nice,' my mother said obliviously.

'He's odd,' I said. 'Very odd.'

'Well, he might make a good friend for you, Luca – a boy not far off your own age. I know it's a little female heavy in this house.'

Luca's face was a picture. It was lucky Mum's back was turned. He hadn't been convinced by the Ade we'd seen today and, now that Ade had left, neither was I. I thought of what Luca had been telling me just before Ade had appeared by the car. The spell that the Vulpecula can cast. I shook my head.

It was just too unbelievable that Ade and Polly belonged to that deadly species. They were messed up, for certain, but that didn't mean they were evil.

I was pretty sure about that.

# CHAPTER FIFTEEN

The girl levered herself up on one elbow, wincing at the pain that shot through her arm. She concentrated on the sliver of light through the stone, the birds cheeping outside, the greeny-brown leaves on a tree-top. It must be dawn.

Or was it a dream? Was she dead? She could be dead.

She had stopped feeling anything – any emotion, that is – a long time ago. How long she couldn't be sure. She had woken up, not knowing where she was – who she was, even. The first thing she'd done was touch her neck. It was bare. She had a faint feeling that something had gone.

The tears had come for a while, but she didn't know what she was crying for. They were the numb kind of tears. The most frightening thing was that she didn't know what she was doing here, how she had got here. Maybe it would come back?

She sat up, holding her knees, noticing how bony they were. She was so thin. And her hair was all matted. It bothered her. She realized, with a kind of bleary triumph, that she was proud of her hair. Pulling her fingers robotically through it she encountered a mass, something sticking to her hair, knotting it. In the semi-darkness it was difficult to see what it was, but as she pulled it out her heartbeat picked up and she was glad that there was not enough light to see properly. She had a hunch that it was blood.

The sound of a dog barking got her up and on her feet. She pressed her face against the cold stone, one eye fixed on the outside.

'Hello?' she whimpered, strength draining from her. 'Hello?'

Only the sound of the birds. She lay back, her hand still on that sticky mass.

'Please.' She felt her breaths coming short. 'Please. Help me.'

# CHAPTER SIXTEEN

'Like I said, the guys were all a little older.' Polly put on her sunglasses, even though it was cloudy and grey. She smiled broadly at me. 'You should come. It's fun.'

'I'll think about it.' I hugged my bag to my chest. 'I'm a bit busy these days.'

'Oh yeah.' She smirked. 'You have me to look after. It would be like taking a chaperone. Kind of uncool really. Hey!' She stuck her hand out at a guy walking past her. 'See you in class.'

He smiled shyly at her, barely glancing at me, as though Polly was the only person he could see. I suppressed the shudder that ran through me.

Polly was looking around her, though I didn't know how she could actually see anything through her black lenses. She was annoying me more and more these days.

'So,' I said, 'your brother was round at our place the other night. Ingratiating himself with my mother.' I watched as she removed her glasses.

'Really?' she said, her lips widening. 'Well, that's Ade. Every mother's favourite.'

'Yeah. He's got that charm thing down all right,' I said casually. 'He almost had me thinking he was decent.'

The smile disappeared from her face. 'He is decent. I told you that.'

'I know what you told me.' It was difficult to keep the ice out of my tone. 'But you're not the most reliable of sources, are you, Polly?'

She studied me, her eyes cold and unforgiving, before that supercilious expression returned.

'You think you're happy, Jane. You think you can hold on to this little relationship of yours. That everything will work out. But things change. People come into your life and they change things.' She cocked her head almost sympathetically. 'You have so much to learn.'

I opened my mouth to respond but she had already turned away, waving at some other hapless guy.

'Gotta go now.' She turned to give me one last fake smile. 'But I'll see you later. We're stuck with each other now – whether you like it or not.'

She flicked her red hair over her shoulder as I

121

watched her walk away, self-entitled and confident beyond her years.

Something about Polly and Ade seemed to hold me in their spell and made me feel powerless to fight it. The moment Polly was out of sight the anger came, but more than that, cold fear.

Why was Polly so vicious and scathing about my relationship with Luca? She had never even met him. How could she know so much about us? It had to be from Ade.

I sank down on to a chair and grappled in my bag for some aspirin. I had another headache coming. I hadn't been able to focus on college work lately, as though there was a fog between me and my coursework. Between everything.

'Jane?' A pair of stockinged feet in sensible footwear stood in my line of vision. I looked up to see Mrs Connelly peering at me. 'Is everything all right?'

I closed my bag, mustering up the biggest fake smile I could manage.

'Everything's fine,' I told her. 'I was just looking for something in my . . .' I trailed off, noticing that Mrs C had removed her glasses. She had beautiful eyes, a golden-brown colour I had never seen before.

'Jane?' she said again, softly. 'Are you sure you're

all right? You don't look—'

'I do feel a little woozy,' I said, realizing it was true. Everything seemed to be slipping out of focus. I tried to get up, but couldn't seem to find my footing, as though the floor was moving.

The last thing I felt was Mrs Connelly's hand gripping my arm before everything disappeared.

'. . . under severe stress,' a voice was saying, faded in the background. I opened my eyes, taking in a set of scales and an empty bookshelf. A light without a shade, a harsh bulb only, hung from the ceiling. I was lying on my back on a bed in the nurse's office. I sat up quickly.

'What happened?' I said. Mrs Connelly had her back to me, in front of her was my mother – and Polly.

My mother looked over at me, smiling but concerned.

'Darling.' She moved beyond Mrs Connelly. 'You fainted.'

'Oh.' I swung my legs over the bed. 'I feel fine now. I must have picked up a virus or something . . .'

'But you haven't been yourself for a while.' This time Polly spoke. Her usual stinging tone was replaced by something much softer and more friendly. 'I've been really worried about you.'

'Really?' I was trying to sound sarcastic but it came out

as something much more submissive. 'You never said.'

'We've both been worried,' Polly went on. 'Ade and I.'

My mother looked at her, then back at me. 'I'm glad someone is looking out for you.' She didn't add, 'At last you have friends,' but it was what she meant.

'I don't need you to worry about me,' I said, regaining my strength. Now my tone was more defiant. I looked around and spotted my bag on the floor by the trolley. I got up and opened it to take out my brush. Pulling it through my hair, I was careful not to look at anyone. I just wanted to get out of there, out of the suffocating atmosphere.

'I've got the car,' said my mum. 'I'll take you home.' She turned to Polly. 'Thank you, dear.'

*Thank you, dear?*

Mum picked up my jacket and started trying to put it on me.

'It's OK,' I said gruffly. 'I can put my own jacket on.' I caught Polly's eye. Now she looked triumphant.

'Feel better soon,' she said. 'Ade is really worried about you.'

'Why?' I said sharply. 'He hardly—'

'We both are,' she cut in quickly. 'You're a friend.'

Both Mrs Connelly and my mother were smiling now, oblivious to my bewilderment.

'Come on then,' said Mum, as though she was talking to a six-year-old. 'Let's get you back home.'

I allowed myself to be led out of the room but my eyes were rooted on Polly's, which were unblinking. She was pulling her long red hair into a single plait.

'I'll call you later,' she said sweetly. 'See how you're feeling.'

Once again I was rendered speechless.

# CHAPTER SEVENTEEN

It was only a small, faint noise, but Luca heard it just the same. He twitched, trying to locate the source, but he couldn't see anything.

*Probably a mouse*, he thought, though not convinced. It was raining again and the hut was damp and misty, the smell of rotting wood getting under his skin. He was sick of this job, which seemed never-ending. Every time they removed another lot of rusting metal, a new lot seemed to appear. Luca had avoided looking too closely at anything, fearful that he would find something else bloody and sinister, like the necklace.

Luca had come ahead of Pete, who had some family emergency to deal with. He'd driven to the training ground at the crack of dawn, through the pot-holed lanes, ashamed of himself for feeling scared. The truth was that he was beginning to feel there was more danger on

Mortal Earth than there was on Nissilum. Back home there were firm rules and a hefty price to pay for stepping out of line. And there was a spirit of cooperation, an iron-fast moral code that everyone who lived there had chosen in return for sanctuary. On Mortal Earth people lived by a different code: as long as they were not found out, they did as they pleased. Or so it seemed.

Through the hut's entrance Luca saw the headlights of Pete's van as it pulled into the grounds. He felt relieved. Pete's pragmatism was reassuring. And despite the fact that his grandchildren were downright odd – if not dangerous – Luca felt an affinity with the old man.

And through Pete, maybe Luca could find out more about Polly and Ade, something that would put his mind at rest. He couldn't believe that evil was related to Pete. He hoped that his fears were only the result of a lifetime spent distrusting alien species.

Pete shone his torch as he approached and Luca squinted in its glare.

'Be light soon.' Pete entered the hut and switched off his torch. 'This place never seems to get any cleaner.'

'Everything OK?' Luca asked.

Pete scratched his head. 'Yeah. My wife was anxious – our grandchildren didn't come home all night.' He shrugged. 'I told her they're teenagers. They're probably out at some party somewhere and lost track of time. But she worries . . .'

'Ade and Polly, right?'

Pete blinked, looking surprised. 'That's right. You know them?'

'I've met Ade through Jane. Polly's at her college.'

'Uh huh.' Pete yawned. 'She's a handful.'

*So is her brother*, Luca thought, but did not say.

'You know they're adopted?' Pete said, stretching. 'Poor kids. Had a terrible start in life.'

'Do you know what happened to their biological parents?'

'Not sure.' Pete looked away, too quickly. 'A bad lot, I heard. Those kids were in a bad way when my son and his wife took them on.'

'I see.' Luca kept his voice level, though he didn't like what he was hearing. He waited for Pete to continue.

'But they're good now. All good . . .' Pete's voice trailed off and he turned his attention to some rubble at his foot. 'It's all in the past.'

'OK then.' Luca took hold of the industrial wheelbarrow in front of him; it was heavy and loaded with bricks. 'I guess you don't know what's going on in their heads.'

'What?' Pete jerked back to look at him, his face

stern, frowning. 'So what could be going in their heads? They're just kids. Heads full of rubbish, more like.'

'Right.' It seemed like a touchy subject for Pete. 'I didn't mean anything by it . . .'

'Ade struggles with being given up by his parents. I see the troubled look in his face. He was old enough to know what was going on, of course. And he and his sister, they've got a real bond. Unbreakable. She hangs off his every word. And he would do anything for her.'

'It must be hard for them – what with your daughter being unwell.' Luca stopped seeing a look of confusion on the older man's face. But Pete quickly recovered himself.

'She's had some health worries over the years, but . . .' Pete seemed to check himself before shutting down. 'They all have their struggles, like anyone else. But they're not doing badly. The boy will be running his own business soon. And Polly, she's as sharp as a tack. She runs rings round me. She'll be fine too.'

'That's good.' Luca felt awkward. There was something Pete wasn't saying, he was sure of that. But before he had a chance to push it, the sound – the one from before – was heard from somewhere in the hut.

'You hear that?' Luca stood perfectly still. 'Sounds like a mouse squeaking. Something alive anyway.' He glanced around. 'Something in pain.'

Pete snorted. 'Not in here. There can't be a living thing left in here. Apart from us.' He shivered. 'And we'll be six feet under soon if we don't work up some heat by finally getting rid of all this rubbish.'

But the sound continued – plaintive, almost like a human whimper. Luca didn't know whether it was his heightened sensory perception, but it felt as though it was meant for him.

'Let's get going, boy,' Pete said gruffly.

Luca picked up the handles of the wheelbarrow again and rolled it outside, where he and Pete lifted it together and threw the contents into the waiting dump.

Behind them the light inside the hut went out. Pete exhaled, squinting. 'Must be the damp,' he said, taking his torch out of his belt. 'You stay put, I'll go and see where the fuse box is.'

Luca watched as Pete stumbled around inside. His unease was growing.

'Pete,' he called. 'Pete?' The old man had disappeared out of sight. 'Are you OK, Pete?'

He waited but there was no answer and the cold air seemed to tighten around him, a low whistling sound coming through the trees. As it died down, Luca heard an audible moan coming, but not from the hut; it seemed to come from everywhere, growing louder, like a chorus of moaning, whispering in a guttural tone.

Luca swallowed looking up at the sky and seeing the moon. It wasn't full, he was safe from that at least, but still he felt the hair on his arms pricking.

His heart thumped as he took a step towards the hut and he chastised himself for being scared.

Stepping inside, there was only darkness and silence. Luca's eyes flickered around, then settled on something glinting in the corner. A flash of fur and angry, beastly eyes, watching him. But he couldn't make out what it was.

'Who's there?' He stood ready to face whatever it may be. 'Whoever you are—'

And then his eyes fell on the figure of Pete, lying motionless under the animal's nose. With a defiant screech, the animal stood on its back feet before rushing headlong past the paralyzed boy.

# CHAPTER EIGHTEEN

There was someone above her. She had heard them – more than one of them – moving around. Lack of food for days had considerably weakened her, maybe even was causing her to hear things that weren't really there. But how could she be sure?

Crawling to the corner of the cave, she felt around for her water bottle. It had barely a trickle left in it now, but she drank it greedily, clutching the bottle as though it were her lifeline.

She stood up, thumping at the roof of the cave.

'Help!' She shouted as loud as she could though her voice was weak and inaudible. She knew she had little time left, that calling for help was pointless. She would die here, in this stinking wet cave.

But then, distinctly – she couldn't be imagining this – the sound of voices, fading in and out. There was someone up there. Someone could rescue her.

But the voices moved away. Whoever it was was going, leaving her here. She listened, her heart in her mouth, praying for them to hear. She resumed her shouting, stretching every vocal cord she had.

A thump above her – like a fallen tree, it seemed so loud.

Then silence.

Tears sprang to her eyes. She was going to die.

She was going to die down here in this stinking cold, wet grave.

# CHAPTER NINETEEN

I lay on my bed looking at the clock. It was nine p.m. and Luca had not arrived home. I told myself that his working hours were erratic – it wasn't a nine to five job. Pete obviously had him working late for a reason.

But he had never been this late before. I didn't feel weird any more. Now all I felt was the adrenalin racing around my body. Pure anxiety.

There was a knock at my bedroom door. Before I could reply my little sister stuck her head round it. 'What happened to you?' she said without preamble. Her hair hung loose, streaky gold, and I realized how tall she had suddenly got, her once rounded cherubic face narrower, the beginnings of killer cheekbones developing. Dot was growing up, and I'd been so wrapped in my own stuff lately, I hadn't noticed.

'I'm touched by your sisterly concern,' I told her. 'And is that my T-shirt?'

Dot glanced down, her cheeks colouring a little, before she looked back up at me, impish defiance on her face.

'You can have it.' I threw a pillow at her, all at once so grateful to be back in ribbing-big-sister mode.

But Dot wanted to talk.

'I feel like we never hang out together any more,' she said, approaching the bed and throwing the pillow back at me. 'You know, like we used to.'

I sighed. 'I know. I'm sorry, Dottie. There's been so much going on. I've neglected you.'

'It's OK.' She plumped down on the bed. 'I'm glad you're happy. I was starting to get worried about you.' She rolled on to her back, her long, unusually dark eyelashes batting over her big blue eyes.

I reached out and tugged gently at a lock of her hair.

'I wish I could go back sometimes,' I said quietly. 'Back to when life was just a bit simpler. When it was just the two of us.'

'And you were lonely.' Dot was staring up at the ceiling.

I smiled down at her. 'Yep. That's true. But it was safer that way.'

Dot rolled back on to her stomach. 'Safer?'

'Yeah. I mean, there was nothing to worry about.'

'Are you worried now?' The concern in her voice made me swallow. I felt as though I was going to cry. 'What are you worried about, Janey?' she went on. 'Is Luca being mean to you?'

'No!' I laughed. 'Luca hasn't got a mean bone in his body.'

*At least not when he's a boy*, I added to myself.

'Yeah, but he is moody,' Dot said tentatively. She looked up at me from under her giant lashes. 'Not in a scary way. Just kind of intense.'

'Suppose,' I shrugged. 'He's just thoughtful. He feels things deeply.'

There was a silence, before we both burst out laughing.

'So what is bothering you, if it isn't Luca?' Dot twiddled her hair. 'You've never ever fainted before.'

'I know.' Suddenly I wanted to confide in Dot. Tell her everything. It would feel so good to unload all the thoughts in my head. But I couldn't. As tempting as it was, Dot was too young to understand. So I hesitated before answering.

'I've just been trying to do too much, please too many people, I guess,' I said at last. 'And it's harder trying to keep it all going than I thought. Things keep getting in the way.'

'Like that red-haired boy,' she said, her eyes fixed on me, unblinking.

'No, he's nothing to do with anything,' I said defensively, a flush creeping over my face. 'Why do you say that?'

'Well, he's totally in love with you,' she said slowly. 'It's so obvious.'

'Nuh-huh.' I shook my head. '*So* not in love with me.'

'Yeah he is,' she persisted. 'I saw the way he looked at you when he came over. It made Luca angry. I could see that too.'

'It's not . . .' I faltered, trying to find the right explanation. 'It's not because of that. Luca doesn't like Ade, because Ade's not . . . very nice.'

'Oh, I could see that too,' Dot said lightly. 'But that's kind of exciting, isn't it?'

'Dot!' I raised an eyebrow. 'Where did you get that from?'

'Everyone knows that. It's like a fact of life or something.' She looked at me then, in such a knowing way, it was as though she was the big sister and I was the little kid, clueless all of a sudden.

The sound of feet thumping up the stairs startled us both and we sat up, just as the door was pushed open and my mother stood, pink-cheeked, staring at the two of us.

'There's been an accident,' she said, trying to catch her breath. 'Down at that training ground.'

'Luca!' I felt my heart speed up, launching myself off the bed. 'Is it Luca? What happened? Is he hurt?'

'No,' she said, putting her arms out to stop me as I tried to run past. 'Not Luca. It's Pete.' She paused, obviously wondering whether to say anything more with Dot in the room.

'Pete?' I stopped.

'He had some kind of attack,' she said, swallowing. 'Luca said it happened suddenly . . .'

'But Luca's OK?' I said, my eyes pleading with her. 'Luca's not hurt?'

'No, Jane.' She tried to take hold of my arm. 'Luca's fine.'

A shadow fell across the doorway. Luca stood pale-faced and shaken, hugging himself, as though he was in shock.

'I don't know what happened,' he said, stepping inside, and I saw his whole body was shaking. 'Pete's gone to A&E. They think he had some kind of heart attack.' He shook his head. 'But he was fine. It doesn't make sense.'

Luca's eyes over the top of my mum's head were trying to communicate something to me that he didn't want anyone else to see. For the first time ever he looked out of his depth, like a little boy. I went to him and wrapped my arms around his shivering body.

'It's OK,' I whispered. 'It's OK.'

I was aware of my mum and my sister slipping past us out of the room. We waited until they were safely in the hall, before I took Luca's face in my hands.

'What did you see?' I said hoarsely, my own body tense and scared. 'What did you really see out there?'

'The good news is that Pete is suffering from a mild concussion and some cuts and bruises.'

My dad walked into the kitchen, a newspaper tucked under his arm. He drew a chair out from the kitchen table and poured himself a large mug of tea. He'd been straight over to the hospital to see Pete the moment Luca had arrived home. It was now nearly one a.m. and we were all up.

I held Luca's hand under the table, still trying to make sense of what he had told me earlier when we'd been alone together in my room. Luca had said that it had seemed so odd. One minute Pete was sauntering towards the hut, fit and healthy, the next he was lying cold on the ground.

'Well, he's old,' I'd said, as an explanation. 'Old people aren't so steady on their feet.'

Luca had screwed up his nose. The shadows under his eyes seemed to grow deeper by the second.

'He didn't make a sound, though. I didn't even hear him fall – it was as though someone caught him, to muffle the sound.'

'Who?' I frowned. 'There wasn't anyone else there, was there?'

'No. Nobody who made themselves visible anyway.' Luca clenched his hands together and I could see they were still shaking. 'But I told you about that sound I kept hearing before all the lights went out.'

'Yeah. But wasn't that a mouse or some night-time creature.' I tried to sound as soothing as possible. 'And an animal couldn't have caused Pete to fall.'

Luca had looked at me then, straight into my eyes. And I saw a flash of fear in his face. Felt his belief that something – something unworldly – had been present.

'You think it's . . .' I didn't know if I could finish my sentence. It sounded too ridiculous. 'One of those Vulc— whatever you call them?'

'The Vulpecula?' Luca sighed. 'Honestly, I have no idea. But I just sense there is something in or around that place. Or somebody trying to send a message.' He put his head in his hands. 'It all seems too much of a coincidence.'

'OK.' I kept my voice steady. 'But maybe there is a much more rational explanation. Maybe there is nothing sinister about any of this. Not even to do with Ade or Polly.'

'Yes. Pete certainly stuck up for them.' Luca relaxed very slightly. 'They can't be that bad. He would know if there was something bad.'

'That's true.' I nodded. I had got up then, hoping that was an end to the weirdness. I felt totally drained. I turned my back on Luca and slipped off my T-shirt and reached for my pyjama top. I was just pulling it over my head when I felt his cool, strong hands behind me on my bare waist. And then his head, nestling against mine. I shivered, this time not from the cold or fear. I tilted my head back, allowing his fingertips to caress me, sending electric impulses shooting through my body.

'I don't want anything to spoil this,' he whispered in my ear. 'Us.'

I turned, my breath coming quickly. 'Nothing will.' I gently pushed his head up to look into his green eyes. 'How could it?'

Luca pushed back my hair; his lips parted, so full and soft, I wanted to kiss him for ever. But he didn't pull me towards him, instead a sadness came over him.

'There are so many bad things out there,' he said. 'I thought once we got here that I would stop feeling it – drop my guard. On Mortal Earth the danger is more tangible. That's what I thought. But now . . . now I know there is something here.'

'But you have no proof of that,' I said. 'Maybe it's just habit.'

'I do have proof.' He shut his eyes wearily. 'I have the necklace.'

And now sitting in the kitchen, trying to make sense of it all, I felt fuggy headed. I yawned, catching my mother's eye.

'I think we'd all better get some sleep now,' she said sensibly. 'Dot was up way too late. She's going to be a nightmare tomorrow.'

Luca and I exchanged a genuine smile for the first time that night. Then I caught Mum's eye.

'You miss your sister?' she asked Luca. 'You must miss her.'

'I do.' Luca nodded, then smiled down at the table. 'A lot.'

'You grow up so quickly.' Mum's eyes ran over us. 'One minute you're running around, hiding in trees, the next you're . . .' She trailed off, exhaustion taking over. Dad put his hand on her arm.

'Jane and Dot are still here,' he said, smiling. 'And Luca.'

'I know.' She shook her head. 'I just – well, I keep

thinking of Pete. I think he dotes on his grandchildren. After his other daughter disappeared . . .'

'His other daughter!' I leaned forward. 'I didn't know he had a daughter who disappeared?'

Mum looked warily at my father. 'Well, it's late, I don't want to go into it.'

'What happened to her?' Luca's voice was sharp like glass. 'And when was this?'

'Oh, not that long ago. A year maybe?' Mum smoothed her hair with her palms. 'She'd be around thirty-two now. A lovely girl. The apple of his eye.'

'But I never knew any of this,' I said. 'Why didn't I know?'

'Oh, darling, it was a while back when you were . . . while you and Luca were apart. She was living with Lydia and Johnny, Ade's adoptive parents. Then one day she just upped and went to live in London and went quiet on them.'

'I wonder why?' I glanced at Luca. He'd gone very pale.

'Nobody's seen her?' he said, not sounding tired at all.

'Last I had spoken to Pete about it, no.'

Dad yawned and patted Mum's hand. 'I'm beat.' He smiled wearily at us. 'And I think we should all go to bed now. Luca can go and visit Pete in the morning.'

'Yeah.' I yawned. 'Sounds like a good idea.'

Mum rose from the table, hesitated, and then looked at the two of us. 'Maybe Luca should sleep in your room tonight. He doesn't look right. You can keep an eye on him.'

I felt my entire body go crimson. I hardly dared look at my father. But when I did, he looked completely unaffected by what my mother had just suggested.

Luca on the other hand, looked like he could hug her.

'Are you sure?' he asked, his fingers brushing mine.

'Totally,' she said firmly. 'You're a good boy. I know I can trust you with my daughter.'

The night was pretty chaste, so my mother was right. Though in fairness this was down to exhaustion on both our parts. Still it felt good to feel the warmth of his body next to me in my queen-sized bed. I lay awake, keeping my eyes open, just watching him sleep. His dark lashes on his cheeks, his lips parted, he looked peaceful at last.

In the morning it would all seem more reasonable. We would go and see Pete and he would tell us he tripped and fell, and now was better. Everything would go back to normal. Ade and Polly were just a slightly odd brother and sister. Yes, Polly was a little malevolent and Ade – well, Ade was an unknown quantity, but after Luca had told me that they were adopted, I began to understand why they might not be so well adjusted.

Not everyone had good families.

I stroked Luca's dark hair, careful not to wake him, and let my eyes wander over to the window. The moon was nearly full – not quite – but nearly full. I glanced back at Luca fearfully. It was not the time for him to contend with a full moon. He had managed so far, disappearing to turn. He had mastered the art of creeping quietly back into the house when it was over, appearing in the mornings, shadowy and weak. My mother tactfully and cleverly diverted Dad's and Dot's attention with small talk, but we both had our hearts in our mouths, wondering at something so violent, so beastly, that was happening to Luca alone. He was so far from home, yet drawn back to his roots, the animal within him would never leave.

Could we sustain this life, he and I?

I shut my eyes, pushing out the future, which seemed so riddled with Luca's past. It wasn't his fault, and I would take him, all of him, because I had no choice. And life, people, weren't perfect.

But sometimes . . . sometimes I just wanted a normal boyfriend.

# CHAPTER TWENTY

The waiting room was packed with mothers and children, pensioners sniffing into their handkerchiefs and hospital staff rushing through, clipboards in hand.

Luca approached the receptionist, who was simultaneously tapping at her computer keyboard and talking on the phone.

'I hope he's OK,' I whispered. Like most people, I hated hospitals. It's that anxious claustrophobia, the smell of overcooked food, and sick people, of course. But on top of that I had this queasy feeling in the pit of my stomach. I don't know why I felt such doom, but I couldn't shake it.

Luca squeezed my hand, just as the receptionist got off the phone.

'We've come to see Pete Henshaw,' said Luca. 'He was admitted last night.'

The receptionist rolled the gum in her mouth.

'Pete Henshaw.' She commenced tapping on the keyboard again and we watched as her eyes narrowed, then a faint frown appeared on her face.

'Oh . . . I . . .' She looked up at us. 'Hold on for one minute, please.'

Taking the gum out of her mouth and flicking it in the bin, she gave us a worried look before moving to speak to an officious-looking senior nurse. Luca and I watched them talk, and then the nurse looked over at us, a perturbed look on her face.

'What's going on?' I murmured. 'What are they talking about?'

'I don't know.' Luca looked tense too. The nurse was approaching us.

'You're relatives of Mr Henshaw?' She eyed us, her face softening slightly.

'No. He's my boss . . .' Luca started.

'And a family friend,' I added quickly, knowing how the bureaucracy worked in these places. 'We're very close to Mr Henshaw.'

'OK.' The nurse removed her glasses. 'I'm sure that's true, but . . .' She looked briefly around her at the hustle and bustle. 'Come with me a minute. We can talk more privately.' She moved around the reception booth, smiling more kindly now, then gestured for us to follow her to an empty room off the waiting area.

I concentrated on her sensible black shoes. The feeling of doom was increasing by the second.

Once we were inside, the nurse closed the door and touched her hair nervously. 'You want to sit down?' she asked in an almost pleading tone.

'No thanks.' Luca sounded curt. 'Is Pete all right? He should be coming home today, isn't that right?'

'Mr Henshaw is not doing well.' She tilted her head to the side in a sympathetic pose. 'He is not recovering as he should be. Overnight he slipped into a state of unconsciousness.'

'A coma, you mean?' The doomed feeling grew until it felt like it was taking up the whole of my insides. 'But how? He just fell over, right? I mean, there were no serious injuries . . .'

'No. But with men of his age – often the most simple of injuries can result in complications. Sometimes there are underlying illnesses that impede recovery.' She trailed off, seeing the incomprehension on our faces.

'I believe his daughter is on her way in to see him.' The nurse's tone became more efficient. 'And his grandchildren.'

Luca shut his eyes. 'Thanks for letting us know. We'll leave his family to it.'

'I'm sure, since he's a family friend that they won't object if you wait for them to arrive.' The nurse reached out for the door handle.

'No,' Luca said abruptly. 'That's OK. This is a private time. We'll come back later.'

The nurse hesitated, biting her lip before speaking again. 'Don't leave it too long,' she said. 'He's very weak.' With an attempt at a warm smile, she opened the door, leaving us rooted to the spot.

As soon as the door had closed behind her, I let out a deep breath.

'I thought Pete was getting better,' I murmured. 'Dad said he was fine.'

Luca sat down on one of the two uncomfortable-looking chairs in the room, chairs designed to compound the anxiety of anyone who used them.

'Luca?' I frowned. 'Don't you think this is ridiculous?'

He shook his head slowly. 'I knew something wasn't right. Pete might not be a young man, but he's fit and strong for his age. And he was just lying there – ' he glanced up at me ' – as though he had been overwhelmed by something . . .'

'It does seem really odd.' I sank down in the chair next to him, wincing at the hard plastic. Maybe we should stick around?'

Luca nodded, then looked past at me through the window in the door. A woman in her early forties was anxiously tying and untying the belt on her coat, as she stood talking to a man in scrubs. Next to her, a man rubbed her back comfortingly. And behind him stood two familiar figures.

Ade and Polly.

'Well.' I puffed out my cheeks. 'Looks like there's no escape now. We have to face them. That must be Pete's daughter.'

'Poor Pete,' whispered Luca. 'He doesn't deserve this.' He looked down at the floor and I saw the ridges of stress indented in his forehead.

'Come on,' I said, getting up. 'This could be our last chance.'

Polly's face darkened as she saw me approach. Her hair was tangled and the make-up round her eyes was smudgy. She'd been crying. I could see that even at this distance. As we got closer, she lifted her hand to her face, rubbing at one eye. If I had been feeling in a less compassionate mood, I would have said it was a deliberate gesture, intended to convince everyone around her that she was deeply upset.

But I *was* feeling compassionate. *Give her the benefit of the doubt*, I told myself.

The doctor had finished talking to them and was moving away, so Luca stepped forward, ignoring the numb figure of Ade, and put his hand out to Pete's daughter.

'I'm Luca,' he said, smiling reassuringly at her. 'I worked – work – for Pete,' he told her. 'I'm so sorry.'

She stared at his hand. 'What are you doing here?' Her eyes flickered at me. 'This is family business.'

'I know,' I intervened. 'But Luca was there when it happened. He – we – wanted to see that Pete's OK.'

'Yes.' She straightened up, and her arm slipped through her husband's in a fortifying gesture. 'I know you were there. And you've got some nerve coming here.'

I caught Ade's eye, thought I saw a brief look of satisfaction in his face, and watched as he moved closer to his sister. The two of them observed us almost petulantly.

'I don't understand,' Luca said. 'I'm distressed for Pete. I wish there was something I could have done.'

'Really?' She sniffed. 'More than you have already, you mean?'

'But Luca had nothing to do with the accident,' I said, trying to keep the anger out of my voice. 'There was nothing anyone could have done.'

'From what my son tells me, your boyfriend is not an ideal employee,' she said coldly. 'In fact, he's got a bit of a temper on him from all accounts—'

'From all accounts!' I spluttered. 'You mean from one account?'

Ade rolled his head just slightly trying to look self-effacing, genuine.

'I never said Luca was capable of killing anybody,' he said calmly. 'It's just . . . well, my first encounter with him was a little hostile. Don't you think?'

'Because you're an asshole,' I blurted, immediately closing my eyes. This was not the place to trade insults. Though it was certainly the time.

'Jane,' Luca calmed me softly. 'Ade's upset. We're all upset.'

'You.' Pete's daughter pointed rudely at him. 'You have no right to be upset!'

'Lydia.' Her husband put his arm around her. 'Just leave it. Don't you want to see your father?'

She opened her mouth, not finished yet. But sense prevailed. 'Yes.' She drew back her shoulders, shaking her husband's arm off her. 'Yes. I want to see my father.'

'Well then.' He nodded at us curtly, and we stepped aside as they walked on, Ade and Polly following as though they were a couple of innocents.

'That was unbelievable,' I breathed as they moved further down the corridor, heading for Pete's room. 'That they could think you had anything to do with Pete's accident.' I stared at him. 'And I can't believe you just stood there and took it.'

Luca looked shocked and paler than ever.

'People say things,' he said quietly. 'When they're upset they just want someone to blame.'

'But it's outrageous. Ade has told her a pack of lies.'

'I don't know. Maybe he does see me as hostile.' Luca looked defeated.

'But he provoked you all night.'

'Yes.' Luca hesitated, before turning to look me in the eyes. 'But the truth is that from the moment I saw him I felt this aggression, this defensiveness. He didn't need to open his mouth. It was already there.'

'Oh.' I stared back at him. 'Well, maybe your senses told you he was a jerk. And you were right.'

'No. It was more than that. It was deeper. It was . . . animal, almost.'

'Animal instinct,' I murmured.

'I don't trust myself around him. What I am capable of . . . Things I don't even realize I am doing.'

'What are you trying to say, Luca? Are you saying you did have something to do with Pete's accident and you just kind of forgot about it until now?'

His eyes were heavy when he answered. 'Honestly . . . I don't know.'

# CHAPTER TWENTY-ONE

'There's post.' Mrs Jonas appeared in the kitchen doorway. 'Mostly junk and bills, but there's one for you, Luca.' She handed him a formal-looking white envelope.

'Thanks.' Luca took it, confused. 'I've never received post before – well, not here anyway.'

She smiled, dumping the rest of the letters on the table and looking up at the clock. 'I have to run, I have some errands to see to. Jack is away all day. Can you make sure you lock up before you go into work?'

'Of course. I am not sure whether I'll be going in to work, anyway,' he told her, the events of the day before – at the hospital – still fresh in his mind.

'I'm sure Pete will need things doing. How was he when you looked in yesterday?'

Luca hesitated. He and Jane had decided not to say anything when they'd got back to the house. The subject had run dry between them. They had been lost in their own thoughts. A little shocked.

'He's fine,' Luca lied to her now, not wanting to get into it. 'I'm going back in again today.' He smiled weakly, frankly not sure what he would find if he did go there. 'He could be home soon.'

'That's great.' Anna picked up her bag and her keys. 'Give him my best when you see him.'

The door slammed behind her and Luca was left alone in the house, the envelope still in his hands. He forced himself to open it.

*Luca*

> *Given the circumstances, we feel it is best that you do not continue to work at Pete's yard. If his condition deteriorates further we will be seeking legal advice on closing down the business and possibly a private sale.*
>
> *In addition, we will be seeking advice on investigation into any part you played in Pete's accident. If the accident proves to be fatal, you realize the consequences for you will be serious.*
>
> *In the meantime, please post your keys through the yard door.*
>
> *I will be in touch in due course.*
>
> *Lydia Ellis (Henshaw)*

Luca felt strangely relieved and heavy-hearted at the same time. He didn't ever have to go back to that place. But he was also being accused of something he would never do. Not if he were in his right mind, anyway.

He looked at the phone, desperately wanting to talk to Jane, but thinking it was better not to drop this news on her when she was at college. It was tricky enough for her there as it was.

Instead he had a long bath, trying to empty his mind, listening to the soothing sounds of the trees rustling and the birds outside. When he dressed afterwards something fell out of the pockets of his jeans as he pulled them on.

It was the small plastic bag, with the necklace still inside it. He crouched, holding it in his hand, and all the good work that the bath had done disappeared.

The necklace. The sounds in the hut. Pete's accident . . . and Ade's intent on proving him guilty somehow. It was all connected. He was sure of that.

But it was Luca's words – his unique sense of danger – against Ade's accusations. It didn't look good for him. The only person who believed in him, who knew he wasn't capable of deliberately and maliciously hurting anyone or anything, was Jane.

Unless Ade worked his sinister magic on her, too.

# CHAPTER TWENTY-TWO

I was determined to keep it together at college. Keep my head down and concentrate on getting on with what I was there for – my coursework. I just hoped Polly would be off, on compassionate leave or whatever. She was the last person I wanted to face.

As soon as I arrived I made a beeline for Ashley and Emma, who were chatting by their lockers.

I poked Emma in the back.

'Hey,' I said. 'Long time no see.'

They both turned around.

'Hey! We thought you'd dropped us,' said Ashley good-naturedly. 'You've been distant lately.' She put her hand on my arm. 'Is everything OK?'

'Of course,' I said brightly. 'And I'm sorry. I kind of got caught up in my own stuff and Mrs Connelly keeps on at me about my mentoring.' I shook my head.

'I think it all got a bit much.'

'No probs.' Ashley closed her locker and ran a hand through her hair. 'But we heard you fainted.' She raised an eyebrow. 'We were worried.'

'Stress, I think.' My tone was dismissive. 'But enough about me. What's been happening with you two? Any gossip to report?'

Ashley and Emma exchanged a secretive look.

'Spill,' I said sternly.

'Ashley's got a boyfriend,' said Polly.

'Really? Who?' My eyes flew from one twin to the other. 'Anyone I know?'

'Well, yeah,' Ashley said coyly. 'It's Ade.'

My mouth hung open for a few seconds, before I recovered. 'But, I thought . . .'

'Yeah. He was a pig that night. But he explained that he gets nervous and it comes over as . . . like . . . just a bit rude. But he doesn't mean to be. And honestly, he's been so amazing. Treating me like a princess.' Ashley's cheeks were flushed with excitement. 'I think I'm in love.' She stopped talking and both girls looked at me expectantly.

'That's great.' I fought to hide my shock. 'I'm glad he's treating you well. So he should.'

Ashley smiled. 'Thanks for hooking us up. I know it didn't seem like such a good idea on our first date. But you know, I'm hoping we can spend time with you and Luca again. Ade really wants to get to know him better.'

'Really?' This time I couldn't stop my eyes narrowing. 'Is that so?'

Ashley stopped fiddling with her hair and crossed her arms over her chest. 'What's that supposed to mean?'

'Well, if Ade wants to be friends with Luca, he's got a funny way of showing it.' I sighed. I really hadn't wanted to think about the odious Ade today, but I wasn't going to let him pull the wool over Ashley's eyes.

'Look.' Ashley glanced quickly at Emma. 'I like Luca and all. But you know he is kind of intense and moody.'

'He's not—' I stopped. Hadn't I heard Dot say exactly the same thing the day before? 'He doesn't mean to be like that. He's just serious. And thoughtful.' I tried to smile at Ashley. 'He's a very good person.'

'If you say so.' Ashley looked at her watch. 'I've got to go.'

'Me too,' Emma said, looking uncomfortable. 'It was nice seeing you, Jane.'

'You too.' I tried to make eye contact with Ashley but she was avoiding it. I pushed my bag higher on my shoulder instead and exhaled. 'Well, let's do something. The three of us. A movie, or—'

'Cool,' said Emma, biting her lip awkwardly.

'Yeah, cool,' Ashley echoed, brushing past me. 'If you can get down off your moral high ground, that is.'

'Ashley!' But she already had her back to me, linking arms with her sister, on her way to her next class.

I watched them walk away for a few seconds, before I moved towards my locker, robotically unlocking it and taking out some books. It felt like everything I thought was right was wrong.

Was Luca wrong too?

I sat through Art barely taking anything in. I couldn't get rid of the heavy feeling in the pit of my stomach. I drifted zombie-like to History, only coming to when my phone rang from my pocket.

'Hey.' It was Luca. 'How are you doing?'

I glanced at the crowd of students squeezing through the door to the classroom and turned away from them, retracing my steps down the corridor. 'You know . . . a little shaken up from yesterday and tired. But I guess I'm OK.'

'You seem weird,' he said, and he sounded anxious. 'Are you freaked out?'

'I'm not freaked out, exactly. It's just so unfair, what Ade said yesterday. And it looks like he's got Ashley in his thrall now too.'

'What do you mean?' Luca's voice sounded tight.

'Well, they're going out.' I sat down on one of the benches that lined the corridor wall. 'He's worked his magic on her somehow.' As I said it I realized how appropriate that word was. Magic. Though good or bad, I didn't know any more.

'That's disappointing,' Luca said mildly. 'Let's hope he messes up and she dumps him.'

'She seems really happy,' I said, frowning at the sight of a familiar figure chatting to somebody at the other end of the corridor. 'I suppose that's a good thing.'

'Listen,' said Luca. 'I have bad news.'

'What?' I tore my eyes away from Polly. 'What's happened?'

'I got a letter this morning from Lydia Ellis. You know, Pete's daughter. A very formal letter telling me that my services were no longer required at Pete's yard.'

'Oh no.' I screwed up my face in sympathy. 'I'm sorry, Luca. That's so unjust.'

'Yes. Though I suppose it makes sense in a way, seeing as Pete's . . . well, that he's not there.' Luca's voice seemed to be getting smaller. 'But that's not the bad news.'

'OK.' I hunched over. 'Well, what is it?'

'If Pete doesn't recover . . . they're going to have me investigated over his accident,' went on Luca. 'They've obviously fallen for Ade's pack of lies.'

'That's ridiculous,' I said, raising my voice. 'They have absolutely no proof!'

'I have a feeling they'll find some,' Luca said dully. 'I wouldn't put it past Ade to rustle that up too.'

'Oh God, Luca. This is awful,' I moaned. 'But you're innocent. I know that, anyone who has any sense knows that.'

There was a few seconds of silence before Luca spoke again.

'I don't know any more, Jane,' he told me quietly. 'I just don't know.'

'Listen. I'm going to bunk class and come home,' I told him. 'I'll be there as soon as I can.'

'I don't want you to miss school because of this,' he said firmly. 'Honestly. I'll be fine. One of us should carry on as normal. I'll see you later.'

'Are you sure?'

'Absolutely,' he said. 'And, Jane, we'll get this sorted out. One way or another we will.'

'I know.' I sounded a lot more convinced than I felt. 'Well, I'll see you later then.'

As I ended the call, I saw biker boots rooted in place in front of me, and long legs encased in dark-grey leggings that led to a leather micro-mini skirt.

I forced myself to look at Polly and saw the familiar

supercilious expression on her face.

'Trouble in paradise?' she asked sweetly, swinging her bag girlishly.

'No,' I shrugged, getting up. 'I'm late for my class, excuse me.'

'What's the matter, Jane? Are you wondering if you can trust your boyfriend?' She opened her eyes wide and innocent. 'Isn't it awful when people you thought you could count on turn out to be so untrustworthy?'

'Well, you're in a better position to judge that than me,' I told her. 'I mean, you trusted your real parents, didn't you, and look what happened to them.' It was a nasty thing to say, but I felt no guilt, not even when I saw Polly's face darken.

'You have no idea what you're talking about,' she spat in a low voice.

'That's true. But something made you like this.' I shook my head. 'This malicious. What has Luca ever done to you and your brother?'

Polly's face brightened alarmingly. 'I feel sorry for you,' she whispered. 'You're in way over your head.' She smiled nastily. 'If you really want to know the truth, then ask your boyfriend.' She stepped aside and I moved past her; my whole body was shaking and that familiar foggy feeling was coming down over my senses.

'Just ask yourself who it really is you're involved with.' Then she added, 'When you think about it, you have no idea what Luca is capable of, do you?'

'I know enough.' I stopped, gripping my bag handle too tightly, as though I were trying to hold on to it and not be swept away. 'And he is good and strong – and he doesn't bear grudges.'

'Uh-huh. I think you're finally getting somewhere.' Her tone was so annoying it was all I could do to force myself to walk on. 'If you try really, really hard, your poor mortal brain will figure it all out – eventually.'

Mortal brain.

I froze for seconds, my back to her. But when I turned, she had vanished as though she had never been there. Confused, I looked around me, and there she was in the distance, pushing through the door at the end of the corridor, just like any other student.

Luca is right. I thought shakily. His instincts were right all along.

# CHAPTER TWENTY-THREE

*Am I dead or alive?* she thought, lifting her hand and pressing it to her chest, feeling the faint beat of her heart. Her mouth was so dry she could hardly feel it, and her skin was covered in a cold, clammy sweat.

She thought someone would come for her. She really thought she would be missed. But maybe this was all her fault. Her fault for coming back, for trying to find them.

Weirdly, her hearing was sharper. The sound of her watch ticking seemed deafening and a drip coming from somewhere further back in the cave was so loud.

She remembered reading that you begin to hallucinate when your body becomes too starved, so when she heard the scratching sound above her head, she didn't react for a minute or two. It would stop in a minute. It was just a dream, or an imagining.

But the scratching sound persisted and then there was

something else, a quick panting sound, like a dog digging for a bone.

An animal. An animal was up there.

What little strength she had forced her up; she put her foot on a large stone and balanced on it, placing her palm on the roof of the cave, seeing that thin crack of light and then the nose, the snout of an animal. A dog?

'Hey,' she called, coaxing. 'Hey, boy . . .'

To her relief the dog started to whimper, sticking its nose as far as possible into the crack. She saw a large, kind brown eye.

She felt tears streaming down her cheeks. She tried to scream, but nothing was coming from her throat.

'Ralph!' came a man's voice from a distance. 'C'mon, boy. C'mon.'

'No . . .' she moaned hoarsely. 'Please, don't go . . .'

But the nose had disappeared. Along with it the kind brown eye.

And her last hope.

# CHAPTER TWENTY-FOUR

I hurried out of school in the pouring rain, my hair already sticking to my face and the back of my neck. I barely cared. I just wanted to get back home. Back to people who were on my side. I hadn't taken in a word anybody had said after my exchange with Polly in the corridor. My few classes had been a blur. The teachers were beginning to notice.

'Everything OK, Miss Jonas?' asked Mr Burns, my new Art teacher, when the lesson was over. 'You seem a little off colour today.' He scratched his beard cluelessly, obviously not wanting to delve too deep in case I started talking about embarrassing 'women's stuff'.

Right then, I really missed Soren Balzac, who had faked the Art teacher role the year before. Mischievous he might have been, but at least I could talk to him. And he had known, as much as Luca, what darkness lurks in every corner.

'I'm fine,' I told Mr Burns. 'I just have to pick up my little sister. I need to run.'

'Fine . . . fine . . . Just checking,' he said relieved, already turning his attention to another pupil. Part of me wanted to turn back to him and scream that everything was not all right, that I didn't understand my life, and I was scared.

I felt really scared.

Outside, I automatically turned in the direction of the bike sheds, where I had locked up my bike, but stopped. It was too wet and I wasn't in a fit state to ride home tonight. I'd need to call my dad . . . or Luca.

I fished my phone out of my pocket and pressed the button to make it come to life, but the screen remained black. The battery was dead.

'Great, just great,' I muttered, as the rain came down heavier. I would just have to get the bus.

But when I arrived at bus stop, just down the road from the school, a sign told me that the service had been cancelled for the rest of the day.

Again, I wanted to scream. Instead, I stood rooted to the spot.

Other students were leaving, walking past me, chatting and laughing. A couple of boys were kicking a football to each other. It was like I was invisible; nobody seemed to see me.

Somewhere in my bag I found a hat, not waterproof, but it might stop me from getting pneumonia. I put it on and pulled my jacket around me tightly, as my eye caught Ashley's pink Mini, driving slowly through the rain in my direction.

I turned away. After our conversation this morning, I couldn't imagine Ashley would be feeling charitable. Better to pretend I hadn't seen her.

But the car horn beeped and I heard the engine stop.

'Jane, get in.' It wasn't Ashley's voice. Of course. It was her new boyfriend. I squeezed my eyes shut, but I would have had to be deaf not to have heard him or the horn, so I turned slowly, summoning as easy-going an expression as possible.

'You're going to catch your death in this rain.' He leaned out of the car window and, next to him, I saw the figure of Ashley, her face tilted towards me too.

'Get in, babe,' she said, and the kindness in her tone would have made me want to cry, even if I didn't feel like it already.

'It's OK . . . I'm . . .' I hesitated, pathetically hunting for a reason why I was standing soaking wet by a defunct bus stop. 'It'll stop raining soon . . . I'll be fine.'

The car door opened and Ade got out. His own hair was a little damp and curling slightly. He smiled and it lit up his face. He looked genuinely concerned.

'Hey. Don't be silly,' he said softly, taking off his jacket and, before I could protest, wrapping it around me. 'We're not going to let you stand here – and you can hardly cycle home in this weather.' He rubbed at my arm in a fraternal gesture. I should have flinched, or glared at him at the very least, but his jacket was so warm, and I felt so tired . . .

'Don't let a misunderstanding break up your friendship,' he said quietly. 'I would never want to come between you and Ashley. She feels the same way.'

I glanced past him at Ashley, who did indeed look a little mournful in the passenger seat. Catching my eye, she smiled tentatively. I smiled back.

'OK. Thanks, that's kind of you.' I opened the back door and got in beside Emma, who grinned good-naturedly.

Ade started the engine and pulled away from the kerb; through the rear-view mirror I caught his eyes staring at me and found myself unable to look away. Instead of the mean, narrowed look I expected, they seemed to glisten slightly. Soft and empathetic.

Ashley leaned forward in the front seat and turned off the radio before turning back to me.

'I'm sorry,' she said. 'About earlier. I know you're upset right now. What with Luca losing his job.'

I tensed. 'How do you know about that?' I tried not to snap. I didn't want to start another argument.

'I told her.' Ade's voice was steady. 'Lydia's taking it really badly about Pete.' He changed gear, clearing his throat. 'She's taken it out on Luca. I told her to rethink it. Honestly. I never meant for that to happen. But it's her illness. You know, the depression. She took one comment from me and made it more significant.'

'That's not exactly what you were saying at the hospital,' I couldn't help myself retort. 'You seemed to be encouraging her to think that Luca is some kind of thug.'

'No.' Ade turned on to the main road back to Bale. 'I was upset too. I'm sorry. I really regret that now.'

'Right.' I tucked my hands between my legs. 'Well, it's too late now.'

'I'm going to talk to her tonight,' he said. 'Make her see that she's totally overreacting.'

I shrugged. 'Whatever.' I stared out of the window at the still foul weather. 'How is Pete?'

Ade's shoulders slumped, dejectedly. 'He's not better, I'm afraid.'

'Oh. I'm sorry.' I sighed. 'I'm so sorry about Pete. We both are.'

'I know.' Ade sounded genuinely convinced. 'You've got a good heart.'

'She has,' Ashley cut in. She nudged him with her arm. 'She brought us together, after all.'

'Yeah.' Ade half laughed, but I could still see his eyes in the rear-view mirror and, though he wasn't looking at me any longer, I had a perfect view. His eyes were dull again.

After what seemed like a lifetime, the pink Mini pulled up at the edge of the track to our house. I pulled down gratefully on the door handle. I couldn't wait to get out of the damp claustrophobic atmosphere.

'Thanks,' I said, one leg out of the car. 'Give my best to Pete.'

'And give my best to Luca,' Ade replied. 'Tell him I'm sorry.'

I nodded, waved at the twins and slammed the door shut. I didn't wait to see them drive off; I wanted to absorb the conversation I'd just had. And prepare what I was going to say to Luca when I got in.

He was still the only one home, lying on the sofa in the living room and watching TV.

I stood in the doorway, smiling at him, his long lean body stretched out, watching some God-awful soap. And then I sneezed.

Luca turned, smiling, pleased to see me. 'You're

soaked,' he said, getting up and coming towards me. 'You should have called. I would have come to collect you.' His eyes ran over my saturated clothing. 'You look like you found a few layers to wear, anyway,' he said. He helped me take Ade's jacket off and frowned.

'What's this?' he said, holding it up.

I felt a stab of annoyance. 'Damn,' I muttered. 'I forgot to return it.' I took a breath and looked up at Luca. 'Ade and Ashley gave me a lift home. And Ade lent me his jacket.'

Luca's face went from smiling to hostile. 'Ade gave you a lift home?' he said icily.

'Yeah.' I shook my head, flustered and unwilling to explain myself. 'It was bucketing. I couldn't ride my bike. And my phone was dead.' I looked defiantly into his hurt green eyes. 'What else was I supposed to do?'

'After what he said?' I had never seen Luca look so hostile – not at me, at any rate. He dropped the jacket and moved back to the TV, tensely pacing around it.

'Luca, don't be silly.' I tried smiling. 'I haven't suddenly gone all Team Ade, if that's what you're thinking . . . I mean, I could hardly say no.'

'You could have said no.' Luca's tone was like granite. 'Easily.'

'It was pelting with rain, my phone was dead, and the

buses were cancelled!' I threw up my hands, exasperated. 'What did you expect me to do – walk home?'

'Of course not.' He rubbed angrily at his hair, making it stand up in comical dark tufts. If this were any other time I would have laughed.

'Look,' I said more calmly, 'I know you may not believe this, but Ade seemed genuinely contrite. He said that Lydia is stressed and ill and throwing out accusations left, right and centre. She took what he said to an extreme.'

'What he said,' Luca echoed me slowly. 'That's just it. We have no idea what he said. And of course he would want to appear contrite – it makes it so much easier to get you on side.'

'On side?' I crossed my arms, getting riled again. 'Why on earth would I be on his side?' I crossed over to Luca, seeing up close how he was shaking again. 'You're my boyfriend. I will always be on your side.'

He stared at me for seconds, before dropping his head, looking down at the carpet. 'You don't understand, do you? This is exactly how they play it.'

'They?' I sighed. 'You mean the Vulpecula?'

Luca lifted his head at the doubt in my voice. 'I wouldn't expect you to grasp this. You don't know what they tried to do to my family.'

'Yes . . . But are you sure that Ade is . . . that he and

Polly are members of this species?' I bit my lip. 'I mean, I thought so too – yesterday and today. And Polly was stirring up a load of trouble earlier. But maybe that's just because she's an angry teenager who got dumped by her parents as a baby.' I paused, lowering my voice to something softer. 'I mean, it is unlikely, isn't it?'

Luca shut his eyes wearily. 'I don't want to fight,' he said quietly. 'The last person I want to fight with is you.'

'Then let's not fight.' I finally shed my own jacket and felt my wet hair. 'All I want to do is take a shower and do something very boring – like watch TV.'

'Great,' Luca muttered, 'because I haven't been watching TV all day.'

I smiled; he was like an adorable petulant little boy, and if I hadn't been wet through I would have hugged him, taken away all his worries.

'Ah, but you haven't been watching it with me,' I said, trying to catch his eye, 'have you?'

A flicker of a smile.

'I know Ade's a jerk,' I told him. 'Believe me, I would never willingly get a lift from him. I think he and his sister are bad news. But maybe that's all . . . Maybe they're just a couple of damaged kids?'

'It's possible,' Luca said reluctantly. 'I suppose.'

I was at the door when I turned back to him. 'Oh and

he's going to try and get you your job back. He's going to talk to Lydia. You see? Everything's going to be OK.'

Luca looked startled. 'He's what?'

'He's going to put things right.' I paused. 'Maybe he isn't so bad after all.'

'Jane!' Mum's voice came from the kitchen. 'Phone.'

I frowned. Beside me Luca stirred slightly from his semi-coma in front of the television. The comedy drama about a bunch of nerdy science boys analysing the battle of the sexes had been pretty stupefying. I sat forward.

'Who is it?'

There was a second or two of silence, then, 'It's Polly Ellis – a friend of yours from college?'

I frowned harder. 'Oh. Tell her I'm asleep or something.'

Mum appeared in the doorway. 'That's rude, sweetheart. She knows I'm talking to you.' She had her hand over the receiver and was giving me a censorious look.

I held out my hand for the phone. 'OK,' I sighed. 'Thanks, Mum.'

'Hey.' Polly's voice was unnaturally chirpy. 'Just calling to see how you're doing.'

'Erm . . .' I shifted, glancing at Luca who was now most definitely asleep next to me. 'Why?'

'Well, I think I might have come across a little strong this afternoon,' she went on. 'You know, a little aggressive.'

'A little.' I shook my head; strangely the events of the afternoon had evaporated into a haze. 'But maybe I was a little hostile, too.'

'Yeah,' she cooed. 'You have a lot on your mind right now. I feel bad that I made everything worse.'

I screwed up my nose, trying to remember exactly what we'd said to each other, but for the life of me, all I could remember was a spat. Like two cats arching their backs or something.

'Forget it,' I said. 'It doesn't matter.'

'It does. And I know Ade feels terrible too.'

'Yeah, well. Let's just put it behind us,' I told her. 'I get that the two of you are trying to make amends.'

'Oh good.' She sounded relieved. 'Because I know it means a lot to him that you think well of him. He really likes you.'

'Yeah.' I moved up and off the sofa, away from Luca. 'Well, I appreciate it.'

'Do you?' she said, more sharply. 'Because it is really important that you know how he feels.'

I fell silent, a whooshing sound in my head. Exhaustion, no doubt.

'Jane? You do know how he feels, don't you?'

'I . . . Uh . . .' I blinked and my eyelashes felt like lead. 'Yeah, I know . . .'

'So . . . that's great.' Polly took an audible intake of breath, like she was smoking a joint, or trying to sound like she was. 'Shall we start over, build a bridge?'

'Of course.' I checked back on Luca, whose head had dropped in sleep. 'I'll see you at college. Bye, Polly.'

It wasn't until I drifted off to sleep that night that her words came back to me: 'You do know how he feels, don't you?' And the ambiguity that was so obvious now made me sit bolt upright, sending Bobby skittering off the bed in fright. He set about a low moan from his new position on the floor.

'Sorry,' I whispered, not wanting to wake Luca. Bobby eyed me suspiciously. Holding my hand out to stroke his ear reassuringly, I got out of bed as quietly as possible and padded over to the window. I looked out at the calm of the night. The moon was almost full. Tomorrow Luca would disappear. The timing was bad. I didn't know what I thought from one moment to the next. Ade and Polly were bad news . . . then they were just a couple of messed-up kids. But Luca wasn't fuzzy about anything. I knew that.

I pushed some clothes off the chair by the window to

sit down and they fell into a heap, something rolling out of a pocket. Sighing, I bent to pick up a pair of jeans – Luca's – and groped for whatever it was: some coins and a small plastic package. For a second, the contents gleamed in the moonlight and I recognized the necklace Luca had shown me what seemed like weeks before. Dirty but still just gold. I shuddered. We never did find out what the deal was with the necklace. But it seemed like Luca had been carrying it around with him.

Still holding the bag, I sat back on the chair, tucking my legs underneath me. I let the chain slither out on to my palm and saw how delicate it was. It looked valuable too. Proper gold. How had it come to be lying in that stinking hut, miles from anywhere? What girl in their right mind would take a walk around the old training ground?

I put it back in its bag, picked up Luca's jeans and shoved it in the pocket. I carefully laid the jeans over the chair and leaned back, shivering slightly in the cool of the bedroom.

Nothing really made sense at the moment. Looking over at the sleeping boy in my bed, I realized that something had already come between Luca and me, something that neither of us could explain. Not yet, anyway.

Could that be the most dangerous threat of all?

# CHAPTER TWENTY-FIVE

When he opened the door to see her standing there, his heart sank. Had she come to haul him over the coals again? Luca steeled himself, but Lydia's expression wasn't hostile. It was awkward, but not unfriendly.

'Is your . . . is Mrs Jonas in?' she asked in a quiet voice.

'Uh . . . No. Sorry – just me.' Luca realized he still had his hand on the door and Lydia Ellis was still on the doorstep. He let go. 'But if you want to come in and wait, Anna's only gone to the shops . . .'

'Thank you, but . . .' She hesitated. 'It was you I came to see.'

'Oh.' He pushed the door wider open. 'OK . . .'

Lydia Ellis stepped through into the hall, looking around. 'What a nice home,' she said, a little wistfully. 'Cozy.'

'Yes. Yes, it is.' Luca smiled warily. 'Come through

to the kitchen. I can make some tea.'

'I won't stop long. But that would be nice.' She looked at him then and appeared to relax slightly.

In the kitchen, she sat at the table while Luca waited for the kettle to boil. He wasn't great at making tea – well, not the kind of pitch-strong tea that mortals drank. He added another teabag to the two already in the pot, to be on the safe side.

Lydia cleared her throat behind him, and turning slightly, he saw her stroking Bobby's ears. 'Beautiful boy,' she murmured gently. Watching, Luca felt such a wave of sadness coming from her, he felt humbled. The poor woman's father was at death's door. He didn't blame her for hating him.

He carried two mugs of tea over and sat down opposite her.

'I'm not much good at making tea.' He pushed hers towards her, along with the sugar bowl. 'I won't be offended if it's not to your taste.'

'I'm sure it's fine.' She took a sip and her eyes tilted up towards his, a spark of warmth, reassurance there. 'Perfect,' she said, setting the mug down again. He noticed how drawn she looked and the faint tremor in her hands.

'I have talked to Adrian,' she began. 'And he feels . . . he has made me see that I have been too quick to judge you – to rob you of your job.' She stopped, sighing. 'Though what will become of the business heaven knows.'

'How is Pete?' Luca said quickly. 'Is he any better?'

Lydia shook her head. 'No. He is barely there.' She swallowed and for one tense moment Luca thought she would burst into tears. But she recovered herself, straightening in her chair and meeting his eye.

'He's been such a good father,' she said then, shakily. 'So patient and kind. God knows he has had to put up with a lot the last few years. I think I took him for granted.'

'I'm sure not,' Luca said carefully. 'He has always spoken so fondly of his family. You mean so much to him – all of you.'

'Yes . . . yes . . . He dotes on those children, of course.' Lydia sniffed. 'A little too much perhaps.'

Luca was silent, interested.

'We tried for so long to have our own.' Lydia was talking into space, her gaze had moved away from Luca. She stared out of the kitchen window. 'Because of what had happened with Eva—'

'Eva?' Luca asked.

'Yes – my sister. She had a baby when she was a teenager. So young . . .' Lydia's voice was barely louder than a whisper now, as though telling him this was somehow forbidden, as though someone was listening who shouldn't be. 'The child was adopted. Eva went away, and then she came back and everything had been done. All the arrangements had been made. She was sweet, innocent Eva again.'

'I'm sorry,' Luca said. 'I didn't know.'

Lydia twitched. She seemed to be having some kind of internal struggle, looking for a moment flustered, almost cross.

'I'm not sure why I am telling you this . . .' Her tone was abrupt. 'I hardly know you.'

'Perhaps you need a stranger to talk to?' he suggested. 'Someone unconnected to your life. But someone who knows Pete?'

She brightened then, looking more relaxed. 'Yes. It is a relief. Things at home are always so intense. Ever since the children came into our lives . . . It has been difficult to think straight.' She frowned. 'I don't know why.'

Luca had a pretty good idea why. Ade and Polly had forceful personalities, to say the least. And Lydia did seem a timid kind.

'We wanted to adopt Eva's baby, my husband and I,' Lydia went on. 'We begged her to let us. But it was too late.'

'How long ago was this?' Luca sat forward.

'Oh, a long time. I forget how long . . .' she said

vaguely. 'The child, wherever she is, will be around fifteen now.' Lydia looked down at her mug. 'The strange thing is, last time I saw Eva she said she was certain that the child had tried to contact her. She had been receiving phone calls at odd times and, when she answered, the caller hung up. Probably wishful thinking.' She looked up. 'I think Eva regrets what happened. She's completely estranged from us now. Punishing my parents for what they did – making her give up the child. That child was her only chance.'

'I don't understand,' Luca said gently, not wanting to discourage her from talking more. 'What do you mean "her only chance"?'

'Well, she can't have any more children.' Lydia shrugged. 'Like me . . . We are cursed, the two of us.'

'I'm sorry,' Luca said uncomfortably. 'But you have Ade and Polly.'

'Yes. Oh yes . . .' She brightened just a touch. 'And I am so grateful to be a mother. Though it hasn't been easy. They run rings around me, I'm afraid.'

Luca smiled wryly. *Not just you*, he thought, *they run rings around everybody*.

'And they have always been odd with Eva,' Lydia went on absently. 'I don't know why. My husband says they are just very protective of me. But I don't know, sometimes,

184

they can be so . . . wild.'

'Wild.' Luca swallowed. He pushed his mug carefully away from him.

'Yes, when they were very young we had a real struggle. They wouldn't talk to us, only ever wanted to be together. One seemed to know instinctively where the other was – or how they were feeling.'

'Well, they say that happens with brother and sister. Twins are often in sync like that, aren't they?' Luca was careful to say all the right things. What good would it do to alarm Lydia? The poor woman looked frightened enough as it was.

'They're not twins,' she snapped, irritated. 'Why does everyone always think that?'

'I'm sorry,' Luca said. 'I didn't mean to—'

'I must go,' she said abruptly, getting to her feet. 'I only really came to tell you that you could keep your job. And I'm sorry for how I was at the hospital. I get a little muddled sometimes.' She stopped, as though regretting speaking, and picked up her bag.

'I'll get your coat,' said Luca.

When he returned with it, he found her dabbing at her eyes with a tissue. 'Mrs Ellis? Are you all right?'

'Yes . . . yes.' She smiled, though it was through teary eyes. 'I feel so up and down . . . And here, I have been telling a stranger more than I should . . .' She took her coat from him and hurriedly put it on, seeming anxious.

'I will look after the yard,' he told her. 'For Pete. I will make sure the business keeps running.'

'Thank you, dear. You're a good boy when you make the effort.' As Luca stared back at her, confused, he saw a strange faded look in her eyes. She looked as though she wasn't quite present. Had she thought he was Ade? He felt all of a sudden very sad for this woman – and worried. She seemed to be under some kind of spell.

As he shut the door behind her, he leaned back on it for a few minutes, trying to take in what had happened and what she had said. And then he felt his skin start to prickle and his heart pump faster and he closed his eyes. It was the time of the full moon again. Just when he needed peace and time to think. Usually he was much more prepared than this. But with everything that had happened he was caught out.

A sharp pain in his chest made him wince and he looked down; the veins in his arms were beginning to protrude. He was glad he was only wearing a flimsy T-shirt.

'Ahh,' he hissed, closing his eyes and taking deep breaths. He glanced at the stairs, only taking a moment to think before he launched himself at them, taking two at a time, a fleeting thought of the near-disaster that had been averted.

If Lydia had left any later than she did, then she would have seen him turning. And any trust in him would have evaporated for sure. He needed to get outside and let nature take over his body. The curse that would never leave him – wherever he was.

# CHAPTER TWENTY-SIX

'So.' Ashley dumped her patent leather bag on the canteen table and sat down happily in front of me.

'So?' I raised an eyebrow, halfway through a bowl of lukewarm apple crumble.

'We're friends again.' Ashley smoothed her hair. 'After last night . . .'

'Yes.' I abandoned the crumble. 'Of course, we're friends. I'm sorry if I—'

'No. Ade explained to me – you know, about why you might be a bit anti him right now. He told me about what happened at the hospital.'

'Oh.' I pursed my lips. 'What did he say?'

'Just that everyone was a bit upset, and he was really worried about his grandfather, and he kind of pinned the blame for his accident on Luca.' She sighed. 'And he knows that was unfair, and he didn't mean for Luca to lose his job, and . . .' She paused. 'He just really wants us all to be friends.'

'Right.' I shrugged. 'Well . . . yeah, sure.'

'And,' she leaned forward, 'he really wants us to include Polly when we go out. She's kind of lonely and I think she feels a bit left out of things.'

'Right.' I couldn't help my nostrils flare slightly.

'I mean, it would be nice for us to be a gang, don't you think? Like in *Friends* or something. Hanging out together.'

For the life of me, I couldn't imagine it.

'OK,' I said, a little inadequately. I looked down at the bowl of cold crumble.

'I know she's weird and, well, I find her intimidating if I'm being honest. But I'm trying to be grown up, you know. Make an effort.' She stopped, a timid smile on her face. 'I want Ade to be happy.'

'Well, I want you to be happy,' I told her. 'And if that means getting on with Ade and Polly then I guess I can do that.'

'And Luca?' she asked quietly.

'I guess—'

'You talking about me?' Polly appeared next to me, dressed entirely in black, her dark-red hair spiralling down her back. She wore a single black flower clipped next to her ear and heavy eye make-up, making the colour of her eyes more vivid than ever.

'Wow,' said Ashley. 'You look amazing. I love that kind of neo-punk Goth thing.'

'Thanks.' Polly's eyes slid to me. 'I thought I'd dress up – to mark a new start.'

'A new start?' I asked lightly, unable to take my eyes off her.

'Yes.' She looked at Ashley and then back at me. 'For all of us. I think we kind of got off on the wrong foot.' She dropped her head slightly, a humble gesture, totally out of character.

But I had had enough of making enemies. I didn't need the aggravation – and nor did Luca. Being friends with Ade and Polly was a win-win situation.

'Well, I think that's a great idea,' I said after a pause. I caught Ashley's expression – she looked delighted.

'I think we should celebrate with a night out,' Polly said, touching the flower in her hair, adjusting it slightly. 'There's this great new club that's opened a little way out of Bale. It's where all the "cool" kids are hanging out these days, apparently.' Her eyes gleamed.

'Sounds great,' I said, trying to keep the sarcasm out of my voice. It wouldn't hurt to make an effort. I looked Polly up and down. 'Is there a dress code?'

Polly cocked her head to one side thoughtfully. 'I bet

you could look pretty hot if you tried,' she said. 'You know, if you wore something other than jeans and a sweatshirt. I bet you'd look stunning.'

I shrugged. 'I'm not really into all that girly stuff,' I said. 'It's not me . . .'

'Yeah.' Polly half yawned as she spoke. 'I get you like the understated look and all that. But sometimes it's good to shake things up a little. Show another side of yourself . . .'

I remembered standing in Vanya's clothes closet in Nissilum, staring at myself, a stranger in the mirror. It seemed so long ago.

'I have so many clothes you could borrow,' cut in Ashley, excited. 'Emma and I could totally make you over.'

Polly smiled tightly at her. 'In pink?' She rubbed at her arm patronizingly. 'No. Leave it to me.' She widened her eyes at me. 'Why don't I come over to your place tomorrow night with some clothes. I think we're about the same size . . .'

'Oh no, that's not necessary,' I said quickly, uneasy at the prospect of Polly in my house.

'I insist,' she said good-naturedly. She grabbed my arm excitedly. 'I want to meet that boy of yours too. If we're all going to be friends for real, I think we should all get to know each other better, don't you?' She trapped my eyes with hers, making it impossible for me to do anything other than open my mouth, speechless.

'I wish I could come,' said Ashley. 'I've never been inside your house, either. I'd love to meet your family. But it's my dad's birthday and we're having a special dinner.'

'Oh well, never mind,' said Polly dismissively. 'You can meet them another time.'

I caught Ashley's disgruntled expression and tried to signal my helplessness through eye contact.

'Fine,' I told Polly eventually, defeated. 'Come over after college tomorrow. But don't bring anything too outrageous – or revealing. It's not my style.'

'Trust me,' she said solemnly. 'I know exactly what you should wear.' She sighed happily. 'I've got to run. Stuff to do. I'll sort out when club night is . . . It's going to be amazing.'

Ashley turned to me once Polly had disappeared. 'She's a little overwhelming, isn't she? I see what you mean.'

'I know,' I groaned. 'And I'm regretting this already.'

'At least she's trying,' Ashley said. 'I just want us all to get along.'

I smiled at her, though inside I felt I had just been ambushed again. Polly and her brother had this way of removing your free will just by looking at you. Some people were like that, I knew. But I couldn't shake the feeling that Ade and Polly Ellis were more than just a couple of strong personalities.

'She's amazing,' gushed Dot, watching Polly. 'She's like Emily the Strange, but with red hair.'

'Polly the Strange,' I said, shaking my head. That was putting it mildly.

'When I grow up I want to look like that,' Dot continued, gazing at Polly's outfit: a black net tutu, a striped black-and-yellow jumper, and purple suede creepers. Her legs were bare and pale and covered in fine freckles. On her head she had wrapped her hair in a black cotton turban-type thing, with a few red tendrils escaping. She should have looked terrible, but she looked amazing.

A footstep on the stairs behind us made me swivel to find Luca, rubbing sleep out of his eyes.

'What's the commotion?' he asked blearily.

'Are you OK?' I frowned.

'I'm just tired. I think I overdid it yesterday. He gave me a meaningful look and I remembered he had turned the day before. It always left him drained and fatigued for a day or two. I took his hand and linked my fingers through his. 'Maybe you should sit this experience out,' I whispered. 'It won't be pretty.' I turned back to where

Polly was still talking to my parents.

'Who is that?' Luca said, craning to see.

'Polly,' hissed Dot, still enthralled. 'Isn't she fabulous?'

Luca and I exchanged a look.

'*That's* Ade's sister?' he said. 'She looks like a cartoon character.' He noted my raised eyebrow and added, 'I've been watching quite a few cartoons lately.'

Dot giggled. 'She's like a gorgeous bumblebee.'

'Dot's smitten,' I said dryly. 'Looks like Polly has another person under her spell.'

Polly broke off her conversation with my mother and realized we were all perched on the stairs, observing her. She waved and grabbed the handles of a large laundry bag at her feet.

'I've got enough for all three of you,' she said, approaching us. Her eyes were trained on Luca. 'You must be the famous Luca?' She dropped the bag next to me and held out her hand. 'I'm Polly Ellis. I can only imagine what Jane's been telling you about me. But pleased to meet you, I'm sure.'

Luca took her hand awkwardly. 'Ade's sister,' he said, nodding. 'I've heard a little about you, yes.'

'Hmm.' Polly's eyes remained on him for a couple of seconds, before she transferred her gaze to Dot. 'And who is this adorable little girl?'

Dot squirmed, delighted. 'I'm nearly twelve years old actually,' she said. 'My name is Dorothy, but everyone calls me Dot.'

'You're so cute.' Polly ruffled her hair. 'You're nothing like your sister.' She flared her nostrils mischievously. 'Not that Jane isn't cute, of course.' She looked down at her bag, then back at me. 'Shall we get started?'

'Polly's giving Jane a makeover,' Dot explained to a confused-looking Luca.

'Why?' He frowned, tugging at my arm as Polly's bare legs were already ascending the stairs. 'Don't let her push you around,' he whispered. 'I don't want some kind of cartoon creation as my girlfriend.'

'Don't worry,' I told him. 'I'm just trying to be friendly. You know, humour her . . . I think it's better that we at least make a show of getting on with the Ellises, don't you?'

Luca hesitated, though he still didn't look happy. 'I suppose so,' he said reluctantly.

'Hey,' Polly called down from the top of the stairs. 'Which one is your bedroom, Jane?'

'I'm not sure,' I said, staring at myself in my mother's full-length bedroom mirror. 'It's a little fitted for me.'

'You look like a nineteen-fifties film star,' said Polly,

lifting my hair up at the front and backcombing it. 'Like Ava Gardner or someone like that.' Still holding my hair, she stepped to the side to look at my reflection. 'You've got better boobs than me; I don't fill out this dress nearly so well. She smoothed the stiff cotton down to my waist, where the dress moulded to my body. The skirt was full and swirly and stopped at the knee. The neck was a loose boat-style and the sleeves were shortish, showing my arms. Though it was grey, it had a sheen to it and I could see it brought out my eyes.

Polly turned back to my hair, pinning it up in a kind of roll on top of my head. She smoothed out the rest of it so that it hung in loose curls over my bare shoulders.

I looked down at my feet. 'I don't have any shoes that will go with this.'

Polly rummaged around in her laundry bag, drawing out a pair of shoes identical to her own. Teddy-boy creepers, dark grey with black piping.

'These with ankle socks,' she commanded. 'Stops you looking twenty years older than you are. I call it film star rockabilly. Glamour with a bit of edge.'

Not at all sure, I sat down on my mother's bed and put on the shoes. They fitted perfectly. How had she known my size was the same as hers? I wondered. Once the shoes were on, I stood and looked at myself again.

'Actually, it is kind of cool,' I admitted. 'Sort of girly, but a bit tomboyish, too, with the shoes.'

'See.' Polly plumped herself down on the bed. 'Aren't you glad you humoured me now?'

I turned sharply. Had she heard what I'd said to Luca on the stairs? How could she have? We'd been whispering . . .

But Polly's smile was not malicious. She collapsed back flamboyantly on my mother's quilt and stretched out her arms. 'He's hot,' she said then, a propos of nothing.

'Who's hot?' I said, touching the hairsprayed quiff on top of my head. It was stiff and weird to the touch.

'Luca.' Polly sat back up. 'I can see what all the fuss is about. And why you're so loyal.'

'I'm not loyal because he's hot,' I said frowning. 'I'm loyal because he's . . . well, he's Luca.'

'Sweet,' Polly said wryly. She looked at her nails. 'Have you two done it yet?'

'No.' I sat down next to her. 'Though we sleep in the same bed together.'

'Interesting,' said Polly, smirking. 'And slightly odd.'

'It's my parents' house,' I said. 'And my little sister lives here too. No way am I doing it under this roof.'

'That must be rather frustrating – for both of you.'

It was frustrating. And I had been thinking more about

it just lately. I didn't want to make it into some big deal between the two of us, but I didn't want to be one of those couples who were more like brother and sister. The longer time went on without us even attempting to lose our virginities, the more awkward it would be.

I sighed. 'We'll do it when the time is right, I guess.'

'Maybe Luca already has,' Polly offered in an innocent tone.

'No. No, he . . . hasn't.' But as I spoke, I realized I had no idea. Luca and I had never talked about it.

'Jane . . .' Polly's face was just centimetres from mine. 'What are you thinking about?'

'Nothing,' I replied, fixated by her weird-looking pupils. Dark and like pinpoints.

She smiled and all I could see was the curve of her pink lips.

'So, aren't you worried that he might start . . .' She sighed, a perfect intake of breath. 'You know, that he might get impatient?'

'Luca's not like that,' I said slowly. 'He's deeper than that.'

'Ooh. Deeper.' Polly started to giggle, until she caught sight of my expression. 'I mean, that's lovely. Special.' She stared hard at me. 'So Luca's special.'

'Yes.' I said, the fog descending. 'He's not like other boys.'

Polly didn't take her eyes off me as she reached up and retouched the cotton bandana thing on her head. I followed the movement of her hands.

'I know that,' she said, and her eyes seemed to sparkle, as though they were made of magic dust. 'I've always known.'

'What . . . ?' I began, desperately trying to regain some kind of sense.

But the door had opened. We both looked up to see Luca standing there.

'Hey,' I said immediately getting up off the bed as if I was guilty. Though of what, I didn't know.

'You look great,' he said carefully, his eyes travelling up and down me. 'Transformed.'

'Doesn't she?' Polly swung her legs over the end of the bed. 'I knew she would.'

I felt naked all of a sudden. Exposed and uncomfortable.

'I'm going to get changed now,' I said, noticing how Luca switched his eyes over to Polly. In a second, I saw something I didn't want to see. Fear shot through me.

'I should get going.' Polly stretched, her arms long and languorous. She eased herself up, and stood, her bare legs making her look a little like a Titian A pink princess.

'I'll leave you to get an early night,' she said, as she loaded a heap of clothes, combs and make-up into her bag. She straightened up and smiled at Luca. 'I think you're expected at Grandpa Pete's place tomorrow. My mum wants things straightened out.'

Luca looked startled. 'Tomorrow? Sure . . .' And then his face lit up, in a way I hadn't seen it do for a while. He was staring at Polly as though all his Christmases had come at once. 'That's great,' he told her. 'I'll be there first thing.'

'Is there any change?' I said. 'Is he conscious?'

Polly shrugged. 'He's still in a coma,' she said. 'Mum's in a state.'

'Is there anything we can do?' Luca asked.

She hesitated. 'You can come to the club night on Saturday. Ade and I need cheering up.'

'Sure,' I said quickly, glancing at Luca. 'We'd like that.'

'Good.' She picked up the bag and swung it over her shoulder. 'I want you to see the other side of us. We're not that bad underneath, you know.' Her eyes brightened a little when she added. 'We're just a couple of mixed-up kids, really . . .'

In an instant she was gone, leaving Luca and me alone in my mum's bedroom.

'I'll see myself out,' she called, halfway down the

stairs. 'I'm sure you two have a lot to talk about.'

As Luca frowned, I sighed, sitting back down on the bed. 'She's an odd girl, all right,' I said. 'The way she said "We're just a couple of mixed-up kids" – it was like she was reciting it. Like she'd heard someone else say it too many times.'

'I know.' Luca sat down next to me. 'I still don't trust either of them. I mean, for whatever reason she seems to be making an effort with you – with me . . . And I'd like to think it was because she regrets how she and Ade have behaved towards us. But I don't buy it.'

'Me neither,' I said, perturbed. 'I don't know what's going on, but I don't think we have a choice. And maybe if we go along with what she wants, we'll find out the truth.'

I looked at him and a ripple of anxiety went through me.

'Keep your friends close . . .' Luca began, reaching out and tugging gently at my hair.

'And your enemies closer,' I supplied. 'Isn't that what they say?'

Luca nodded, looking at my dress. 'But if we have to go to this club night then you should really wear that – you look beautiful.'

'You think?' I tried to hide my smile. 'It's not

a bit too much?'

He leaned forward and kissed my shoulder. His arm crept around my waist.

His lips moved to my neck, kissing me gently, and my body leaned into his.

'Luca?' I said in faux protest, but still a little taken aback. It wasn't like him to be so . . . amorous.

'Every time I look at you,' he whispered, his breath hot and sweet in my ear, 'I just want to . . .' He half sighed then, his hand moving closer to my breast.

'Luca.' I wriggled away from him, flushed. 'I want to . . . do it, too. I mean,' I felt my face ablaze, 'I really want to. But we can't.'

Luca stopped touching me and, for a second, he looked irritated, but I could see him wrestling with his instincts. 'I know.' He sighed. 'It's OK. It's difficult here with your family.'

I nodded, biting my lip. I felt all kinds of things, but inadequate came top of the list. I wanted to feel right about it, but the truth was it wasn't just the fact that we were under my parents' roof. It was something about Luca. He seemed changed somehow. More aggressive. I had glimpsed another side of him.

'But we need to . . . We can't go on just kissing and skirting round it.'

'I know,' I said, my heart thudding, because I had disappointed him somehow. That's how it felt, anyway. 'And we will. Soon. Just . . . not now.'

Luca held my gaze, the usual softness in his eyes replaced by something sharper, harder.

'Of course.' He got to his feet. 'You're right.' He put his hands in his pockets and I could see how tense he was. 'I'd better get to bed. I have an early start.'

'OK,' I said quietly, the beginnings of desperation growing in me. 'But you can stay here, in my bed. If you like.'

He half smiled, but it looked forced. 'Thanks. But I think I'll sleep in my room tonight. You know, where there's no distraction.'

'Right. Yes,' I said, standing there in my stupid dress with my stupid backcombed hair. 'Well, I'll see you in the morning then.'

Luca moved towards the door, turning just as he got there. 'Probably not. It'll be practically dawn when I get up. We'll talk tomorrow though . . .' He tried for a reassuring tone, but it came out flat.

Before I could reply he was gone, the door silently shutting behind him. Looking at the clock I saw it was barely nine. I sank down on the bed, closing my eyes. It felt like a quiet catastrophe had just occurred.

# CHAPTER TWENTY-SEVEN

'Your teeth are fluorescent,' said Ashley, swaying precariously in front of me. She stuck her straw into her mouth then drew back, her nose wrinkling. 'I have no idea what I'm drinking, but I'm pretty sure it's not the alcohol-free cocktail I ordered.' She frowned down into her sickly-looking pink drink. 'I think Ade's trying to get me drunk.'

'Uh-huh.' I smiled, taking her glass out of her hands and putting it on the counter, accidentally nudging the arm of a tall girl dressed entirely in leather.

'Careful,' she said sharply, swinging round to give us the full benefit of her heavily made-up face. She had a thick layer of foundation on and her eyes were barely discernable in the midst of all the black eye-liner. 'I hope you two babies have ID?'

I rolled my eyes at Ashley, who let out a shrill giggle.

'Haven't you got a horrible pink bedroom somewhere you need to get back to?' said the girl, sneering and reaching up to touch her heavily lacquered short hair. I had a sudden urge to poke at it, though the fierce look on her face was a pretty good deterrent.

'Excuse me for breathing,' murmured Ashley, then hiccuped.

I shook my head and, taking her arm, steered Ashley away from the bar, into the crowds who were swaying to some droning nouveau punk that the DJ was playing.

'Have you seen the others?' I shouted over the noise. 'Luca went to the bathroom ages ago.'

Ashley blinked. 'That's true. And Ade was talking to Polly over there . . .' She stabbed into a corner of the vast room with her finger. 'But he's not there any more.'

I nodded, trying not to feel worried. I had to chill out. We were supposed to be having a good time. But Luca had been gone an awfully long while. I took off my denim jacket. It was baking hot, but I had just felt too self-conscious in my dress.

Ashley's eyes widened when she saw it. 'Amazing dress, Jane. You look . . . amazing.'

I couldn't help laughing. 'So, to be clear, I look amazing, right?'

'You do.' She swayed forward.

'Ashley,' I said, grabbing her arms. 'I think you are drunk. Someone must have given Ade the wrong drink. Here . . .' I glanced around, looking for somewhere to take her. 'There's a free area over there. Let's sit for a while.'

But Ashley had gone pale. 'I think I'm going to be sick,' she said, putting her hand over her mouth. 'I think there was alcohol in that drink.'

'You don't say,' I muttered. 'OK. I'll take you home. I just need to find the others.'

'No need,' said Ashley, hiccuping again. 'Ade's here.' She waved at him.

'What's going on?' Ade suddenly appeared so close beside me that as I turned I nearly buried my face in his faded black T-shirt. I could see his pecs and his strong, lightly freckled arms against the dark cotton. I turned quickly back to Ashley.

'Ashley's not feeling good,' I said, trying to keep the disapproval out of my voice. 'I think she needs to go home.'

'You OK, honey?' he said, stroking her hair. 'Want me to get you a cab?'

I swivelled, to properly express my disdain with hostile eye contact.

'Maybe you should take her?' I said glaring at him.

'I was going to suggest that, too,' he said calmly.

'Of course you were.' I put my arm around Ashley. 'When she was passed out on this disgusting floor, no doubt.'

'Don't be mean to Ade,' said Ashley shakily. 'It's probably better he doesn't take me. My dad will only go ballistic anyway.'

'Hey.' I felt a hand on my back, moving up to squeeze my shoulder. I relaxed. Luca.

'I think we should all go, actually,' I said. 'Luca, Ashley's not feeling great.' I looked pointedly at Ade. 'I think someone gave her the wrong drink.'

'I'll take her home,' Luca said without hesitation. 'And then I'll come back . . .' He paused, realizing Ade was standing next to him. 'Or Ade can . . . I don't mind.'

'That's good of you, mate,' said Ade, smiling broadly at both of us. 'Are you sure you're OK to do that?'

'No problem,' said Luca. He looked reassuringly at Ashley. 'I'll go and call a cab.'

'Wait!' I walked after him, tugging at his T-shirt. 'You shouldn't be the one taking Ash home . . .'

Luca reached his hand back to take mine. 'Well, I don't trust her with him,' he said, stopping and glancing back at Ade. 'I want to see she gets home safely.'

'I don't think he'd hurt her,' I said, confused. 'I mean, he wouldn't, would he?'

'I'm not taking the chance,' Luca said. 'I need to borrow your phone to call for a cab.'

'I don't want you to go.' The words flew out of my mouth before I could stop them.

'Why?' Luca moved out of the way of a couple pushing past us. 'Are you OK?'

'I just . . .' My eyes darted around me. 'I don't know . . .' The truth was, I was irritated that Luca hadn't even thought that leaving me alone with the unchivalrous Ade was a heinous idea.

'Jane.' He stepped closer to me. 'It'll be fine. I won't be long.' He smiled reassuringly. 'And Polly's around somewhere, isn't she?'

'Yeah.' I sighed, trying for a less lame attitude. 'Sorry. I'm just not particularly—'

'Not particularly what?' A voice came from behind. Polly moved around me, managing somehow to fit between Luca and me.

'Nothing.' I smiled as brightly as possible. 'How are you doing?'

Polly shrugged. 'I'm not feeling too great. I was just wondering if I could get a lift back with Luca and Ashley?' She turned slowly to Luca. 'If that's OK?'

Luca made some kind of eye contact with me. 'What about Ade?'

'He's fine,' she said vaguely. 'He's chatting to a couple of guys who are going to give him some electrician work. They're talking business or something.'

'OK.' I fought a little rising panic. 'I guess I'll just hang out here, then. Unless I come with you?' I knew I was testing Luca, to see if he'd insist that I leave with him.

'I'll be back before you know it,' said Luca obliviously, his eyes anywhere but on me. He was putting on his jacket, patting his pockets for his wallet.

I couldn't say anything, not now. Why was he being so uncharacteristically uncaring? I nodded wearily, noticing the catlike smile on Polly's face.

She pouted at me. 'You have to stay here and show off that dress. Besides, we can't all abandon Ade. He wants to talk to you, too.'

'Really?' I looked at Luca, expecting, hoping for, a thundercloud to appear above his head. But he looked perfectly serene. I felt like I was going to cry.

Never had I wanted to be slouched in front of the TV more with Luca than I did then. And Polly looked perfectly OK to me. In fact, she was glowing. Suddenly I had to get away from them.

'I'll go and get Ashley.' I practically threw my phone at Luca.

I walked back into the dark noisy hall, my eyes darting

around, finally locating Ade, his auburn hair a little damp and curling, pushed back off his face. He was deep in discussion with a couple of no-hopers.

I tapped him on the shoulder.

'Where's Ashley?' I shouted.

He frowned then shrugged, far too nonchalantly for my liking.

'In the Ladies, I think,' he shouted back. 'Is your noble boyfriend taking her home then?'

I nodded, crossing my arms in a totally stand-offish gesture.

'Does that bother you?' he said, not shouting now, his face closer to mine. I caught the whiff of alcohol on his breath and was too aware of his body. He was big. Not fat, but big-built, strong-looking. He grinned and his teeth shone white.

'Why would it?' I shrugged. 'He's kind.' I lifted my chin defiantly. 'You should maybe think about being a little kinder yourself.'

Ade set his face in an exaggerated contrite look. 'You *are* bothered,' he said, putting his hand on my arm. 'What, are you two joined at the hip?'

'Did I say anything about being bothered?' I snapped, pushing his hand off me. I was so hot I felt like I was on fire; I could feel the sweat on the back of my neck.

'You look absolutely stunning, by the way,' said Ade, and the heat grew more intense. 'I hope your noble boyfriend has told you that tonight?'

'Of course he has,' I said calmly, though I was lying. Luca hadn't said a word, just raised an eyebrow when he'd seen me at the beginning of the evening in all my club regalia. I'd tried not to mind about that, but of course I had. Luca hadn't been the same since the night he'd come on to me so strongly. Part of me thought that it was because I had knocked him back, but another, bigger part of me knew something was wrong.

'He's a lucky lucky boy,' said Ade, who seemed to have forgotten about his no-hoper companions and was giving me the full force of his attention. 'I just hope he knows that.'

'Yeah, well . . .' I swung round, staring at the door of the ladies' toilets. 'When I want your opinion on how Luca should feel, I'll ask for it.' I craned my head over the heads of a couple snogging. 'I'm going to go and get Ashley out of there. Something might have happened to her.'

'Can't take her drink,' said Ade, shaking his head.

I was about to move but stopped and turned to him. 'She didn't want any alcohol,' I said, slowly. 'Weird that she ended up with some, don't you think?'

He held my gaze. 'The bar staff here are rushed off

their feet. They mixed up my order. It happens.'

'Sure it does,' I said sarcastically and set off to get my friend.

The Ladies was packed with girls re-doing their make-up and swigging from contraband bottles of vodka or whatever. All of the cubicles were empty. I checked each one of them all the same.

'Has anyone seen a blonde girl in a blue stretchy dress?' I asked. 'A little drunk, maybe?'

A hard-looking girl with short peroxided hair made a face. 'Plenty of them,' she said airily. 'Take your pick.'

'No, my friend was in here. I thought she was in here, anyway.'

'You mean Barbie's best friend?' said a girl with poker-straight dark hair. 'I saw her. She staggered out of here about ten minutes ago.'

'Oh, yeah?' the short-haired girl laughed unpleasantly. 'She went to find the rest of her pretty pink friends, probably.'

There was a collective titter from her gang of mates.

'Thanks,' I said wryly, pulling open the door.

Ade had disappeared when I emerged back into the hall. I sighed heavily and marched off determinedly to find Luca. When I rounded the corner I saw all three of them: Ade, Polly and Ashley, huddled together.

Luca was patting Ashley's back awkwardly.

As I approached, Ash lifted her head, her mascara streaked down her cheeks. *Horror Barbie*, I couldn't help thinking.

'Ashley,' I said, stepping close to her. 'I came to find you, but you'd—'

'Yeah eventually,' she said, sounding sober now. 'Thanks for just leaving me, Jane.'

'But I thought. . .' I glanced quickly at Ade. 'I thought Ade was looking out for you.'

'Ade was talking business with his . . . his . . . those people,' she said, her voice rising in pitch. 'But you just walked off and left me – following Luca . . .' She looked between Polly and Luca. 'What is it? You can't leave him alone for a second? Scared he'll run off?'

My mouth dropped open. 'No!' Polly and Ade were looking at me knowingly, smug almost, while Luca watched the scene awkwardly.

Ade put his arm around Ashley. 'Ash, you're upset. Let's get you home.'

She shrugged off his arm. 'And you're as bad,' she said, uncharacteristically bolshie. 'You don't want me. I can see that now. You haven't taken your eyes off her all night!'

I eyed Luca, waiting for him to explode. But there was

nothing. Not a flicker of anything. What was going on with him tonight?

'That's just silly,' I said. 'You had a drink and you're imagining things.'

'She's right,' said Ade, stroking her arm. 'You've got this all wrong.'

Polly tossed her hair impatiently. 'Look, let's just go. The whole night is a disaster.' I saw her roll her eyes at Ade. 'I should have known.'

'What's that supposed to mean?' I glared at her. 'Don't pretend you didn't design this yourself.'

Polly smiled, a slow catlike smile, and in the midst of my annoyance I caught Luca gazing at her, riveted.

'You really need to watch that paranoia of yours, Jane,' she said. 'I think you're losing it.'

'Luca?' I addressed him finally. 'Are you just going to stand there?'

Luca exhaled, looking more irritated than sympathetic.

'I came to find you,' I repeated to Ashley. 'I'm the one who cares around here.' I shot a furious glance at the other three. 'And actually, I'm going to take you home in that cab. The others can stay here.'

Ashley looked uncertain, but I could see some sense returning. 'Would that be OK, Ade?' she said.

'Of course.' He squeezed her a little too tightly and

looked distinctly unconcerned that she was leaving.

'You'll find your own way home, I suppose?' I said to Luca. I couldn't bring myself to meet his eye. 'I'm not coming back here.'

'Jane,' he said quietly. 'What's the matter with you tonight? You've been in a strange mood since we got here.'

I was going to retort that it was him who'd been weird, but I really didn't want to have a row. Not with Polly looking on, relishing that prospect.

How had I ever thought she was on my side? I couldn't wait to get home and tear the stupid dress off. It had caused me nothing but grief since I'd put it on.

'I'm not getting into it,' I said eventually. 'And don't wake my family up when you get home.'

With that, I took hold of Ashley's hand and half dragged her out of the club.

# CHAPTER TWENTY-EIGHT

'Don't you think you should have gone after her?' Luca turned on Ade, who was watching Ashley disappear with Jane.

Ade sighed. 'You know what girls are like,' he said. 'They seek refuge in each other in times of trouble.'

Luca frowned at this statement; he was trying to figure out what Ade meant exactly when he felt Polly's eyes on him. Not for the first time that evening he felt a little more of his free will slip away.

'*We* can still have fun,' she said softly. 'You look as though you could do with some fun.'

Luca bristled at the subtext to her words. 'Jane *is* fun,' he said defensively. 'She's being a good friend, that's all. She's been worried about Ashley all evening.' It was a pointed response, directed more at Ade than Polly. 'You've hardly been the model boyfriend, Ade.'

Ade laughed, stroking his chin arrogantly. 'You don't know much about the female of the species, do you, Luca? Girls need to be kept on their toes. All this chivalrous, lovey-dovey nonsense. It's emasculating.' He drew up his shoulders, suddenly looming over Luca in an almost animal-like stance – a deliberate gesture to assert his dominance.

Luca was thankful that the full moon had just passed. This kind of display would have tested all his instincts if the time had been right. He took a breath, deciding to ignore the obvious provocation. But he was beginning to register that he had not in fact been all that chivalrous that evening. In fact, he had behaved in a way he would never normally behave. He had been dismissive, disrespectful to Jane. Why hadn't he gone with her and Ashley? He should have insisted on it. He felt a surge of sadness and anger at himself. And along with that a fear: that his natural personality was been warped somehow. Gradually, subtly – by Ade and his sister.

He had to get a grip on this situation. Recover himself, if he could. He hated any acts of unkindness. Hated that he had been insensitive to a girl he loved more than anything.

'Where I come from, the male protects the female,' he said calmly. 'There is no game.' Out of the corner of his

217

eye he was conscious of Polly's expression, intense and sultry, and was aware of a tingling on his skin. He moved slightly away from her.

'I think that's adorable,' she said, and in a subtle movement touched his arm, her fingers moving down it. Long, elegant fingers, skin like alabaster. 'I wish we had been raised with that code.' She glanced at her brother. 'But Ade is trouble. Always has been. Always will be.' She laughed, her fingers digging slightly into Luca's flesh. 'And the truth is we girls like a steely quality to our men. Someone to keep us in order from time to time.'

Luca closed his eyes, as though that would shut out the effect she was having on him. He had come so far. He would ruin it all if he wasn't careful. The music seemed to be getting louder now and people were pushing past the three of them.

'Looks like the band has come on stage,' said Polly coolly. 'Shame Jane and Ashley had to miss it.'

Luca glanced into the hall, a leather-clad band of girls were tuning up their instruments on the small stage. A lead guitar struck up and the crowd inside surged forward.

'You want to go and watch them play?' Polly asked, seeing him watching the girls moving provocatively on stage.

He shrugged. 'Not really my thing . . .' Though he

couldn't take his eyes off the band.

'Come on,' Polly purred, and this time he felt her cool hand in his, her fingers stroking his palm. 'It might help you relax.' As he turned to her, he saw the subtle pink of her lips against that perfect pale skin and her eyes, intense and seductive.

'OK,' he found himself saying. 'Maybe just for a bit. He was certain a look had passed between brother and sister, but his head felt too full of alien thoughts to care. Suddenly he felt like dancing, like letting go. Letting all the stress leave his body.

Inside the hall, Polly swayed next to him and he found himself mimicking her movements, their hips touching. Then in a subtle movement she was behind him, her arms around his waist, her body pressing up against his. He felt himself tense for a second, but then he was drawing her hands closer around him and allowing them to slowly stroke his stomach. Behind his, her body felt strangely soft and yielding, as though she wasn't afraid of it. He shut out an image of Jane, who was so cautious about hers.

As the band's first track ended in a dramatic guitar riff, he knew he should disentangle himself and move away from Polly. But he couldn't. Then he felt her mouth against his ear, her breath heavy but sweet.

'Aren't you glad you stayed?' she whispered.

Luca was silent, but he shut his eyes, knowing he wanted to turn and kiss her. Not just kiss her . . .

What was happening to him? He had to get out of here.

He turned to tell her, to push her away, but her face when he met it was so startling beautiful, and the desire in her eyes so undeniable, that he couldn't speak. He stared at her, feeling his pulse quicken.

'It's OK,' she said breathlessly. 'Just relax . . .' She tilted her chin to look up at him and tugged gently at his T-shirt, pulling him close to her. He made a feeble attempt at resistance but he knew it was useless. He leaned into her, his lips moments from hers.

'Such pretty green eyes,' she whispered and then she kissed him, surprisingly softly, and though he tried not to reciprocate, he felt something primal take over. Before he knew it, he was kissing her back. Hungrily, passionately, his hands all over her body.

'Hey,' someone said nearby, 'get a room.'

And then he was lost in the noise, consumed by the crowd, by the heat, by Polly. But as he ran his hands through her hair, pushing it back off her face as he kissed her, a pain appeared from nowhere – it felt like a stabbing in his heart – getting more intense. And then a million images flashed through his face. His father's . . . his sister's . . . Jane's. The betrayal in their eyes . . .

He pulled back, gasping a little. 'I've got go,' he told her, finally pushing her away from him.

A real or contrived look of hurt appeared on her face. Her bottom lip pushed out unhappily. 'But we were having such a good time,' she said, and her words were so clear even though the noise from the band was almost deafening. 'Don't go . . .'

'No.' He shook his head, feeling trapped. Not just literally by the people hemming them in, but by something coming from Polly. He looked away from her, knowing that every time he did, she sucked him in and rendered him powerless. Keeping his eyes on the back of the hall, he registered a new feeling. One of revulsion and self-loathing.

Jane. He had betrayed her.

'Luca,' Polly pulled at his arm. 'Come on. You know you were enjoying yourself. You wanted it . . . You wanted me.'

Finally, the fog in his head evaporated and when he looked at her he saw the hardness in her eyes. Determination. Steel.

'I don't want you, Polly,' he told her. 'I never did.'

To his surprise, he saw her eyes fill with tears and that

221

determined bottom lip actually wobbling.

'Fine,' she said quietly. 'I obviously misread those signals.' She rubbed at her eyes with her sleeve.

'Look,' he said, confused, still unable to move with the surrounding bodies. 'I've got a girlfriend. And I love her. I should have gone home with her. I don't know what I was doing just now, but it was wrong. And you know that.'

Polly nodded, dropping her head, sniffing loudly. Then she took a deep breath and looked up at him again.

'Maybe you should ask her how much she loves you?' she said seriously, staring hard at him. 'How committed she is to you.'

She was talking rubbish. Luca would have rolled his eyes if he were that kind of person; instead he stared impassively back at her.

'You don't believe me?' Polly went on. 'Maybe you want to know the real reason Ashley was so off with Jane earlier . . .'

'Ashley was drunk . . .' Luca began.

'Not that drunk.' Polly spoke knowingly. 'Funny how such a sweet harmless girl could get into such a snit over someone she dotes on. Someone she trusted so much. Don't you think something happened to make her change?'

'I have no idea what you're talking about.' Luca's voice was cold. 'And I don't want to know.'

'Not even if it's about your girlfriend and my brother . . .'

'What?' Luca felt his jaw tighten. 'Jane is not Ade's biggest fan. I would have thought that was obvious.'

'Oh, Luca.' Polly smiled patronizingly. 'You're a little naive, aren't you? The tension between those two . . .' She hesitated. 'It's so intense. It's like this rare chemistry between two people. Jane knows it's there and she fights it with hostility. It's like I said, us girls want a real man deep down. They want a few hard edges.'

Luca literally felt his lip curling. 'Is that what you want? Because you were all over me just now. Despite the fact that I am so "unmanly".' His tone was acid. In that moment he felt such deep loathing for this manipulative creature.

'Perhaps the chemistry is right between us,' she said, unaffected by his hostility. All traces of hurt had disappeared. 'I bring something out in you that Jane doesn't. Have you thought of that?'

He blinked. Somewhere inside him he wondered if she was right. And he hated it. Hated to think he was anything like her selfish thug of a brother.

But the prospect of Jane being so aroused by Ade was

even more hateful. More than that, it was devastating. Luca breathed deeply, intent on not rising to this bait. He had to get out of here, away from the two of them. Back to Jane.

The band had left the stage and the crowd were chanting for an encore, but some of it had dispersed and Luca saw a clearer path out of the hall. He untied his jacket, which he'd wrapped around his hips, and put it on.

'I really am going,' he told Polly. And before she could protest he pushed past her, tagging on to the back of a group leaving. He was aware of a terrible thirst and, glancing at the bar, saw only a few people buying last drinks. He just needed some water.

He headed over and leaned against the counter. The sole barman was in conversation with a tall figure and, looking sideways, Luca realized that it was Ade. He sighed and turned away. He couldn't bear to look at him.

He was counting the change from his pocket when the barman spoke to him. Luca looked up to see a glass of clear liquid being pushed over to him.

'Water?' said the barman, grinning. 'You look like you need it.'

'Thanks,' said Luca. He downed it in one. And putting it back down, looked again to his right. Ade was staring at him, a glass in his hand. He raised it, smiling in an oily way.

'Cheers,' he said. 'You finally extricated yourself from my sister's clutches, I see.'

Luca said nothing; he turned to go. But as he did so, he felt his vision blur and the sounds around him became muted, indistinct. He shook his head, but everything was hazy.

'Are you all right, mate?' he heard someone say behind him.

And then nothing. Everything stopped.

'Luca?' Another voice, female, and a hand on his shoulder. He looked up, realizing he was leaning against the top of the bar, holding on to it for dear life.

Polly's face swam in front of him and then there was another taller figure behind her, his red hair swept back, and deep blue eyes looking into his own.

'He's out,' one of them said. 'Let's get him out of here.'

# CHAPTER TWENTY-NINE

'You're all right.' His voice was kind and she felt him lift her up. An angel had come for her.

She felt a hand lightly tapping her cheek, then harder, like a slap. She felt her eyelids flutter. She made a sound, like a whimper.

'Ow,' she moaned.

'I'm sorry,' he said, whoever he was. 'You've got to stay awake, love. Try and stay awake.'

And then he lifted her up, carried her in his arms, and she heard him shouting to others. As she opened her eyes properly, she saw the hole above her, revealing the night sky . . . the stars glinting . . . the tops of the trees. There came the caw-caw sound of a bird. She tried to keep her eyelids open, but she had no strength. She just fleetingly saw the men standing around. One in a uniform, the other dressed in a fleece and jeans. There was an animal barking and sniffing around her.

'We need to get her to hospital,' said the man in uniform – a policeman. 'God knows how long she's been down there.'

'What's your name, sweetheart?' said the man holding her. She summoned all her strength to look him in the face.

'Are you my dad?' she asked him, hoping. 'Have you come to get me?'

Her rescuer hesitated. She watched him glance at the others and a slow, sad expression came over his face.

'Just try and stay awake, sweetheart. You must stay awake.'

But she was already slipping back into the darkness; she couldn't hold on any more.

It had finally come. The end had finally come.

# CHAPTER THIRTY

I woke up fully clothed and with only a vague memory of the night before, with that feeling you have when your brain is adjusting to consciousness and dreams merge into reality. What seemed like a nightmare turns out to be only that.

I sat up, putting my hand to my face. An awful feeling rested in the pit of my stomach. My bedroom was deathly quiet, even the birds outside seemed to have stopped singing. It felt like an omen.

Thudding heart. I pushed back the duvet and got out of bed. I caught sight of myself in the mirror; my hair was like a dark haystack, the backcombing wasn't a good look in the cold light of day. I grimaced and undid the zip on my dress. When it was off, I tossed it to the other side of the room, repelled by it.

Creeping down the corridor to the attic staircase, I

hesitated at the foot of the stairs, not wanting to see him, but knowing I must.

An old feeling, one of loneliness and isolation, was settling back deep down inside me.

I pushed open the door to his bedroom, half expecting to find him lying there in his bed with Polly draped over him. I shut my eyes, preparing myself. And only as I heard the door creak wide open did I let myself open them.

He wasn't there. The bed was made, typically immaculately. But Luca wasn't in it. I swallowed, craning, trying irrationally to see the shape of his body under the covers.

He had stayed out all night with Ade and Polly. God only knew what they had done to him. I began to see how Luca's mood – so unlike him – had started the night Polly had come round for my makeover. It was no coincidence. He was behaving like . . . like the two of them.

I felt my eyes blurring with tears. Perhaps Polly was right about one thing. I was losing it.

Downstairs in the kitchen the clock said it was not even half past six. I stared down at the tea I'd made myself. I should probably have showered, dressed and headed out to find him. But a new emotion was overtaking concern. I was angry. Angry with him for not coming home. Luca was so reliable and strong. I had come to see him as my rock. But right now he was exhibiting very unrock-like behaviour. I expected better of him. Someone was coming down the stairs. I hoped it was my mother, though I didn't feel like explaining what I was doing, sitting alone at this time of the morning.

To my relief, she appeared in the doorway.

'Jane?' She wrapped her dressing-gown closer around her. 'I thought I heard someone get up. But on a Sunday morning – I knew it wasn't Luca going in to work.' She sighed, went to the fridge and took out some juice. 'What's going on?' she said, with her back to me. 'What are you doing up?'

'I couldn't sleep,' I said, then faked a yawn. 'But maybe I will go back to bed.'

Mum shut the fridge door and turned, the carton of juice in her hand. 'How was last night?' she smiled. 'You went out with that nice Polly and Ade, didn't you?'

I couldn't help the shadow that crossed my face. I fiddled with the handle of my mug, avoiding Mum's gaze.

'It was OK,' I said, trying not to sound too dismal.

'Hungover?' Mum put her cool palm on my forehead. I wanted to grab her hand and hold on to it for ever. I couldn't answer her. There were no words to describe how I felt. None that were appropriate for this time in the morning anyway.

'Where's that boy of yours – still asleep?' She shook her head, oblivious. 'I'll make some more tea. You can take one up to him.'

As she moved to fill up the kettle, the feelings I had been holding tightly back brimmed over. The lump in my throat was almost painful as I tried not to cry, but I couldn't stop the tears coming. I *had* to stop, I couldn't let Mum see this. I had to get a grip.

'I always forget whether Luca has milk or not,' Mum was murmuring. 'Or is it green tea he has?' I felt her turn to me to supply the answer, as I always did, because she could never remember.

'Jane?' Mum slammed down the kettle and came quickly, her arm slipping around my shoulders. With one hand she drew my face round to face her. 'Darling, what on earth is the matter?'

'Mum . . .' I croaked. 'It's all such a mess.'

She pulled me up and put her arms tightly around me. Just smelling her familiar smell, made me cling to her like a life-raft.

'Tell me what's happened,' Mum said softly into my hair. 'Have you and Luca had an argument? It can't be that bad.'

231

I shook my head, half buried in her dressing-gown. 'Luca didn't come home last night,' I whispered, almost hoping she wouldn't hear me, because I didn't want to hear the words out loud.

Mum gently pulled me away from her and lifted my chin.

'Did you get separated at the club?' she asked. 'Perhaps he got caught up with that Polly and her brother?' She smiled. 'He'll be fine. They seem like such a nice family.'

'Huh . . .' I smiled weakly. 'Yeah. They seem like a lot of things.'

Her forehead wrinkled in a frown. 'What do you mean?' she said, a little sharply.

'Just that they're not that nice. They're weird and manipulative. Something about them seems to cast a spell over . . . well, over Luca anyway.'

Mum's frown dissolved and her face took on a more knowing look.

'I see,' she said, sighing.

'What do you see?'

'Try not to be . . . possessive, sweetheart. It's good that you and Luca are making friends. You shouldn't feel threatened by it. Perhaps you need to learn to share. It's normal.' She sighed again. 'It's not healthy to spend all your time with each other. Having friends is healthy.'

'I know that!' I snapped. 'Believe me, this isn't adolescent jealousy, Mother.'

'Ssh,' she soothed, stroking my forehead. 'You're overtired.' She turned and looked up at the clock on the wall. 'Leave it another hour or two. If Luca hasn't phoned, or come home by then, Dad will take you out to look for him.'

It was 6.45 a.m. Time seemed to be dragging this morning. I wasn't sure I could wait another minute, let alone two hours.

I had to stay calm, though. If I got all riled up about Luca, then Polly and Ade would have won. It may have been a little superficial to think that way, but it was the only way I could hold it together.

'I'm going outside,' I told Mum, who was looking at me warily. 'Take Bobby for a walk or something.'

'Good idea.' She smiled, patting me on the shoulder. 'Everything will be OK, sweetheart, you'll see.'

I wasn't convinced of that, but I smiled back at her. No point in worrying my family. After all, there could be a totally innocent explanation for all this.

Outside, the crisp air lifted my spirits. Bobby was overjoyed to be taken for his first walk of the day so early. I guess he figured he'd fit in a few more than usual today.

I bent and scratched him behind his ears, those doleful eyes blinking at me. 'I can rely on you, can't I, Bob?' I pressed my head against his, hoping to gain some kind of strength from him. And good old Bobby stood patiently, waiting for me to finish whatever it was I was doing.

'OK.' I took a deep breath, stood and snapped the lead on to his collar. 'Let's go.'

Leaves crackled under my feet as I led Bobby through the woods, up the hill. I hadn't done this in a while and, with a sharp pain, I remembered how I used to when I first met Luca. I shut my eyes and strode on, Bobby panting at my side.

When we reached a familiar clearing, I rewarded him by releasing him from his lead. He bounded off excitedly.

'Not too far,' I called, smiling at the sight of the big dog lumbering through the trees. Bobby was getting old – he wasn't moving as fast as he used to.

A sudden sharp breeze picked up and the leaves flew up in a flurry. I looked up at the sky and saw the clouds moving quickly and the colour turning from blue to grey and a kind of pinky-grey – the sun struggling to be seen amongst all the movement.

'What's happening to us?' I whispered. 'Why can't we go back to how we used to be. Go back to Nissilum . . .' I realized in that moment how much I wanted to be lying by the river where the Water Path was – where it all began for us. I pictured Dalya's mischievous expression: curious, intelligent. I shut my eyes, letting the breeze stroke my face, and all of a sudden it felt like everything was slowing down. My thoughts, time . . .

I snapped my eyes open. The woodland trees had disappeared, with their brown leaves hanging on for dear life in the face of autumn's work. In their place was the bountiful green foliage of different, bigger trees. Oaks. A rush of breath came up my throat and I looked down, knowing I would see the water, gurgling on its way to a sea somewhere.

I was back. Back on Nissilum. But how?

It looked like the Water Path was deserted, and so incredibly peaceful, but I sensed something behind the trees. I peered at them. Something was there.

And then from behind two large oaks, walked a figure I recognized. A little taller, fuller in figure, but the same lustrous dark hair and dark eyes, coming towards me, with a cautious smile on her face.

'I don't know how I got here,' I told her, smiling back.

'I do.' She reached me and I saw she was not a child any more, she was a young woman. With a waist and a bust and at least three inches on me.

She sighed happily and then her arms were round me. She smelled like Luca used to – woody and clean.

'I brought you back,' she said, drawing away. 'I mean, you thought of me, I felt it intensely. You had a picture of me in your head and you wanted to be back here, at this very spot. And it was so powerful, that I pulled you here. All the way here.'

'I'm so glad,' I said and felt the tears coming again. I shook my head to be rid of them. 'I can't tell you how good it is to see you.'

'Is there something wrong?' Dalya's eyes were anxious.

'Oh, Dalya,' I breathed, relief flooding through me. 'I don't know what's happening. Luca is . . . different. He's under some kind of spell.' Unlike my mother, I knew Dalya wouldn't dismiss my fears.

She looked thoughtful, tucking her hair behind her small ears. 'My father is worried, too,' she said after a bit. 'Luca came to see him a few weeks ago asking a lot of questions . . .'

'Yes. I remember. He told me.' I sighed. 'The Vulpecula.'

Dalya's eyes widened. 'You know about them?'

'Bits.' I shrugged. 'I know they're supposed to be extinct. And that there was a big drama between your breed and theirs.'

'Ulfred hasn't told me everything,' she admitted. 'But

enough to know that if we – if any of us Hunters – come into contact with them, there is an old grudge they are harbouring.' She paused. 'Up until now we thought we were safe. That they had all died out. But then Luca said . . .' She stopped, probably not wanting to voice her fear out loud.

'I think they are living on Mortal Earth,' I said seriously. 'I have no proof, nor does Luca. But I think he was right all along. He had this feeling and he found something – a necklace covered in blood. It was miles from anywhere, in a place that no one in their right mind would go to. Not anyone who wears a necklace like that, anyway.' I looked up at her. What had been a paranoid fantasy seemed to be getting horribly real.

'So what does Luca want to do?' Dalya asked.

'I don't know. Not any more.' I swallowed, before adding, 'The thing is, I think they have already worked their evil on him. And I don't know where he is. He didn't come home all night.'

Dalya stared fearfully at me. 'I don't understand.'

'We went to a club with this brother and sister we've got to know.' I shuddered. 'Ade and Polly. Beautiful, eerie-looking redheads. They're adopted. Apparently. They have this strange aura about them and some kind of power. It's like whenever I am near them, I can't think straight. And I left Luca with them last night.' I put my hands over my face. 'I should never have done that.'

'Jane.' Dalya gently pulled at one of my hands. 'We need to speak to Ulfred. Maybe he will know what to do.'

'I hope so,' I whispered, a pit of anxiety forming again in my stomach. 'I hope it is not too late.'

# CHAPTER THIRTY-ONE

Luca was in the back seat of Ade's car, lying across the width of it. He opened his eyes, and the headache hit him like a mallet. He sat up . . . The rest of the car was empty. It was daylight outside, though he had no idea where he was. The car was parked in a small clearing next to a gate. To the right of it was a large empty field, sad-looking, despite the blue sky.

He rubbed at his head gently. It still hurt. And he felt so weak, a horrible taste in his mouth.

A shadow fell across the passenger window. He saw it out of the corner of his eye. When he turned, he saw Polly, still wearing the clothes she'd had on the night before. She'd taken off all her eye make-up and her face looked ethereally naked – almost childlike, the colour of her eyes stark against that porcelain skin. She pressed her face up against the window, then opened the door.

'Here.' She held out a plastic bottle of water. 'Drink.'

Luca stared at the bottle, then shook his head. 'I don't think so.'

Polly crouched down and he saw she was wearing Ade's jacket. Her long red hair hung in spirals. She gathered it up in one hand and coiled it into a knot at the back of her head in a skilled, swift motion. With her hair off her face, he could clearly see her prettily pointed chin and wide cheeks, two angular yet elegant ears.

Luca thought he was going to be sick.

'You really should drink,' Polly said, as though she was genuinely concerned. 'You're dehydrated.' She shook the bottle a little.

Luca didn't move to take it from her. 'Where's your brother?' he asked instead. 'And what are we doing here?'

She unscrewed the cap on the bottle and took a long swig. 'It's just you and me, I'm afraid.' She got to her feet and put one long leg into the car, followed by the other. Once she had shut the door, she sat, holding the water bottle, staring in front of her. In profile, her lips pouted beautifully. Luca looked away, determined to keep his wits about him.

'I know who you are,' he said eventually, shifting subtly away from her as he spoke.

'You do?' She turned to him, her eyes wide. 'And who is that?'

'The Vulpecula,' he said, staring straight into those eyes.

Polly's expression told him nothing. She simply screwed the cap back on the bottle. Then she sighed.

'I don't know what you're talking about,' she said. 'But then, I am feeling a little worse for wear.' She smiled. 'It was fun last night, wasn't it?' Her delicate nose twitched a little. 'Once you started to relax.'

Luca tried to recall the events of the night before. He remembered dancing with Polly – her hips against his body, her arms . . . He stopped thinking, knowing that she was doing it again. She was removing all his rational thoughts, leaving only basic, primal thoughts. Desire. He became very aware of her legs next to his.

'Well, it's been nice talking to you,' he said, refusing to look at her. 'But I have to get home. Jane will be going out of her mind.' Thinking about Jane, he felt a mixture of guilt and dread. To his surprise and his dismay, he didn't feel anything else. He shook his head and reached out for the door handle to his left.

'Don't go,' Polly said softly. 'It's so peaceful here.'

'I feel terrible,' he said, his back to her. 'What happened last night. It was wrong.'

'You didn't seem to feel like that at the time,' she said. 'I know when a boy wants me. And you wanted me. Last night – and this morning, for that matter.'

'This morning?' He jerked round to face her. 'Nothing happened this morning!' But the truth was he couldn't remember . . . He felt cold with a kind of panic. Had something else happened?

She put her cool hand on his, her long graceful fingers beginning to twine with his. He tried to pull his hand away, but found he couldn't. Flashing into his head came images of Polly's naked arms around him, her pale, taut body pressed against his. Had that happened? Or was she making him think it did?

'I know how long you've been waiting for Jane,' she whispered. 'Didn't it feel good not to hold back any longer – to be free?' Her lips curled into a conspiratorial smile.

Luca realized her face was changing, her mouth shifting, expectant, her teeth flashing – and a sudden visceral quality came over her expression. Her nose twitched again and her eyes narrowed out. She seemed to be smiling, but it was more feral than that. It was a hostile baring of teeth. The kind of stance a wild animal takes with its prey.

Somehow he found the strength to pull his hand

from under hers and open the car door.

Once he was out, he knew only that he had to get as far away as possible from Polly. He started to run, his legs like lead, a whooshing sensation in his head – the ache giving way to a now familiar fuggy feeling.

'Don't worry,' Polly called after him from the car. 'I won't tell Jane what we did. Your secret is safe with me.'

Slowly, the further he got from her, the stronger Luca began to feel, until finally he was running, bounding down the rough country road, blood pounding in his head. He ran for miles, gaining ever more strength, hoping that he would reach somewhere familiar and find his way back to Jane's house.

Out of nowhere a truck rounded the corner, driving slowly, but still a shock. Luca stopped suddenly, panting. He held out his hand for the car to stop, seeing with relief the familiar driver.

'Luca!' Jack Jonas stepped down from the truck, an expression of simultaneous relief and confusion on his face. 'What's happened? I've been driving round everywhere looking for you.' He came towards Luca, putting his hand on his arm. 'Never mind. Questions later. Let's get you home.'

In the car, Luca found himself trying to hide the shaking overwhelming him.

'I lost track of time,' he said. 'And before I knew it, it was morning . . .'

Jane's father stared ahead. 'I understand,' he said. 'Though it's a long time since I was in that kind of . . . predicament.'

'Nothing untoward happened,' Luca supplied quickly, 'if that's what you're thinking.'

Mr Jonas looked almost amused. 'Untoward? No. You're a good lad, Luca. I trust you.'

Luca nodded relieved, but the guilt he'd felt earlier grew in dimension. How was he going to explain this to Jane? Would she ever believe he had done nothing wrong? As Luca stared up at the morning sun outside, he realized he had absolutely no idea if he had betrayed Jane or not. But the thought that he had broken his precious code of honesty and trust, something he had been raised to believe in wholeheartedly – the thought that he might have destroyed that, was devastating.

They may not be admitting who they were yet, but the Vulpecula had found a way to wreak revenge on the Hunters: by sabotaging the most precious thing in Luca's world.

He turned and looked behind him at the fields – half expecting Polly to be in pursuit, relieved when all there was was empty landscape.

But as he turned, Jack braked suddenly, swearing under his breath.

'What the—' he started, and Luca paled at the sight in front of them.

Jack stopped the engine and got out of the car. Luca stayed where he was, glaring at the figure in front of the car.

Ade stood, his T-shirt a little torn, with what looked like scratches across his face. His skin was paler than ever. Though Jack was talking to him at the side of road, Ade's eyes were rooted on Luca inside the truck.

Luca stared back. Whatever game Ade was playing, he looked like he had Jack's sympathy.

Mr Jonas moved back to the driver's side of the truck, opening up the door; he shook his head at Luca. 'Poor kid's been attacked.'

'Attacked?' Luca stiffened, unable to keep the sceptical look off his face. 'By what?'

Jack puffed out his cheeks. 'A group of drunken lads apparently – it happened after you all left the club last night.' He looked over at the boy. 'Well, you were there, I guess you must have seen it happen.'

Luca frowned. 'I . . . No . . . I didn't see anything.' He bit his lip. He couldn't remember anything that had happened after he had passed out after that glass of water

– which hadn't been water, obviously. The next thing he remembered he had woken up in the back of Ade's car.

Not that he could let Jack Jonas know that. Whatever Ade was up to, Luca would have to go along with it if he was going to avoid awkward questions.

'Is he OK?' he asked, trying to inject some concern into his question.

'Superficial I think.' Jack glanced back at Ade. 'He has a black eye and he seems a bit out of it.' He sighed. 'Lucky we found him.'

*Or he found us*, thought Luca wryly.

Jack was regarding Luca with faint disapproval. 'You kids should take care of each other better,' he said. 'I guess it's easy to get carried away, drinking and . . .' He paused, clearly not wanting to get into what Luca might have been doing with Polly that was so distracting.

'Ade disappeared . . .' Luca began to protest but it looked as though Mr Jonas wasn't particularly interested in the details anyway, he was busy getting a blanket out of the back of the truck.

'I'm going to bring him back to the house,' he said. 'The last thing Lydia Ellis needs to worry about is her son getting involved in a brawl of some kind. We can clean him up and get him home.' He stepped away from the truck and passed the blanket over to Ade.

246

'You're coming with us,' he told him paternally. 'You look as though you could do with a bath and something to eat.'

Ade rubbed at his bare arms. 'I don't want to be any trouble,' he said, lowering his eyes humbly. 'I just need a lift back into Bale. I can get home from there.' He drew the blanket over his shoulders, clutching it to him a little pathetically.

'No trouble,' said Jack gruffly, pushing back the front seat and beckoning to the boy to get in the back. 'We'll see you right.'

# CHAPTER THIRTY-TWO

Dalya left me by the Water Path while she went to fetch Ulfred and, I had to admit, the serenity of the place was a welcome relief. It was almost impossible to feel troubled while I sat by the burbling water, the clean air pushing all muddy thoughts out of my head.

It seemed a lifetime before she returned with her father. At the sight of Ulfred, tall, bearded, twinkly-eyed, I nearly cried. It was like seeing my own father after a long time. I stood and waved a hand in greeting. He nodded formally in return.

'Jane,' he said. 'It is good to see you. How have you been?'

I smiled. 'Fine, thank you, Ulfred.'

'And Luca?' He pursed his lips, concerned.

'I don't know. We've been going through a strange time lately. Luca, he is—'

Ulfred nodded. 'He came to see me not so long ago,' he cut in gently, getting straight to the point. 'We talked of the Vulpecula. At that time I didn't seriously believe that they were living somewhere.' He sighed. 'But I realize now that Luca's instincts should always be taken seriously.' He looked kindly at me. 'You're worried about the boy, aren't you?'

'Yes.' Now that I was talking to people who weren't going to laugh in my face at my fears, I felt a surge of emotion hit me. All the weird, unsettling events of the past few weeks were coming to roost. 'I think he's in danger. They were trying to get to him through me. I see that now.'

'Tell me about "them",' said Ulfred. He settled his large frame on a flat rock by the river. 'How do they behave?'

'Well, they're clever . . .' I began. 'I mean they're sharp-tongued and sometimes vicious in what they say. But the main thing is the effect they have. They just sap all the strength from you so you can't fight back. Worse than that, they somehow channel your thoughts so that you think they make sense and that the things they say are right and that you are wrong.' I stopped. It all sounded so flimsy.

But Ulfred's expression had turned grave and he began to pace agitatedly in front of me. 'This is not good,' he said anxiously. 'That is exactly how the Vulpecula operate. It has to be them.' He channelled a fearful look at Jane. 'And they have found him. They have Luca in their sights.'

'But why Luca? Why would they have a specific vendetta against him?' I could feel my heart rate increasing, not at all sure I wanted to hear the answer to my question.

Ulfred hesitated. 'A long time ago we – the Hunter breed, or a member of the breed – made a pact with the Vulpecula. We would assist their transition to Nissilum, where they could reside, under the pretence of redeeming themselves, living wholesome, non-predatory lives, but in reality to cause a violent and catastrophic war with all that live here. Toppling the Celestials as rulers and instating themselves as some kind of despotic governing force.'

I swallowed an almighty lump in my throat. 'But they didn't, did they?'

Ulfred shook his head. 'No. They were betrayed by the Hunter who had promised them dominion. And they were forced out. They can only remain here if they are invited, officially, and that never happened.'

'Betrayed,' I murmured, knowing what he would say next.

'And they have clearly been waiting for their chance for revenge. Over centuries of bitterness. Waiting for one of us to cross to where they are free to roam. Mortal Earth.' He looked up at me and I could have sworn there were tears in his eyes. 'And now Luca has done just that. While he is on Mortal Earth he is an easy target for them. They will use him to barter with us here to carry out the plan that was thwarted all that time ago. Luca must come home. He must come home if he has a chance . . .'

'Come home?' I said. 'For how long?'

Ulfred had been looking thoughtfully down at the ground but he raised his head at my question.

'Indefinitely,' he said carefully. 'The Vulpecula won't go away. And there is only one way of truly defeating them, of destroying them, that I know of. And that has great consequences in itself.'

'How? What would destroy them?' I asked, my heart in my mouth.

'Fire. They are terrified of it, of course, but it is their souls that need to be burned, until they crumble. Any other death does not properly kill these creatures. They can rebuild themselves. But if their souls are destroyed then finally so are they.'

I stayed silent, thinking.

'But, Jane.' Ulfred's voice was quiet. 'I will not let my son endanger himself that way, either. He must come home if he is to be truly safe.'

251

* * *

I arrived back in the woods to find Bobby waiting patiently in the clearing where I'd left him. He stuck out a paw in friendly greeting and I grasped it miserably. I needed all the comfort I could get, because every way I looked the future was bleak. I clutched the dog to me.

'We'd better get back, Bob,' I said. 'I need to make sure Luca is OK.'

As we approached the house, I saw Dad's truck was parked outside, the door open. Dad came out of the back door and Bobby rushed up to him ecstatically.

'All right, boy.' Dad rubbed the dog's head.

'Hey.' I walked across. 'Is Luca back?'

Dad stopped cuddling the dog. 'Yep. I found him out near Bale. I think he had a rough night. Had a little too much to drink – nothing serious. More than can be said for the other kid.'

'The other kid?' I frowned. 'What other kid?'

'Lydia's boy – Adrian. Got into some kind of fight. Luca was a little vague on the details.' Dad smiled in the way he did when he was trying to put a good spin on things. 'Still, they're both back home so no harm done.' He shut the truck door and reached out his arm to draw me to him. 'You OK, Janey?' he said, as I nestled into him, glad of the warmth and the safety of one of his hugs. 'You don't seem yourself lately.'

'Well, my boyfriend stayed out all night,' I said, my voice muffled against his sweater. 'But apart from that . . .'

Dad stroked my hair, the way he used to do when I was small.

'Boys will be boys, sweetheart. Try not to build it up into anything more than it is.'

I nodded, steeling myself for seeing my boyfriend. And the odious Ade. I would have to pretend everything was OK in front of my parents. Act as though I wasn't spooked.

Dad took my hand. 'Shall we go in?' He began to lead me to the house when Luca appeared in the back doorway. My father let go of my hand.

'I'll leave you two to it,' he said quietly. 'Go easy on the boy.'

As he disappeared inside, pausing to pat Luca's shoulder, I kicked at the ground with my boot.

'You're really angry with me, aren't you?' said Luca, coming towards me.

I shrugged. 'Not any more, no.' I lifted my head to look at him properly. 'I've figured it out now.'

Luca stared at me expectantly. 'You have?' He came a step closer.

'Yeah.' I stayed rooted to the spot, not ready to totally forgive him yet. 'It's Polly. She has that effect on people.

She just seems to . . . overwhelm you. She did it to me too. Kind of steals all your energy. All your free will.'

It was Luca's turn to kick at a stone on the ground. 'You're right – she does. I'd like to say I know exactly what happened after you'd gone. But one minute I was . . .' He hesitated. 'One minute I was drinking a glass of water, the next I was lying on the back seat of Ade's car in a field miles from nowhere – and the sun had come up.'

'You don't remember anything else?' I probed. 'Did you . . . ? Did she . . . ?'

'I don't know,' he said quickly, and there was a defensive edge to his voice. 'I told you – it's like I was drugged or something.'

I watched him, the uneasy feeling that he wasn't telling me everything creeping over me. I reminded myself to keep to the important facts and not let any of those other paranoid thoughts get in the way.

'I don't think they need to drug us,' I said after a bit. 'I think they have more sophisticated brainwashing techniques than that. Centuries-old skills.'

Luca frowned. 'You seem very clear about that.'

'I saw your father,' I said bluntly.

'How?'

'This morning – I took Bobby for a walk. I was so . . . so out of my mind with everything. When you didn't come home I . . .' I swallowed, dratted tears threatening again. 'I didn't know what to think – what to believe. All I knew was that I wanted to be somewhere peaceful – with happy memories attached to it.' To my annoyance a tear slipped out and down my cheek. I wiped at it quickly.

'Jane.' Luca's arms were around me before I could go on, and he pulled me close. 'You know, I would never do anything to hurt you, not deliberately. You're the most important thing in the world to me.'

I looked down silently. They were words I longed to hear and I wanted to wallow in them, but I had to tell Luca about my meeting with Ulfred. Somehow I had to tell him everything, he had to know.

'So.' I took a deep breath. 'I thought about the Water Path, and then I thought of Dalya, wishing I could see her again . . . And the next thing I was at the Water Path, with Dalya walking towards me.' I smiled. 'So grown up all of a sudden.'

I looked up at Luca, who smiled fondly. I knew he missed his little sister and it was painful to hear about her second hand. I took hold of his hand.

'I told her I was worried about you and she knew instantly that she must get Ulfred. That he would know what to do. So he came, and we talked about Ade and Polly and what they're like, and he said that their behaviour sounded like the Vulpecula. He didn't even seem surprised.'

Luca bit his lip, still holding my hand. I could see thoughts turning over in his head. 'What else did he say?' he said eventually.

I shut my eyes, really not wanting to tell him, but knowing I had to.

'He says that you should go home,' I said quietly. 'Get away from Mortal Earth. It must be you they want – and they can't cross through into Nissilum. Not any more.'

Luca paled. 'Go home,' he murmured. 'For how long?'

'For good,' I said swallowing.

'I can't do that,' he said firmly. 'There is no way I would leave you.'

'I don't want you to go. It's like the worst thing I could possibly imagine. But if you stay here you'll always be in danger. They'll always be lurking, getting back at your family through you.'

'Is there no other way?' Luca stared helplessly at me. 'No other solution?'

I looked away from him. It was so tempting to tell him that if he set fire to Ade and Polly, burning their souls in their bodies, then they would finally go away. But I had to keep quiet about that. Apart from anything else, Luca could soon be on a real murder charge. Adding arson wouldn't help matters. It wasn't a viable solution.

'Jane, is there another way?' he persisted.

I finally turned back to him, tears burning my eyes. 'No,' I said blankly. 'There is no other way.'

Ade had bathed and was sitting talking to Dot at the kitchen table. I stifled the urge to order him to get away from her. Luca and I had just agreed, after I'd dropped my bombshell, that we needed to act as though nothing was wrong. We couldn't let Ade know what we knew. I did a cursory sweep of his cuts, which were healing already, and the giant bruise over his left eye. Had he really got into a fight? Or had he roughed himself up to make it look as though he had? I wasn't going to ask.

'Hey,' he said croakily. 'We wondering where you'd got to. He half smiled, half winced at the two of us. Luca put his arm around me confidently.

'Ashley got home OK,' I said, and it took everything I had not to say it with a sarcastic note. 'She'll have a bit of a hangover this morning, but she'll be OK.'

'Good. I'm glad.' He made a show of valiantly sitting up straighter. 'I didn't behave very well, did I? I should have insisted on taking her home myself.'

Luca and I said nothing. The obvious answer to that hung in the air like a lead balloon.

'Oh, girls don't like to be viewed in an undignified manner,' said my mother chirpily. She bent to inspect Ade's wounds. 'You're looking better already, young man. Next time, try not to rise to the bait.' Straightening up, she gave him one of her lecturing looks, before turning back to me. 'You took a long walk, darling. Bobby's as happy as a sandboy, dead to the world in his basket.'

'I needed some time with him,' I said, opening the fridge and taking out a pint of milk. I poured some into a glass and replaced the carton in the fridge. 'It felt good to be out in the fresh air.'

'I think Luca thought you were going to dump him . . .' she said, faux-seriously, 'but it looks like the two of you have sorted things out.' She smiled at us.

Out of the corner of my eye, I could see that Ade was watching us. Probably gutted that we hadn't split up and that whatever nasty plan he and Polly had set into motion wasn't working.

'Luca told you how we all got a bit carried away,' he said lightly. 'Lost track of time, isn't that right, Luca?'

Luca nodded, shrugging in as laddish a way as he was capable of. 'Yeah. It was fun. But I should have called.' He looked at me, as if to say, 'Sorry about that'. I shrugged back.

'He's home now.' I put my arm round his waist. 'That's

all that matters.' I took a breath. 'So you got into some kind of fight?'

'I did.' He nodded wearily. 'Stupid. Just some kids out for trouble.' He hesitated. 'One minute I was walking out of the club with Polly and Luca, the next thing, they'd skedaddled.' He raised an eyebrow at Luca. 'Thanks for that.'

I could practically hear Luca's teeth grinding.

'Yeah, sorry, mate.' Luca said. 'But you seem fine now.'

Mum was bustling around the kitchen. 'I don't want to seem rude, Adrian,' she told him. 'But I'm about to start on Sunday lunch. I need you all out of my kitchen.'

Any minute now she was going to invite him to stay for the meal. I had to do something.

'I'm sure my dad can give you a lift home,' I told Ade lightly, 'and be back in time for lunch.'

'Of course. Yeah. I'll get off then.' He got to his feet.

'Don't you want to stay for lunch?' Mum asked turning with a half-scraped potato in her hand. 'You're very welcome.'

'Stay!' pleaded Dot. 'Don't leave me alone with the lovebirds.'

I swiped at her. 'Hey!'

'I'll come another time.' Ade patted her head. 'I promise.'

*Please don't*, I thought, exchanging a relieved look with Luca.

'Come again then,' Mum said brightly. 'It's so nice that Jane and Luca are making friends. And bring your sister with you.'

'I will.' Ade cast a satisfied look at me, then put his coat on excruciatingly slowly.

'I'll see you out,' I said, wanting to look as normal as possible. 'Dad!' I yelled. 'Ade needs a lift home.'

My father appeared in the doorway. 'So soon?' He looked around at us all, before picking his car keys up from the kitchen counter.

I followed Ade and my father out to the yard, tugging on Ade's jacket as Dad got into the front seat of the truck.

'I'm sorry things got a bit . . . weird last night,' I said softly, putting all my acting skills to the test. 'I wish I could have stayed.'

Ade looked surprised. 'I thought you hated me,' he said. 'I'm such a terrible boyfriend, after all.' He raised an eyebrow.

'Yes, well.' I bit my lip, aiming for sexy. 'You know what they say . . .'

'What do they say?' Ade's intense blue eyes narrowed and, for a moment, I forgot I was acting. He seemed to pull me to him, just with a look.

I flared my nostrils subtly and the thudding in my chest nearly drowned out what I said next.

'There's a thin line, isn't there?' I looked straight into his eyes. 'Between love and hate.'

# CHAPTER THIRTY-THREE

She sat up in bed, blinking in the bright lights. A man was sitting by her bed; a remote control device of some sort was sticking out of his belt. As she stared at him, a burst of static came out of it. The man clicked a button of some kind and smiled attentively at her.

'How are you feeling?' he said.

'Uh.' She swallowed, her throat as dry as the Sahara desert. Turning to her side she saw a jug of clear liquid.

'Water?' the man asked. He leaned forward and took hold of the jug, upended the empty glass next to it and poured her some water. 'Here.' He held it out to her and she took it, drinking greedily.

She sank back against the pillows, feeling her body hydrate slowly. The light seemed more bearable now.

'Where am I?' she asked after a minute or so. 'What is this place?'

'You're in hospital,' he said gently. 'Do you remember why you're here?'

She shook her head, anxious, knowing that something awful had happened.

The man took a deep breath, running his fingers through his short blond hair. Though she was confused, she could see he was good-looking. He looked a little like somebody she knew – Jason, her ex-boyfriend.

'Jason,' she said suddenly.

'Jason?' He cocked his head. 'Who's Jason?'

'My boyfriend,' she murmured. 'A long time ago.'

The young man stared at her for a second, weighing up whether this sudden development was relevant. Then, clearly deciding it wasn't, he cleared his throat.

'Do you know your name?' he asked, leaning forward.

She thought for a few seconds, on the brink of saying no, but then it came to her.

'Olivia?' She answered him with a question. She couldn't be sure.

'Olivia.' He nodded, taking a notebook out of the top pocket of his jacket. 'That's good.' He scribbled the name 'Olivia' down in the notebook, then looked back up. 'What about your surname?'

She stared at him, frustrated. 'My mum – she calls me Livvy,' she said.

The man's pen hovered over the notebook; he didn't write that down. Instead he stared at her. 'Who is your mum? Do you remember her name – where she lives?'

She shut her eyes, shaking her head. 'She's dead.'

'What?' The man dropped his notebook. 'What did you say?'

'I think she's dead, I don't know.' She wanted to help the man, she wanted to give him something.

'Is there anything you remember?' he began again. 'We found you in a cave. Someone had tried to bury you alive.'

A flash of something. Faces, laughing at her. A boy, grabbing hold of her arms . . .

'Olivia . . .' The detective said her name and it sounded strange – as though Olivia was the girl she had been a long time ago. He leaned further forward. 'Is there something, anything, you can tell me?'

'They're still out there,' she told him clearly, with certainty. 'The people who did that to me – they're near here. They live here.'

The detective looked at her for a long minute and then he unclipped his remote control device and held it in his hands.

'I need to speak to my superiors,' he told her, getting to his feet. 'I won't be long.'

# CHAPTER THIRTY-FOUR

'Well done.' Mum smiled at Luca and took away his cleaned plate. Luca was obviously getting used to the food here on Mortal Earth and it pleased her no end. She looked down at my plate. I'd hardly touched my breakfast. Sighing melodramatically, she moved to the sink and turned on the radio.

Dot was sitting next to Luca, leafing through an old family album. Luca leaned over it, a smile spreading across his face. He looked up at me and then over at my mother. 'Is that you, Mrs Jonas?' He pointed at an early photo. Mum peered at it.

'Oh God, yes . . . I wasn't much older than Jane in that photo.' She smiled absently. 'My mother took it . . .'

'You look just like her.' He studied both our faces. 'Or she looks just like you.'

Mum laughed. 'Don't – Jane looks horrified!'

'Let me see.' I took the album off Dot. 'I guess so . . .' I looked up at Mum. 'You look so young, Mum.'

'Those were the days,' she said wistfully. She looked at all three of us seated around the table. 'You children should savour this time in your life. Before you know it you'll be over the hill and clearing your kids' breakfast plates away.' She stared pointedly at Dot, who was picking at a plate of egg and bacon.

My dad wandered in and washed his hands, then leaned in to the radio, turning up the volume to listen to the news.

'Police are still interviewing the girl found trapped in an underground cave five miles west of the town of Bale,' said the newsreader. 'In a statement issued this morning they say that suspicious motives are suspected, but that at present the girl, known only as Olivia, is suffering from shock and amnesia. We will bring you more news on that story as we receive it.'

I looked sharply at Luca as my dad turned away from the radio, shaking his head.

'They found a girl in an underground cave?' Dot said, looking horrified.

'Upstairs, young lady, time to get ready for school,' said Mum firmly, looking in a disapproving way at my father. As soon as Dot had left the room she frowned at him. 'She'll be having nightmares for weeks.'

'That's awful,' I breathed. 'Who would do that?'

'There are some bad people out there,' said Luca flatly. Getting up, he filled himself a glass of water from the tap. As he drank I noticed his hands trembling slightly.

'They didn't say exactly where it was they found her,' I said after a pause. 'I wonder if it's around here?'

Dad shook his head. 'No police up here lately . . . We'd know if she'd been found somewhere near. Besides, there are no underground caves in the mountains. It has to be flat land.'

Suddenly the image of the necklace flashed into my head.

'Like the army place . . .' I said slowly. I hardly dared look at Luca.

'Could be.' Dad sat to put on his boots. 'I'll ask around in town.' He glanced up at Luca. 'Want a lift in to Pete's place?'

'Great. Thanks.' Luca looked as though the last thing he wanted to do was go to work, but he attempted a smile. 'I've got some paperwork to see to at the yard.'

'I'm not going in to college today,' I said quickly. 'I'll come down to Pete's with you. Give you a hand.'

Mum raised an eyebrow. 'You're not going in?'

'I only have one class,' I told her, then adjusted my

expression to something a little tremulous and uncertain. 'And I feel kind of freaked out about that girl – Olivia. It could have been anybody.'

Mum rubbed my shoulder. 'I know. Her poor parents.'

'They haven't come forward, it seems,' said Dad. 'No one reported her missing.'

'Well, maybe she's not from around here,' I said. 'They'll hear it on the national news.'

'Terrible.' Mum sighed. 'Well, maybe it is a good idea you don't go in.'

I nodded. I wouldn't have gone in anyway. I wasn't sure I could face Polly after Saturday night. Her loaned dress was still crumpled up in a heap on my bedroom floor, but she could wait to get it back. Today I wanted to be alone with Luca.


'Are you sure you shouldn't have gone in?' Luca said, hanging up his coat. He picked up a handful of letters that had mounted up over the past few days. 'It's not much fun around here.'

I shrugged. 'I didn't want to be apart from you.' I felt myself blushing. 'I mean, not today, not after that girl Olivia being found . . .'

'I know.' Luca sighed and dropped the mail on the large table. 'It bothers me too.'

I looked over at him. 'Are you thinking what I'm thinking?' I said carefully.

Luca locked eyes with me. 'It does seem like another coincidence that probably isn't a coincidence.' He breathed out slowly, then went back over to his coat and rifled around in the pockets.

Luca came forward and dropped the crumpled little plastic bag on the table next to the mail.

'Do you think we should go to the police?' I asked, avoiding his eye. 'It might be Olivia's. It might jog her memory, or something?'

'It might.' Luca stared at it, his forehead creased as he thought. 'But there's something I need to do first.'

'The army training ground.' I sighed. 'I thought about that too. I'll come with you.'

'No.' He shook his head. 'I don't want you there. I want you to be safe.'

'Nothing's going to happen. It's the middle of the day,' I said softly. 'And I don't think you should go alone.'

'OK.' He sighed, then looked at me, a half-smile there. 'I must admit, that place – well, it scares me too. It's so full of . . . of darkness. Like an evil enclave of some kind. The kind of place where dangerous forces gather.'

'We'll be back before dark, easily,' I said, 'if we go now.'

'I'll take Pete's van.' Luca picked up the letters and stuffed them into the pocket of his coat, which he put on. 'Right then,' he said, sounding sturdier than I knew he was feeling. 'Let's go.'

A line of crows greeted us as we pulled through the gate into the training ground. I shuddered in my seat. Looking sideways at Luca, I saw a faint tic of tension in his cheek.

We parked outside one of the huts and got out of the truck reluctantly.

'Which one have you been working in?' I asked.

'This one.' Luca pointed at the piles of rubble outside the hut. 'An endless task, it seemed. Like a bottomless pit of rotting wood and rusty old metal.'

'You found the necklace in there? We should go and see if we can see anything else.'

Thankfully the ground inside the hut was mostly cleared. Luca had been back after Pete's accident and done some work. I knelt down and felt hard wood, creaking slightly, probably rotting too. Luca walked around, stamping on it with his boots. Nothing sounded out of the ordinary. Not until he got to one of the curved corners and his foot went straight through an ancient floorboard.

'Luca!' I went quickly to him. 'Is your foot all right?'

'My foot's fine,' he said, bending and wrenching up the broken board. It came up easily, as did the one next to it. Luca glanced up at me. 'Well, this looks like it's been moved before. And carefully put back in place,' he said quietly.

'Oh.' My heart picked up speed as I peered over his shoulder and saw it, the hole like a well, black and earthy. It was more like a chute.

Perfect for pushing a body down.

Luca straightened up, his shoulders tense. 'It definitely looks like some kind of pit,' he said.

'It might lead somewhere,' I said. 'Somewhere bigger.' I glanced behind me nervously. The sky was gathering storm clouds. It seemed ominous. But then, everything about this place seemed ominous, not least the creepy earth clad beneath us.

Luca was just standing there staring down.

'Maybe we should tell the police about this?' I touched his arm.

'No.' He was firm. 'We need to piece this together ourselves. If we tell them then whoever did this will know we know.'

'You mean Ade and Polly.' I finally said it. 'Because that's who you think did this, isn't it?'

He shook his head slowly. 'Honestly, I don't know.

Why would they do that?' He turned to me. 'But on the other hand, we don't know who Olivia is either – or what she might mean to them.'

'It is odd. If they are the Vulpecula, they wouldn't be interested in a mortal. What vendetta would they have against her?'

'They are driven to succeed,' he said. 'And maybe that means that whoever gets in their way is in trouble.' He looked back down into the pit. 'Maybe Olivia got in their way.'

# CHAPTER THIRTY-FIVE

She touched her T-shirt – a new one someone had bought her – along with some jeans and a hooded sweatshirt. She tried to remember what she had been wearing before . . . before the awful thing had happened, but this strange fog seemed to cloud out her memories of anything before she came to in that disgusting dripping cave.

But she kept thinking about her mum. And the face that kept coming into her head wasn't one she knew. The mother who had brought her up, fed and clothed her. It was another face. She had seen her, this woman. But she didn't know how or where. She scrunched up her eyes, as though that would help jog something. But nothing.

The door to the room opened. A woman in a suit came in, carrying a thin file. She walked towards the table where Olivia was sitting and sat, smiling reassuringly at her.

'Olivia,' she said gently. 'How are you feeling?'

'Better,' she said. 'I want to go home now.'

The woman placed her palms on the table. 'And where is that?' she asked. 'Home?'

Olivia shrugged. 'I'm not sure.'

'Olivia . . .' The woman sat up straight. 'Is there anything you can tell me – anything that might help us find who did this to you?'

Olivia concentrated, her eyes boring down on the table. 'It was a man,' she began. 'I think it was a man – or a boy. He wasn't old.'

The woman turned on a tape recorder. 'Can you say that again, Olivia, for the tape?'

Olivia repeated herself, already doubting what she remembered. 'I mean, someone strong . . . overpowered me. But . . .'

'But what?' The woman looked intently at her.

'I was going to say – I just felt I couldn't fight back . . . I was so weak.'

'But there was a man – a boy with you?' The woman raised one eyebrow. 'Can you remember what he looked like?'

'Blue eyes.' It suddenly came to her. 'Cold eyes.'

'That narrows it down,' murmured the woman, half-heartedly writing something in the file.

Olivia shook then; out of nowhere she started to shake uncontrollably. So hard that the table rattled.

'Olivia . . .' The woman snapped the file shut, alarmed. 'Olivia?'

She could feel its silkiness and the visceral panting sound it made as it brushed against her. It was almost as though it was here now.

She hugged herself, finally looking the woman in the eye.

'An animal,' she said. 'It was some kind of animal.'

# CHAPTER THIRTY-SIX

'Are you feeling better?' Mrs Connelly closed her office door and moved to sit down at her desk. She gestured for me to sit too.

'Much better thanks,' I said, smiling. 'I think I've just been overdoing it a little lately.'

'I see.' A flicker of disapproval appeared in her eyes. 'You know you need to prioritize things better. Your college work is very important. It's vital that you give it as much attention as possible if you want to get the right grades.'

'I'm aware of that.' I'd been in her office two minutes and already she was winding me up. 'But I need to talk to you about Polly. I think you should assign someone else to look after her from now on.'

'Polly feels the same way,' Mrs C said smoothly. 'I gather the . . . the dynamic between you is a little difficult?'

One way of putting it. I took a subtle deep breath.

'Polly has her own difficulties to deal with.' Mrs C paused. 'Her grandfather is very unwell. I believe the doctors don't feel he will recover. It's a matter of days . . .' She closed her eyes, in a show of respect.

'I'm sorry to hear that.' I tried not to let my mind run away with this information. The implications for Luca – and for me.

'Yes, it's the last thing that family needs at the moment, what with the police swarming all over them.'

'What?' I stared at her.

Mrs Connelly cleared her throat. 'It's not public knowledge yet – I only got the phone call this morning. But apparently the girl who was found in the cave – well, she turns out to be related to the Ellises.'

I opened my mouth to speak, but no words came out.

'Clearly they are very distressed and I would appreciate it if you kept this information to yourself,' she went on.

'Of course.' I nodded. I just wanted to get out of there and talk to Luca. 'I won't say anything.'

'Good.' She beamed falsely at me. 'Now, I expect you've got a class to go to.' She stood up and waited as I picked up my bag in a kind of daze.

'Polly is a special girl,' she said as I reached the door. 'Very bright and very sensitive. I think you should remember that and not do anything to upset her.'

I frowned, reaching out for the door handle, and turned to look back at her. All friendliness had disappeared from her face and in its place was an undeniable look of hostility. With her hair scraped back and her eyes narrowed to mean slits, Mrs Connelly had a mean, vulpine look to her. Any retort I was going to make evaporated.

'Of course not,' I said. 'I understand.'

Ashley and Emma were subdued when I ran into them at the lockers. I hadn't spoken to Ashley since Saturday night. I felt guilty about that, but I just couldn't face pretending that I supported her relationship with Ade. I'd had too many other things on my mind. Still, when I saw her, looking pale and unhappy with her sister, I knew I should try and be a better friend.

'Ash,' I said softly, opening my locker. 'How are you?'

'Fine.' But her eyes were not meeting mine. 'Just a bit tired.' She glanced at Emma, who was looking sheepish. 'I haven't slept too well lately.' She yawned. 'And now I have to get to my next class.'

'I'm really sorry about what happened on Saturday,' I said, stuffing some books in my bag. 'I just don't want you to get hurt.'

Finally Ashley looked at me. 'Is that right?'

'Yes. Of course it is.' I closed my locker. 'I was trying to look after you. I know it all got a bit weird, but—'

'Are you sure you weren't just trying to get in between me and my boyfriend?' she said.

'I've got a boyfriend of my own,' I said, my voice rising. 'I have no interest in yours.'

She stared at me, clutching her bag to her chest. I saw the blank look in her eyes and the shadows beneath them.

'Perhaps you should make that clearer to Ade then.' She paused. 'He seems to be under the impression that you've got a bit of a thing about him.'

'What?' The ridiculousness of that statement was so obvious to me that I could hardly find the words to go on. But I made a valiant effort. 'I think Ade's been spinning you a line.' I tried to sound as calm as possible. 'For whatever reasons. But I can promise you I am not even slightly interested in him. I don't even like him – or his sister.' I took a deep breath then. I must as well let it all out now. 'And I'm telling you, Ashley, the best thing you could do now is dump him. Get as far away from him as possible.'

Ash looked disbelievingly at her sister then back at me. 'Unbelievable,' she said coldly. 'At least before you were subtle about your feelings. Now you've just totally exposed yourself.'

'That's so not true,' I said. 'Whatever you think – or Ade has made you think – it's all part of some plan—'

'Oh for heaven's sake!' Ashley shook her head. 'Will you stop with all this mysterious plan rubbish. I mean, are you so sad that you have to create drama when there is none?' She tugged at Emma's jacket. 'Come on, Em, let's go. We're going to be late.'

Emma gave me what I thought was a sympathetic look, but her loyalty to Ashley was always going to come before the truth. I watched them go, my heart sinking further and further.

What a mess. Ade and Polly had succeeded in turning everyone against me. They'd even tried it with Luca. I shut my eyes. But I still had Luca. He would never betray me.

Students were hurrying past me, rushing to lessons, and I knew I should move too. I had History followed by Art. But everything in me wanted to cut college and go home. Back to safety. I remembered Mrs Connelly's face: a mixture of warning and dislike. She had it in for me too. I wondered whether Polly might have worked her magic on the head, along with practically everyone else.

I dropped my bag and felt in my pockets for my phone. As I dialled I hoped that Luca had decided not to go in to

Pete's place and was at home. The phone rang for ages and I was just about to end the call when he picked up.

'Luca?' I said. 'Is everything OK?'

'Sure.' He sounded a little guarded. 'Are you OK?'

'I'm not sure.' I hesitated. 'I've got some news. I think I'm going to come back home. My head's too full of all this stuff to focus on studying anyway.'

'You want me to come and pick you up?' he said. 'I've got a couple of things to do, but I could be there in half an hour.'

'That would be good.' I frowned as I heard the sound of the phone being muffled or something. 'Luca?'

A couple of seconds passed before he spoke. 'I'm here. Listen, Jane. Polly's here. There's bad news. Pete's . . . He's dead. He died this morning.'

I opened my mouth, conflicting thoughts running through my brain.

'Jane – did you hear what I said?'

'Yes . . . Yes . . . That's terrible news . . . Is Polly OK?' I didn't add, 'And what is she doing in my house?' It wasn't the time. Though after what had happened the day before at the training ground, I couldn't believe Luca had let her in.

'What do you think?' he replied, uncharacteristic sarcasm in his tone.

'No, of course . . . Look – I'll make my own way home . . .' I said, trying not to cry. Whether from shock, or the fact that my world felt like it was crashing down around me, I didn't know.

'If you don't mind,' he said. 'Look, I've got to go. I'll see you later, OK?'

'Yes. Sure. I'll see you in a bit.' I hung up, staring at the phone.

A bell went off. Recognizing it, I sighed, stuffing the phone back in my pocket. A fire alarm was all I needed right then. But I followed the surge of people heading outside, half dazed by the conversation I'd just had.

Typically, as it always does when a fire alarm goes off, it was raining outside. Once I had my name checked off by my tutorial group's fire monitor I found shelter underneath the bike shed's roof, and huddled my coat closer round me, watching the students filing out of the main building. Amidst the last people to leave were the twins, deep in conversation. Emma had her arm around Ashley, as though she was comforting her. Another time I would have gone over to find out what had upset her, but not now that I was Enemy Number One.

I was just turning away to make room for some students who wanted refuge under the corrugated roof along with me, when my eye caught the final person to come through the main doors. Tall, auburn-haired, his hands in his pockets and a dark look on his face.

Ade.

Instinctively I moved back, trying to hide myself, and watched as he trailed after the twins, his head down. He couldn't see me, I was sure of that. I breathed out and all of a sudden spots of rain were mixing with tears on my face.

Someone had lit a cigarette and, though I didn't smoke, I wished I did right then. I breathed in the acrid smell instead, letting myself cry here, where no one had noticed me.

'Here.' A hand held out a tissue in front of my face and I blinked, shaking my head. 'Thanks but I'm fine,' I said, concentrating on staring straight ahead.

'Take it,' said the owner of the hand. And at the sound of his voice I turned, disbelievingly.

Ade's smile was kind – and a little sad too. I wasn't going to let that sway me though. Apart from his sister, he was the last person I wanted to see.

'I'm sorry about your granddad,' I said flatly. 'But please leave me alone.'

'Sure,' he said, putting the tissue back in his pocket. 'Sorry I bothered you. I can see you want to be alone.' He looked up, just as a fresh bout of rain pelted down from the sky. All around us people were taking shelter where they could. It looked like I was stuck with him for a few minutes at least.

To say there was an awkward silence was a massive understatement. I prayed for the rain to stop.

'I know you hate me,' Ade said eventually, as we watched two of the tutors rushing around with clipboards. 'And I don't blame you. I'm a jerk. I've always been like that. I just can't seem to behave myself.' He laughed shortly. 'You should hear my mother on the subject.'

I said nothing, but sneaked a sideways look at him. There was no supercilious smile there. His face looked closed off – like he was genuinely upset. I frowned, annoyed that I might be feeling sorry for him, and looked away.

'And Polly's always been this wilful, fiery girl. My parents let her get away with murder. Trying to compensate, I suppose.'

*And what about Olivia?* I thought. *How does she fit into your happy little family?* I wasn't going to get into that now. I wanted to find out more about this poor girl before I said anything to Ade. Odd that he hadn't mentioned it though.

'Yeah, well. That's no excuse,' I said eventually. 'Whatever pain you're going through – you have to abide by some kind of basic principles, you know. It's called being a member of the human race.' I bit my lip, wishing I hadn't said so much; I was certain he was sneering at me now, whether he showed it or not.

'You're a breath of fresh air, you know that?' he said softly. 'So strong. Moral. Smart.' He paused. 'And really beautiful.'

'Yes,' I sighed, irritated. 'I've heard this routine before, Ade. This flattery bullshit.' I turned to him. 'And it's not going to work. I know you and your sister are trying to come between me and Luca. After Saturday night, I am sure of it.'

'Is it working?' he said, one eyebrow raised, and he looked so comical it threw me.

'What?'

'Are you single yet? Can I have you?'

I shook my head at the sheer gall of him. 'No.' I crossed my arms resolutely over my chest. 'I am very much not single.' I looked away then and a shadow seemed to cross over my heart. I couldn't be certain of anything any more.

The rain had stopped and so had the fire bell. The fire engines that had parked outside were pulling away. It was a false alarm and the tutors were herding students back inside.

'You going back in?' said Ade.

I wrinkled my nose. It was on the tip of my tongue to tell him to mind his own business. But something made me respond. 'I don't know what I'm going to do,' I said. 'I just want to be alone, if you don't mind.'

He stared at me for a few seconds. 'Of course,' he said, and I glimpsed a genuine sadness in his eyes. 'I'll see you around then – I hope.'

I barely nodded. All of a sudden I wanted Ade to make me feel better. Even if it was fake – and he was totally bad news. The truth was I didn't know who to believe, who to trust any more. If Ade really was part of the Vulpecula, then he and Luca were deadly enemies, and I knew whose side I was on. But what if Luca was wrong? What if Ade and Polly were just two ordinary mortals?

If they were, then there really would be nothing standing in the way of Luca's and my happiness – our life together. And maybe Luca found that prospect more frightening than anything else . . .

I opened my mouth to tell Ade to stay, but instead I lifted up my coat collar and shifted my bag on my shoulder. 'See you around,' I said, turning to the college gates.

# CHAPTER THIRTY-SEVEN

Luca wanted Polly out. When he'd first seen her trudging up the track towards the house, he'd been tempted to hide. But something about her demeanour had made him soften. She looked crestfallen, vulnerable.

'It's all so messed up,' she said, looking small as she sat in the kitchen. 'Grandpa Pete was the only sane person in our family. And now he's gone. My mum's going to fall apart.' She looked up at Luca, her blue eyes damp and tearful. She'd scraped her red hair back into a severe ponytail and her face looked scrubbed and free of make-up. It was hard to see her as anything other than a lost child when she looked like this. And Luca had been trained to be kind to those in distress.

But there was something else, of course. Whenever Polly was near him, she rendered him incapable of clear thought, she seemed to blunt any sharp edges he had, any sharp thoughts.

'I know I shouldn't be here,' Polly went on, looking down at the table. 'Jane doesn't trust me. And nor do you.' She raised her face to him then, as though daring him to deny it.

He crossed his arms over his chest and saw Polly's eyes flicker over his strong slim arms for a second. 'I'm so sorry about Pete,' he said eventually. 'I can't imagine . . .' He checked himself. 'I mean, I have not lost anyone yet. I don't know how I'd feel if anything happened to someone in my family.'

She nodded. 'It's strange about families, isn't it? Even if you don't like or understand them sometimes, they're yours. And you'd stand by them, whatever. Loyalty –' she sighed '– loyalty is the most important thing of all.'

Luca half smiled. He would have agreed with that once, but now . . . Now he knew that loyalty could be misplaced. He thought for a second before replying.

'It can make you do things you don't really want to do.' He looked at her. 'It can be destructive.'

Polly stared at him, a hardness coming to her expression, and he wondered whether he'd gone too far. She couldn't know that he knew. He had to play it more innocent than that.

'You've heard about that girl turning up?' she said, almost casually after a pause.

Luca frowned. 'I don't know . . .'

'Olivia – the girl they found nearly buried alive,' she said, shifting in her seat. 'She's claiming to be our cousin.'

'And she isn't?' he said stupidly. His mind was turning this over rapidly.

Polly's lip curled. 'Don't get me wrong, I feel sorry for the kid. But she's obviously gone mad. Hardly surprising considering she's been starved of food and fresh air for so long.'

Luca willed his beating heart not to be audible, because it sounded deafening to him.

'She had some kind of epiphany apparently.' Polly's tone was dry. 'Talking to the police, she said that her family were called Henshaw and they lived near where she was found.'

'But you've never seen her before?' he asked. 'Or heard of her?'

'Well, of course not,' she said edgily, casting him a hostile look. 'My mother went straight to bed as soon as she arrived.'

'The poor girl is traumatized,' Luca said. 'If she really is related to you or your mum, then a DNA test will prove it, surely?'

To his horror, Polly started to cry.

'I'm sorry, I didn't mean to upset you,' he said

awkwardly, moving towards her and hovering by her chair. 'I just meant it will rule it out, that's all.'

Polly's head snapped up angrily. 'You think my mum should go through all that? My grandfather's just died and this girl has the audacity to muscle in on our family. It's disgusting.' She rubbed at her eyes, then put her head in her hands. 'Everything is so awful,' she sobbed. 'Everyone hates us, Grandpa Pete's dead and we have to deal with this now.'

Luca put his hand tentatively on her shoulder. He was torn, he realized, between wanting to comfort her and feeling distinctly troubled by what she was telling him. If this girl thought she was related to the Ellis/Henshaw family, then Ade and Polly couldn't have been responsible for trying to kill her, could they? But then if only some of her memory had returned, perhaps that explained it. As he looked down at Polly, crying into her hands, he wondered whether her anger was actually due to what Olivia knew, even if she didn't realize it yet. Whatever the truth was, Olivia was in trouble too.

Polly stopped crying, pulling up her shoulders.

'You think I'm a drama queen, I know,' she said sniffing. 'And I guess I don't blame you. But when you've had to fight for attention all your life, it kind of makes you act up on a regular basis. You know?'

And as she looked up at him, an expression of pure sorrow on her face, it tested all his willpower not to hold her. Or was it that fragile, needy look she was giving him that was zapping all rational thought? He pulled away, subtly, and felt enormous relief when the phone rang.

When he heard Jane's voice, he felt glad to be drawn back to reality. To a real girl he loved. Though a headache was starting up and he found it hard to focus on what she was saying.

By the time he hung up he knew only that he had let her down. Glancing back through to the kitchen, he saw that Polly was applying make-up to her face using a small compact mirror, looking for all the world like a girl without a care.

# CHAPTER THIRTY-EIGHT

I found my own way home. Slowly. I was in no hurry to listen to Luca's explanation for how exactly he had come to be entertaining Polly in my house.

When I got to the back door, I heard the sound of my family gathered in the kitchen, my mum getting dinner ready, my little sister getting Dad to help with her homework. I opened the door carefully and then crept along the hall and up the stairs, relieved to reach my bedroom.

I threw myself on the bed and sank my head into the pillow. I had this feeling that I'd never had before with Luca, that something had changed between us. Something subtle, but it had altered the dynamic. Like a kind of power imbalance. Luca was no longer the benign and devoted boyfriend. He'd turned into someone I felt wary of – someone I could no longer trust completely. It was only a feeling, but it felt like an instinct. And instincts are so often right. I was pretty sure of that.

It was still raining, but more softly now. I heard the dog whimpering outside my bedroom door. His animal sense told him I was inside and it was seriously tempting to let him and take comfort from his lumbering, warm body.

But I just lay there instead, anger and sadness swirling around in my head.

A car pulled up outside the house and I shut my eyes. Luca was home. I levered myself up on my elbows and I caught sight of Polly's dress, still lying in a heap on the floor. I took a deep intake of breath, a fresh surge of anger preparing to come over me. But anger wouldn't help. It would only drive Luca away.

I got up and checked myself in the mirror, stripping off the shirt I'd been wearing all day and changing into a clean striped T-shirt. The little burst of activity brought some colour to my cheeks, and though my hair was still damp, it would do. Berating myself for bothering to make an effort, I unlocked the door and found Bobby panting patiently in front of it.

'All right, boy.' I scratched his head and he pushed his head affectionately through the bottom of my legs. At least someone still loved me.

'I'm not sure if she's back,' I heard Mum saying. 'If she is, she must have crept in.' She laughed. 'You two haven't fallen out, have you?'

Luca said something indistinct and then I heard his footsteps on the stairs. I had half a mind to go back into my bedroom and slam the door.

But he was in front of me before I could move, his face set in an exaggerated contrite expression.

'This is getting to be a habit,' he said, biting his lip.

'What is?' I sighed, passive-aggressively crossing my arms over my chest.

Luca gave Bobby a wary look as the dog stood guarding me, before he replied.

'Me disappointing you.' Luca rubbed at his hair. 'I'm totally messing up here, aren't I?'

I shrugged. 'Go and tell it to Polly,' I told him sulkily.

'Jane, you know there's nothing between Polly and me,' he said, holding out a hand, which I ignored. 'But you also know that there's something about Ade and Polly that strips a person of strength.' He stopped, staring at me.

I thought about Ade and how only an hour or so before I had been on the brink of hugging him. It was crazy but Luca was right. One minute we suspected them of murder, the next we were drawn to them, as though they really were just a couple of troubled kids.

'I know.' I gave a heavy sigh. 'It's totally distracting us from our investigation, too. When I heard that Olivia is saying she's related to the Ellis family, my first thought was that she was telling the truth and they were lying. That the two of them did something to her, but didn't succeed in wiping all of her memory.' I gave him a half-smile. 'They must be so angry.'

'You could say that,' Luca said archly. 'I've had to deal with her full spectrum of emotions this afternoon. Sad . . . angry . . .'

'She came on to you, too, didn't she?' I eyed him beadily. 'Don't try and lie, Luca. I know what she's capable of.'

It was Luca's turn to sigh. 'She . . . Well, she tried to, I suppose.' He paused, looking me up and down. 'But there's really only one person I want.' He took a step closer to me, treading carefully past the dog.

'Luca . . . I . . .' I began warily. 'I don't know what's going on, I'm afraid.'

With one finger he stroked my cheek. 'I know. But I'm here. You don't need to worry.'

'But that's just it.' I looked up at him and suddenly my eyes were swimming with tears. 'It's you, Luca. It's you that I'm afraid of.'

Luca almost gasped. I could see the shock in his face. Half of me wanted to take it back, tell him I was kidding, I couldn't stand to see the look of hurt there. But something stopped me.

'Ade and Polly – they've ruined everything,' I said. 'These mind games they're playing – I haven't got the strength to resist them. I just don't know how.'

'We have to be strong, united, Jane.' Luca finally spoke and for the first time he sounded more like a man than a boy. 'United. This is what the Vulpecula do. They send people mad if they let them.'

'I don't think I can,' I said. 'You need to go back to Nissilum, Luca. Where you'll be safe at least. It's the best thing for you – for us.' I took his hands in mine and clasped them tight. 'And I'm going to the police. They may not believe me, but at least they'll know my suspicions.'

'That's very dangerous,' Luca said quietly. 'You'll be on your own. And the police can't keep up with the Vulpecula. It's pointless.'

'Maybe not. But they can force Mrs Ellis and Olivia to take DNA tests. At least then they'll know she's connected to that family.'

'Jane, slow down,' Luca said. 'You can't do this by yourself. You need me here to help you. At least I know how to play the Vulpecula—'

'But you don't!' I felt exasperated. 'You obviously don't. And you're not safe here. It's you they want to get at most of all. I don't know what the deal is with Olivia, but that's another issue.'

'OK,' he said quietly. 'I'll go home. If it's what you really want.' He searched my eyes.

None of this was what I wanted, but it was time I stopped being so lame about what was going on. If that meant being apart from Luca, then so be it.

I nodded, hoping the tears wouldn't come again. 'And I need you to give me that necklace,' I said steadily.

'The necklace?' He frowned.

'I'm taking it to the police. They can test the blood on it. And they can find out who it belongs to. And who tore it off Olivia's neck.'

Luca shut his eyes, but I knew he realized it was futile to refuse. I also knew that what I was doing was virtually telling him he was useless, unnecessary. That this was one thing he couldn't fix.

'I'm sorry,' I said. 'I never wanted it to be this way. But I won't let you stay here and get hurt by them.'

'When will I see you again?' he said, swallowing.

'When this is over,' I told him.

Luca nodded and, sensing that something sad was

happening, Bobby whimpered sympathetically at our feet.

'So this is goodbye then.' I saw that familiar tic of tension in Luca's cheek and my heart lurched for a second. I held out my arms and he moved into them, clasping me tightly, burying his head into my hair.

'I love you – you know that, don't you?' he whispered. 'Always.'

And the tears that I had been holding back started to fall. I wanted so much to say those words back to him, but I had to hold them back.

'Goodbye,' I whispered back. 'Goodbye, Luca.'

# CHAPTER THIRTY-NINE

'So we're going together,' said Ashley, flicking her hair over her shoulder. 'To the half-term party, I mean. I was sure he'd say no because, you know, he's kind of not into the whole coupley thing . . . But he said yes, immediately!' She clapped her hands together gleefully. 'I can't wait to show him off.'

From my seat at the other end of the canteen table, I forced a mouthful of salad into my mouth. It tasted like sand. I dropped my fork and took a gulp of Coke. Then I allowed myself a small peek at the gaggle of girls around Ashley.

In any other situation I would have been pleased for her. But this wasn't good. I knew there was no point in saying anything to her. Apart from the fact that she wasn't actually talking to me, anything I said would be analyzed as jealousy.

Maybe there was a way I could stop it from happening. I didn't want to upset Ashley. But better safe than sorry.

'Mind if I sit with you?' A familiar yet timid voice spoke in my ear. I glanced down at a pair of porcelain-pale arms holding a tray of food. My heart sank.

'Free country,' I said, putting down my Coke.

'I wanted to talk to you, anyway,' she said quietly. And I was forced to turn and face her. She was wearing some kind of Amish get-up. A grey shirt buttoned to the neck, tucked into a long shapeless skirt. Her hair was coiled in a prim bun at the back of her head and her face was unusually free of make-up. Her eyes, bare without the eye-liner, looked stark and a little red-rimmed.

It was an impressive gesture of humility, I had to give her that.

'I'm sorry,' I said. 'About Pete.'

Polly half smiled in acknowledgement. 'Thanks,' she said with what looked like some effort. She peered past me at Ashley and her friends, still shrieking with delight.

'What's that all about?' she asked, frowning.

'Ashley's going to the half-term party with your brother,' I told her in a flat tone. 'She's kind of excited about it.'

Polly rolled her eyes, though there was amusement, not malice, there.

'Good for her. It seems she's achieved the impossible.' She picked at a chip and dunked it into some ketchup, then put it whole in her mouth.

'Does Ade really like Ashley?' I said, a little surprised by my own forthrightness. 'I mean, is he genuine?'

Polly finished chewing, then dabbed at her mouth with a tissue. 'Who knows?' she shrugged. 'He likes you more. But then you already know that.'

'Not going to happen.' I bristled, very much aware I was sitting next to a potential murder suspect. 'He's not my type.'

Polly picked up her burger and nodded. 'I forgot, yeah. You're more into the shy, retiring type.'

It was an insult and she knew it. At least, I think she did. Yet again Polly was clouding clear thoughts.

'I have to go,' I said. 'It's been nice chatting with you.'

'Don't go,' she said abruptly. Her expression was intense as she stared at me. She had pushed away her plate of food and her pale hands were folded into each other in a childlike pose.

'I have to. Well . . .' I hesitated reluctantly. 'I only have a few minutes.'

'I know no one likes me,' she said. 'I know you don't think much of me either.'

'Polly.' I had been hovering, half off my seat, but I sat

301

back down. 'What's going on?'

She frowned anxiously. 'Too much. We've got some girl hanging around saying she's, like, related to us or something. My mum's gone mental again – won't speak to anyone.'

'Olivia.' I nodded. 'I heard. Why do you think she's saying these things?'

Polly shrugged miserably. 'I don't know. I guess she's a little bit disturbed or something.'

'She *has* just been literally holed up in a cave for God knows how long,' I said. 'She's hardly going to be in her right mind.'

'I guess . . .' Polly breathed out slowly. 'I just wish she'd leave us alone. My mum doesn't need this. Not now.'

I sighed. 'Well, get a test then. Put the whole thing to rest.'

Polly's jaw visibly tightened. She looked away then, silently indicating that the direction the conversation was going was not to her liking.

That figured. I checked my watch.

'I really have to go now,' I said. 'But maybe there's someone you can talk to. Someone who might understand.'

Polly turned slowly back to me. 'I thought I had someone who understood,' she said. 'I mean, who really listened to me – got who I was. But I haven't seen him for days and I think he's abandoned me – just like my real mum did. Just like everyone does, in the end.'

'Who understood you? Your brother?' I felt just a smidgeon of tenderness for her. She looked so lost.

Polly's pale-pink lips trembled slightly and she shook her head quickly. 'No . . . not Ade.' She looked up at me, 'Luca. He understood. We talked for hours on Saturday night. That's why he was out all night. He was listening to me.'

'Luca.' Any tenderness evaporated. 'Luca understands you?'

'I think he knows what it's like to be an outsider – you know, apart from his real family, trying to fit in.' She looked up at me from under her pale lashes. 'I'm sorry – that must sound like I'm trying to get with him, but he was just a friend to me. A proper friend.'

I stared at her. I couldn't decide whether this was just another malicious joke, or if Polly genuinely believed what she was saying. Three months ago I would have dismissed it, but I couldn't be sure any more. Who knew what Luca had kept secret from me But I knew one thing. I couldn't rise to it. There was too much to lose.

'Yeah, well,' I told her. 'Luca's gone, I'm afraid.'

Polly's forlorn look turned decidedly steely.

'Gone? Where?' She almost glared at me.

I shrugged. 'Who knows?' I lied. 'We're over. It's over. He said he wanted to travel. He left a few days ago.'

'I can't believe that,' she said. 'He just . . . left you?'

I nodded, a studied sanguine expression on my face.

'To be honest, I'm relieved,' I told her. 'There was always a weird kind of vibe about Luca. A little bit dangerous, you know?'

'Uh-huh.' Polly looked gripped. 'Dangerous. Yeah, I get that. Are you sure he didn't tell you where he was going?'

'Positive,' I said firmly. 'We didn't exactly part on the best of terms.'

'Wow,' said Polly, and she stared down at her untouched food. 'I guess some people turn out to be wrong. You know, not quite who you thought they were.'

'I guess so.' I sighed again, rechecking my watch. 'Look, I really have to go.' I got up and swung my bag over my shoulder. 'I'm glad we had this talk. I think I understand you a little better now, too.'

'You do?' Polly still looked dazed. 'Cool.'

'See you around – maybe at the half-term party?'

'I don't think so,' she said. 'But Ade will be there.'

'Great,' I said, inwardly noting to give him a wide berth.

'I have to be somewhere too,' said Polly. 'My mum is

supposed to be planning Pete's funeral, but she's not exactly with it at the moment.'

'I'd like to come,' I said, without thinking, 'to Pete's funeral.'

'I'll talk to my family,' said Polly. 'I think Mum wants a private do – but I'll see.'

'Yeah,' I said, turning to head for my next class. 'You do that.'

# CHAPTER FORTY

Luca looked in on his sister, fast asleep, though still clutching one of her precious books. Her feet were nearly sticking over the end of the bed, she'd grown so much since he'd last seen her. He smiled. His heart was full of lead and he couldn't imagine ever feeling again that freedom, that happiness that he'd felt with Jane. But seeing his sister made coming home a less dismal prospect.

He moved away from the doorway. He was uncertain where to go, sure that his old bedroom would be full of household clutter.

'Luca?' Dalya's voice, bleary came from her bed. 'Is that you?'

He stepped inside the bedroom. 'Ssh. Go back to sleep,' he said.

Dalya sat up. 'What's happened?' she said. 'Luca?'

He sat down at the end of her bed. 'Everything is

going to be fine,' he whispered. 'I just came back for a visit. That's all.'

Dalya gave him a shrewd look. She reached to her side and turned on her bedside lamp.

'Something's happened,' she said. 'I know it has.'

Luca sighed. 'It's nothing. Just a bit of trouble on Mortal Earth.'

Dalya rolled her eyes. 'Not more trouble.' She sighed. 'Is this about the Vulpecula?'

Luca hesitated. It had always been pointless trying to keep anything from Dalya. And it was so tempting to unburden himself to someone who knew him so well. But she was still his little sister. He didn't want her to know everything.

'I had to leave,' he said. 'Jane and I – we . . . well, something went wrong.'

'Wrong?' Dalya was wide awake now. 'But you two are so close. What on earth could have happened?'

'It does have something to do with the Vulpecula – I think.' He sighed deeply. 'But I can't think straight any more . . . I don't know whether it's just wrong between us, or whether something bad has got to us.'

'Luca, this is not like you.' Dalya looked alarmed. 'You have always been so clear-headed. You love Jane. She loves you.'

'Yes. Yes, I do.' He put his head in his hands. 'Of course I do. But something has changed.' He stared at her – a woman, but still young, still unaware of the complications that can tangle up a relationship. 'Dalya, it's so hard to be a good person . . . a good man. It is so much harder than I thought it would be.'

Dalya shook her head impatiently. 'But you have always stood strong – and you are stronger than this. I don't see what is so complicated that you can't work it out.'

He knew she was right. There was nothing wrong with him and Jane. What was wrong was something intangible. Like a thick, evil mist covering all rational behaviour.

'I'm frightened, Dalya. Jane is in danger. We're both caught up in this old vendetta. But it's done something to us. Played with our minds. One minute we can be full of determination, the next we're helpless, submissive, under the spell of something . . .' He trailed off, his forehead creased with worry.

'You need to speak to Father.' Dalya drew closer to him. 'Ulfred needs to be aware of what is happening on Mortal Earth. He can help . . .'

'But will he?' Luca shook his head. 'Jane is not his flesh and blood. And while I am here, she is the only one in danger. I'm not sure he would help.'

Dalya was silent. She reached across and took his hand. Her natural empathy, as ever, strong in times of crisis. He squeezed it back, comforted. Looking into her dark eyes, he realized just how much he had missed her sharp intelligence, her knack of getting right to the heart of a problem. He was proud of her.

'You have grown into a fine girl,' he said quietly. 'Truly.'

An impish smirk appeared on her face. 'Are you paying me a compliment, brother?'

'Don't let it fill your head.' He let go of her hand, grinning, glad of the familiar, familial dynamic. Dalya wrapped a shawl around herself and yawned.

'And how is Lowe?' Luca hardly dared ask what his brother had been up to.

Dalya rolled her eyes. 'Thank the Celestials, he is away on a hunting expedition with his horrible friends. He will be gone for weeks.' She sighed contentedly at the thought. 'Freedom.'

'Don't judge him too harshly,' Luca said smiling. 'He is a mass of adolescent confusion.'

'Is that what they call it?' Dalya said, dry as a bone. 'He is driving even Henora to distraction these days. He has his sights set on some girl – a young Hunter who came to visit with the parents a while ago.'

'Lowe is in love?' Luca laughed. 'Thank the Angels for

that. It may bring out a more tender side of him.'

'I doubt it.' Dalya shook her head, looking down at her quilt and then back up at him, her expression turning more solemn. 'I really don't wish to talk about his silly infatuation. I am worried about you, brother. You must ask for help.'

'Yes. I know. And I will talk to Ulfred, I promise. But not tonight.' He felt horribly sad; the prospect of losing Jane again was unbearable. He got up from Dalya's bed. 'Is there anywhere I can sleep tonight?'

Dalya stared at him as though he were simple. 'Of course, silly! Your bedroom.'

'You mean Henora hasn't filled it with needlework baskets and laundry to iron?' he said, more jovially than he felt.

'Henora has kept it as you left it, like a creepy shrine to her favourite child,' Dalya whispered in a ghoulish tone.

Luca smiled, glad at least that his mother had not cut him from her thoughts. 'I am going to sleep then,' he told his sister. 'I could sleep a thousand weeks.'

Dalya got up suddenly and threw her arms around him. 'I will all your happiness to return. And your fears to disappear.'

'Thank you, Dalya,' he said, hugging her tight. 'I'll see you in the morning.'

# CHAPTER FORTY-ONE

'You don't look very dressed up,' Dot said as I appeared in the kitchen. A cut-off denim mini, leggings and some vintage cowboy boots was hardly making an effort – though I was wearing a silky black sleeveless T-shirt in a pathetic bid for glamour. It had been too big for me a year ago but now fitted me a little too well. As I looked down I saw my cleavage was a lot more visible than usual. I swiped playfully at Dot and moved back out of the kitchen to examine myself in the full-length hall mirror. I'd gone for understated with my make-up and let my long hair dry naturally, backcombing it just a little.

'Rock chick,' Dot decided. 'Isn't that kind of over?'

'Who cares?' I said, shrugging. 'I don't. At least not about what anyone at the college thinks of me, anyway.'

Turning back into the kitchen, I caught the look that

passed between my mother and Dot. Wary yet sympathetic summed it up.

'What?' I said.

'Are you sure you're OK, darling?' Mum said, coming towards me. 'I mean, you don't have to go along to this half-term party thing. It's not been long since Luca left. You must be feeling a little vulnerable still.'

'I think she should go,' Dot said confidently. 'You shouldn't let men affect your self-esteem, should you?' She sighed in a knowing manner.

Mum and I exchanged an amused look.

'What do you know about it, madam?' Mum tousled Dot's blonde curls.

'It's obvious. If one boy doesn't want you, then there'll always be another one round the corner. I heard Mrs Ashcroft telling Miss Connor that outside the staff room yesterday. Mrs Ashcroft is married, so she must know what she's talking about, right?'

Mum laughed. 'I suppose she must.' She pursed her lips at me. 'I think your little sister has a fine career as a relationships counsellor ahead of her.'

'A fine career as a busybody more like.' I fake-glared at Dot, but I wasn't mad. I'd told my family that it had been Luca's decision to go, not mine. It was easier somehow; it meant I didn't have to explain my reasons. Though I did feel a twinge of guilt. Luca didn't deserve to be the bad guy. Even if I didn't trust him any more.

'I'm fine, Mum,' I reassured her. 'It's not exactly my thing, but I think I should go. It doesn't look good on uni applications if you're an antisocial weirdo. I need to at least look like I'm normal.'

'Of course you're normal.' Mum was wearing an expression I hadn't seen since Sarah Forrest had bullied me relentlessly at my old school. I couldn't put her through that kind of worry again.

'Kidding!' I said. 'Now, is someone going to drive me to this party or what?'

I heard the music coming from the main school auditorium as I got out of Dad's car, tugging at my skirt, wishing I could get right back in and go home.

'Want me to pick you up later?' Dad asked, leaning over the passenger seat towards me. 'Or are you getting a lift with your friends?'

Friends? What friends exactly? But the new, older, less afraid Jane shook off the response that the younger Jane would have made.

'Yeah. I'll tag along with somebody,' I told him. 'But I probably won't be late.'

'Enjoy yourself,' he said, and it felt a little like an order.

'You deserve to have some fun.'

Slamming the car door shut, I waited until his rear lights had disappeared before I turned and walked through the college gates. Luca had left his leather jacket behind and I wrapped it around myself, like a comforter, breathing in the smell of him that still lingered in the battered old leather.

'I miss you, Luca,' I whispered to myself as I strode in the direction of the music.

Inside the auditorium, the lights were dimmed; a DJ stood up on the stage playing some Dubstep track, while a few confident students were already on the dance floor – no one I knew though. Perversely I wished that Polly had come. At least there would be a fellow outsider to keep me company.

But then she wasn't an outsider like me. She was a very different kind of outcast. And if I thought about it for two seconds, given all that had happened, I didn't want to be anywhere near Polly Ellis.

I scanned the room and finally saw Ashley, her arm draped around Ade's shoulders, sitting at one of the small tables at the side of the auditorium. I squinted to check his expression. Slightly bored summed it up, though as Ashley bent to whisper something in his ear, he did smile, if a little half-heartedly. Ashley straightened up, coiling a lock of hair in her fingers, as though she was nervous. I saw her eyes travel about the room and then catch sight of me.

I lifted a hand in an attempt at a friendly wave, hoping she wouldn't blank me. She hesitated before waving back and I thought I saw a look of relief in her face. Emboldened, I walked over, cutting past the moving dancers, and arrived at their table.

'Is this seat taken?' I spoke in a determinedly bright tone as I pulled out an empty chair.

'Jane – great you could make it.' Ade leaned forward and shrugged off Ashley's arm. I couldn't help but see her slighted expression, but I pretended I hadn't, for the moment at least.

'I thought I'd check it out.' I barely looked at him, instead focusing all my attention on my friend. 'And I'm so glad you're here,' I told her. 'I feel like I don't know anyone else.'

Ashley smiled, grateful for the gesture. 'Well, you can put that right tonight maybe?' She grinned – and it was genuine. I grinned back. 'Though you'll never be able to hear anything over the music. It's way too loud for talking.'

'Luca isn't with you?' Ade asked casually. Turning back to him, equally casually, I couldn't be sure if he was being sarcastic or not. Had Polly not told him that Luca had gone?

'Not tonight.' I bit my lip. 'Not his kind of thing, I guess.'

Ade picked up the bottle of beer in front of him and took a swig. 'I wonder what is his kind of thing?' he said. 'He's a hard one to get to know.'

*And you'll never get the chance*, I said inside my head. *Not now, not ever.* Outwardly, I shrugged good-naturedly. 'He's a little shy,' I said. 'And very private.'

'Uh-huh.' Though I was determinedly not looking at him, I could feel Ade's eyes boring into me.

'Actually, I think I might dance,' I told them, unzipping my jacket. I looked at Ash. 'Want to come with? I feel stupid on my own.'

Ashley hesitated, clearly wanting Ade to give her some sign that he cared what she did. I wasn't surprised to see the look of complete indifference on his face. He just reached out for his beer again and stared straight ahead of him.

'OK then,' Ashley said with a hint of a sigh. 'But I really don't know how to dance to this kind of music.'

'Neither does anyone else,' I told her dryly, 'so we'll fit right in.'

I saw Ade's lips curl up into an appreciative smile at

that remark and cursed myself for making it. The last thing I wanted was for him to pay me more attention than Ashley. I tugged at her hand, half dragging her to the middle of the dance floor.

'You look amazing,' I shouted over the noise. 'Really pretty.'

Ashley smiled and looked as though she was going to cry for a second. 'Thanks, honey,' she said, squeezing my hand. 'I was beginning to wonder if I should have worn something different.'

'Why?' I frowned. She did look great – in a Party Barbie kind of way. She wore a hot-pink bodycon dress that looked a little like a neon bandage, but she had the figure for it, anyone could see that – even if she had gone a little overboard on the bronzer.

Her face fell, just a little. 'I don't know. I think Ade thinks I look a bit tarty,' she said.

'Did he say something?' I stopped moving.

Ashley didn't reply for a second, turning her head slightly away from me, as though she was embarrassed.

'His exact words were "Decided not to hang on to any mystery then?"' She finally looked at me in the eye as she spoke. 'Kind of mean, don't you think?'

My instinct told me to walk back to Ade, grab his beer and upend it all over him, but I needed to be careful. I had alienated Ashley before by being down on Ade. I had some bridges to build.

'Well, maybe he thought it was funny?' I said softly. 'You know what boys are like. They're tactless sometimes. And when they're nervous, they say stupid things.'

Ashley continued to stare at me. 'Luca doesn't say things like that, though, does he?'

I opened my mouth, again, carefully selecting my words. 'Yeah, well, Luca is exceptional,' I told her. 'He's not the norm.' And as I said it, it hit me, like a punch in the stomach. Luca was exceptional. He was the bravest, kindest boy I had ever met. And I had just lost him – maybe for good.

'Jane?' Ash put her hand on my face. 'You're crying! Honey, what's the matter?'

At the kindness in her words, I realized more tears were coming and, though I fought hard to stop them, I couldn't.

'I'm OK,' I said, shaking my head, as if that would work. 'Really. I don't know why I'm crying . . .'

'Come and sit back down then,' she said gently.

But as I turned to see Ade staring straight at us, his eyes focused particularly on me, I knew there was no way I wanted him to see me crying.

'I'll be fine,' I said as briskly as I could manage. 'I'm just going to the Ladies. I must have mascara all over my face. I'll see you back here in a minute. I'm OK, really. Don't worry.'

'You're sure?' She hugged me and, as she tucked her blonde head against mine, I heard her whisper. 'You know I am always here for you, Jane. I'm your friend.'

'I know.' I hugged her back, realizing I didn't want to let go. But I did, eventually.

'See you in five,' I said, turning for the exit. 'Don't go away.'

I had washed my face and put on some tinted moisturizer. At least I looked normal – except for my eyes, which looked kind of dead and sad. Like a melancholy grey sea under an overcast sky.

I sighed, reaching into my bag for some eye-liner, when suddenly the lights went out. The bathroom was pitch-black and I could only just make out my eerie reflection in the mirror. I felt for the light switch, pressing it up and down repeatedly – but nothing.

There must have been a power cut. The music had stopped too. I groped for the door handle and stepped outside. There was no sound coming from anywhere.

Odd.

The corridors were deserted as I crept along them,

my heart in my mouth. The place was eerie at night; all those abandoned classrooms, the sound of a loud clock ticking like a bomb coming from one of them.

'Ashley!' I called, my voice echoing. 'Ashley!'

A sound made me turn to look back down the corridor, but there appeared to be nothing. Nobody. I took a step backwards.

'Is anyone here?' I waited, my hands curled up in my pockets. I wanted to get out of here, but I couldn't leave until I'd found Ashley at least. Something was wrong.

And then, as if in slow motion, a silhouette began to appear around the corner. Not human. Bigger than a dog, but elegant, with a sharply pointed head and a gazelle-like body.

I blinked. I couldn't be seeing this. An animal inside the college.

I couldn't make out any features; the creature, whatever it was, was still a silhouette against the moonlit window at the far end of the corridor. I swallowed.

'What . . . ?'

The animal's finely pointed ears pricked up and I glimpsed its imperious snout and, then, against the dim light, the almost amber colour of its coat.

The animal seemed to be changing before my eyes, the body shrinking and altering its position. I peered, in spite of my fear, and saw it stand upright.

It was not an animal. It was a human. I felt as though I was going to black out.

'Who is it?' My voice was reedy, scared.

'Don't be frightened,' a familiar, almost mocking voice told me. 'I'm glad you came.'

'Where's Ashley?' I said more forcefully. 'What have you done?'

He laughed. 'Ashley,' he repeated. 'I had almost forgotten about her.'

'I don't know who you really are –' I tried to stop the shaking come through into my voice '– but I'll just forget about everything . . . if you tell me where she is.'

'It's not that simple, Jane.' He took a step closer to me.

'What do you want from me?' I crossed my arms protectively over my chest. 'It's like you've singled me out.'

'Perceptive.' He moved even closer and I saw the vivid contrast of his hair against his flawless skin. 'But it isn't exactly you we want . . .'

'Then who?' I played innocent; I knew exactly who he wanted.

'He's big enough to take care of himself,' he said. 'And he has known this time would come.'

And then he was standing right next to me, so close I

321

could feel his breath on my face. His eyes, glinting and sharp, made my skin tingle. It wasn't the first time this boy had had this effect on me. He reached out then and touched my hair, so softly, tenderly, that I relaxed my arms a little.

'I don't want your help.' He took a strand of my hair, twisting it gently in his fingers. 'I've only ever wanted one thing from you.'

'What?' I breathed.

Didn't I already know what he was going to say? Hadn't I known all along the price I had to pay?

Positioning himself so that he was looking right into my eyes, he waited a few seconds so that I could take in his full mouth, the cool blue of his stare.

'You, Jane,' he said. 'I want you.'

# CHAPTER FORTY-TWO

There was a distinct silence at the table. Dalya, her nose deep in another book, was going to great efforts not to notice the atmosphere.

Henora placed a platter of bread on the table then sat, her lips pursed a little.

'You're back for good, then?' Ulfred grabbed a roll and immediately tore off a piece with his teeth. He smiled at Luca, more than a hint of sympathy there. 'Perhaps it is for the best.'

'Perhaps.' Luca could think of no reason, right then, why it was for the best. 'But it isn't for good. Just until Jane finishes her studies and the trouble has died down.'

Henora's eyes narrowed. 'Trouble?'

Luca exchanged a look with his father.

Ulfred cleared his throat, clearly uncertain as to whether to speak the truth in front of Dalya. 'There is an unwelcome . . . presence on Mortal Earth,' he told Henora. 'Luca was not entirely safe there.'

Dalya lifted her eyes from her book. 'I know all about it, Father,' she said crisply. 'There is no need to be cryptic.'

Henora raised an eyebrow at her daughter before turning to Ulfred. 'Please enlighten me,' she said. 'It appears I am the only one in the dark about this.'

'The Vulpecula.' Ulfred spoke tensely. 'They have returned, it seems. Unfinished business.'

Henora visibly paled. 'Heavens.' She stared at Luca. 'They came after you?'

'They're trying . . .' Luca told her. 'They're clever. Jane and I have been caught up in some kind of telekinetic warfare.'

Henora looked confused.

'The Vulpecula use their minds to catch their prey,' Ulfred said. 'They will also use physical force. But they are squeamish creatures. They prefer not to get their hands dirty. They'll try as hard as possible to succeed without bloodshed.'

Luca thought of Olivia, of the necklace. If the Vulpecula were responsible for her ordeal then she must have tried to resist their mind games. He decided not to mention Olivia; he wanted to figure out that mystery by himself.

'You must never go back,' Henora said, anxiously. 'The Vulpecula have an old grudge against the Hunters. You are in grave danger if you return.'

'Jane is in danger too,' Luca couldn't help himself from saying. 'Perhaps not in the same way, but through her connection to me she is vulnerable.'

'Well.' Henora clasped her hands together. 'Jane must take care of herself. She is a mortal and they are not interested in her.' She lifted her chin. 'And nor should we be. Not any more.'

'Mother?' Dalya's eyes widened. 'That is cruel.'

'It is survival,' Henora told her. 'And the girl is in greater danger if Luca stays.'

Dalya shook her head. 'But—'

'Enough!' Henora ordered. 'This is Luca's home – where we, his family, can protect him. We must unite at times like this, not get caught up in sentiment.'

Luca knew that arguing with his mother was pointless. Better to keep quiet and work out his own plan of action. Nevertheless he signalled gratitude to his sister with a look.

'How close is Jane to this brother and sister?' Ulfred asked thoughtfully.

'She's not,' Luca said. 'Not really. But they keep trying to get close to her. They are very persuasive when they want to be.' The image of Polly flashed into his head, dancing behind him closely, her hands running over his chest. Sitting here, with her safely on another world, he felt nothing, but he remembered how he had felt at the time. Torn. Tempted. Was Ade working a similar routine on Jane? Was he with her right now, telling her she was better off without her boyfriend? Luca didn't believe Jane would talk to Ade about him, or that she would reveal where he was. But Ade, like Polly, had a habit of stripping away your conscience.

Ulfred nodded. 'Well, they won't hurt her. If you trust that she will not betray you then they will realize in time that intimidating her is futile.'

'I hope so.' Luca knew that if there was any possibility of Jane being hurt, if she was in danger, then he could not stay here. 'But there is a risk,' he added. 'There is always a risk.'

'If only there was some way we could get rid of the Vulpecula for good,' said Dalya. 'Then Luca and Jane wouldn't need to be apart.'

As she spoke, Luca noticed a strange look pass between his parents and he frowned.

'Is there a way?' he asked boldly. 'Because if there is, I must know.'

Ulfred shook his head a little too quickly. 'No. There is

nothing you can do, except stay here, keep as far away from them as possible.'

Luca stared at him. There was something Ulfred wasn't saying, he was sure of that. But Ulfred was stubborn once he had made a decision. Luca would just have to live with it.

Or find out the truth for himself.

# CHAPTER FORTY-THREE

'Did you cut the power?' I said to Ade's shadowy figure. He was leaning up against the lockers, a streak of moonlight from the window illuminating half of his face.

'This is an old place,' Ade said softly, 'with ancient wiring. Too much excitement on a night like this and the whole lot dies.' He breathed in, almost contentedly. 'A metaphor for life, don't you think?'

'No.' I glanced at the doors to my left. Through the glass panels there was still no sign of life. 'Where is everybody?'

'They're still here.' He smiled. 'They're just being a little quiet right now.'

My head snapped back to him. 'What have you done to them?'

Ade frowned. 'You're so suspicious of me – why is that?'

I couldn't give away what I knew, but it was so tempting. I glared at him in the darkness. 'Because you're a jerk,' I said childishly.

Ade sighed. 'Always so defensive.'

'So,' I said, ignoring that, 'you never did tell me where Ashley is. What have you done, locked her up in the college basement?' Once the words were out of my mouth, I couldn't take them back. I just had to hope that Ade didn't make the connection.

'Now, why would you say a nasty thing like that?' he replied, as though he was hurt.

I shrugged. 'Listen, Ade. It doesn't matter how much you pester me, I'm not interested in you. Not now, not ever.'

'Of course, you have a boyfriend,' he said, moving away from the locker and taking a step towards me. 'I forgot.' He looked around him. 'But where is Luca? Is he unwell?'

'Uh-huh.' I bit my lip.

'You're lying.' Suddenly Ade was right in front of me and, close up, I noticed a fine reddish-gold down on his face. I swallowed, trying to stop my revulsion turning into something else. Because for the life of me, I wanted to touch him. I blinked and stepped backwards to lean against the wall.

'Luca has left you. Polly told me. Did you think she wouldn't?'

I said nothing, concentrating on keeping my wits about me. Ade's eyes were piercing me, their colour vivid even in the dim light.

'But we find that a little hard to believe . . .' Ade cocked his head to the side and his voice was slow, as though he was talking to an idiot. 'Because Luca worships the ground you walk on, doesn't he? How could he just leave you?'

'It's none of your business.' I spoke at last. 'And he hasn't left me. He's just gone away for a bit.'

'That's right. He's gone travelling,' Ade said sceptically. 'Poll did mention that.'

'So why are you asking?' I snapped.

'Jane, don't be testy.' Ade sighed. 'I'm just worried about you, that's all.'

'You don't give a damn about me,' I whispered. 'I know what you're doing. I know who you are. And I know what you've done.' I stopped. I had said too much. Ade's eyes narrowed to dark slits, and his breathing was suddenly heavier. I waited, my heart in my mouth, for him to do or say something vicious. But he just stared at me and, though I tried not to engage with him, I felt as though my head was locked.

Suddenly the overhead lights flickered into life and I flinched.

'Looks like the electrics have been sorted out,' Ade said conversationally, as if what had just happened had never happened. He yawned and we heard the music starting up again, coming from the auditorium.

'Excuse me.' I pushed past Ade, heading for the doors. 'I'm going to find my friend.'

As the doors swung shut behind me, leaving Ade behind them, my body caught up with the shock, my legs trembling and my heart thumping. But I kept walking, down the corridor and through the next set of doors, heading for the auditorium. What had passed between me and Ade was enough for him to know that I was on to him. And that I was almost certainly lying about Luca's whereabouts. I needed to grab Ashley and leave – as quickly as possible.

Walking back into the auditorium, it looked pretty much exactly how I'd left it, ten minutes before. A few more students were on the dance floor and couples seated at the tables against the wall were chatting, just as though the power cut had never happened. I even saw Ashley, talking to some boy, her back to me; she was throwing her arms out, animated, happy. I frowned, but marched towards her, still intent on taking her home.

'Ashley,' I said. 'Are you OK? What happened with the lights?'

Ashley looked at me, confused, her smile fading just a little. 'What?'

'The power cut?' I prompted, as her companion, giving me an odd look, moved off. 'It happened while I was in the Ladies. Pretty scary, huh?'

Ashley wrinkled her nose, grabbing my arm. 'I didn't notice any power cut,' she said. 'Was there a power cut?'

'I . . .' I stared at her, but she looked perfectly genuine. 'I thought . . .'

'There you are,' came a voice behind me, and I saw Ashley's face light up. 'I've been looking for you everywhere.' Ade moved past me and put his arms around her. 'Would you care to dance?' he asked her, nuzzling her neck in front of me. Ashley let out a pleased giggle.

I swallowed. I had no rational explanation for what had just occurred. But I had the sickening feeling that Ade had somehow conjured that whole situation up to freak me out. And he had succeeded.

Ade pulled Ash away to the centre of the dance floor and, as he turned her around, his eyes met mine, a glint of humour there, along with a flinty sharpness.

I had given myself away.

# CHAPTER FORTY-FOUR

Things were coming back. Olivia huddled down underneath the thin quilt and stared up at the overhead light. The hostel didn't provide much in the way of home comforts; a single bulb swayed a little from the ceiling.

Olivia rolled over on to her side, a black, bleak feeling coming again. She closed her eyes and a flash of a red dress, a pretty made-up face, someone stroking her, passed through her head.

She knew it was the early hours of the morning. Tomorrow she would go back. Back to the house and ask Lydia Ellis again if she recognized her. She'd seen the fearful look in Lydia's face, a look of recognition perhaps, but mostly denial. Olivia had little to go on but an instinct. No one had come forward for her. Not even after the national news bulletin. She was alone in the world.

Except, she was convinced, for Lydia Ellis.

There was something in that house, something that reeked of badness. Lack of love. The girl, with her old-fashioned coiling red hair – she had looked at Olivia as though she was dirt on the floor. More than that, she had seemed spiteful, resentful. Her body twitching in the doorway as Olivia had sat talking to Lydia.

And the boy. He hadn't been exactly friendly either. The two of them had seemed anxious around her, concealing it badly with arrogance. Olivia didn't know much, but she had a rare perceptiveness when it came to character, to behaviour. On the streets, she had seen enough weirdos to know.

Olivia gasped. *She had lived on the streets.* She remembered that.

Excited at this sudden unveiling of something about her past, Olivia reached for the pen and the paper that the policeman had given her. So that she could write things down, things she remembered. She scribbled the words 'London' and 'streets'.

Olivia had no money. She had one more night in this place and then she was back. On the streets.

Olivia dressed in the dark. She needed to get out. She sprinted down the scruffy stairwell, passing the two young guys manning the desk, who barely saw her she was through the main door so quick.

Outside, it was chilly, but she barely felt it. She had to get to the house, where she knew Lydia was sleeping.

# CHAPTER FORTY-FIVE

'Go for a drive?' Ashley echoed, frowning. 'But why? Aren't you having a good time?'

Ade stroked her cheek with his finger and I looked away. Standing at the makeshift bar, he had been all over her. It was difficult not to look. Partly in revulsion, partly in a kind of hostile jealousy, I turned my back on them both. I wasn't going to play this game.

'I just thought it would be nice to be alone together,' I heard him say, just loudly enough. 'But if you'd rather stay here, that's fine.'

Ashley made one of her kitten noises, a cross between a mewl and a whimper. 'No. It's not that. I just, well . . .' I glanced over to see her gesturing at me with her eyes.

'Don't worry about me,' I said. 'I was thinking of heading off anyway.'

My watch said ten-thirty. I wanted to go home. I

336

should have called a cab a long time ago. What had stopped me?

'I'll take you.' Ade put his arm around Ashley. 'We'll all leave together.'

I was about to refuse – the last thing I needed was close proximity to Ade Ellis. I'd had enough of that for one evening. But seeing Ashley's innocent expression jolted the obvious chain of thoughts in my head.

I couldn't leave her alone with him.

And Ade was looking at me challengingly, daring me to say no. Did he know I would have to say yes?

'Thanks, that would be good,' I said lightly. 'But Ashley's house is nearer.'

Ade gave a twitch of a smile, but squeezed her shoulder. 'Looks like we're not going to get that alone time after all,' he said. 'But I suppose that can wait.'

Ashley looked almost relieved. 'Sure.' She smiled at me, then at him. 'It can wait.'

No light on country roads often makes for cosy companionship. Not so tonight after Ashley had been dropped off home. Still sitting in the back of his car, I was glad of the distance from Ade, deliberately avoiding looking up in case I saw his eyes in the rear-view mirror.

He'd hardly pulled away before he was turning back to

me. 'Alone at last,' he said in what seemed like a jovial tone. 'I was beginning to think it would never happen.'

'Eyes on the road,' I said flatly. 'And please don't start that again.'

'You're afraid of me,' he stated in answer, 'without your boyfriend to protect you.'

'Not so.' I yawned, though the last thing I was feeling was sleepy. 'I'm just a little tired of your mind games.'

There was a stark silence and, forcing myself to catch his reflection, I saw a granite-like set to his eyes.

'Mind games,' he echoed softly. 'I see.'

'You see what?' Despite my determination not to react, I was fighting irritation. And nerves. And on top of that a mounting sense of déjà vu. I'd endured a similar car ride to this a long time before. With Evan – Raphael, as he really was. I could hardly believe this was happening again. Someone with a vendetta on their mind and me caught in the middle of it. Once again, Luca was nowhere to be seen.

Though it was me who had sent him away. It had been a mistake. A stupid, childish mistake.

Ade was taking his time to respond. A car flashed past us on the other side of the road and the headlights illuminated his profile, his sharp cheekbones, his large, intimidating frame.

'Not everything is in your mind,' he said at last, cryptically. 'Some things are real. An intelligent girl like you – you know that. Perhaps you've been kidding yourself it was all your imagination?'

'What are you talking about?' I snapped, and my hand moved towards the door handle – though what good would that do me in a moving car? 'You talk in riddles, you and your sister. Stupid riddles.'

'But they're riddles you have begun to make sense of.' He paused, turning slightly. 'Even though you are putting up this pretence, it's been clear to me from the start that you are attracted to me. I can smell it.'

I exhaled, to conceal the adrenalin that was starting to pump through me.

'You are so arrogant.' I tightened my grip on the handle. 'And you're wrong. How many times do I have to tell you? Luca is—'

'Luca's gone,' said Ade icily. 'Apparently where no one can find him.'

'Just for a bit,' I said. 'He's coming back.'

'Oh?' Ade turned down the road to Bale. 'Is he?'

The relief I felt at seeing the familiar shops, even Pete's locked-up yard, was palpable within me. There was only a little while to go and I would be home, where my parents and my little sister were. And the next morning I would go to Nissilum. I would go and get Luca.

But Ade was slowing the car down, creeping to a stop. He pulled up outside the diner and switched off the engine.

'I'm starving,' he announced. 'How about some food?'

I shook my head quickly. 'I ate before I came out. I just want to go home . . .'

'But I haven't finished talking to you yet.' Ade's voice was stony. 'And I like talking to you, Jane.'

I closed my eyes, summoning every bit of strength I had. How could I have been so stupid?

'So,' Ade whispered, 'talk to me.'

Outside, there seemed to be a rustling and I realized how deserted the streets were. Looking out, I expected the bright lights of the diner, but the windows were black. A jolt of panic hit me as the street lights buzzed and flickered.

'Ade. Stop it.' I levelled my gaze at his eyes in the mirror, with real effort.

'I can't. It's not that simple . . . There is a long, long history that you cannot be expected to understand.' He tapped the steering wheel and I saw through the front seats that his hands were quivering. I knew that the car door was locked. I felt myself sweating.

'I do understand,' I said, watching Ade take a hand off

the steering wheel and move to the key in the ignition. 'But it isn't Luca's fault.'

Ade dropped his hand and his shoulders slumped slightly. 'He is in Nissilum,' he said, his voice, his words, sounding crisp and forbidden, 'where he is safe?'

'So there's no point,' I said, leaning forward. 'There is nothing for you to gain from me. It isn't me you want.'

'But he wants you – he loves you, doesn't he? He would never want anything to happen to someone he cherishes – someone he crossed worlds to be with.'

I swallowed, hot and cold at the same time. 'He has made his choice.'

'His choice?' Ade turned to face me properly. 'Or yours?'

# CHAPTER FORTY-SIX

Luca was helping his father chop wood when he felt a pain like lightning strike through him. He dropped the axe and bent over, gasping.

'Boy?' His father stuck his axe in the block and moved quickly to him, his large hands taking Luca by the shoulders. 'What is it?'

Luca sank to his knees, feeling a great pressure mounting in his brain. He held his head in his hands.

'I'll fetch your mother,' Ulfred said anxiously.

'No!' Luca lifted his head and saw the shock on his father's face. Ulfred put his hand out to touch his forehead, crouching down to be level with him.

'What is it?' he pleaded. 'Are you ill?'

'I have to get back,' Luca managed, feeling driven yet weak at the same time. 'There's something happening on Mortal Earth – to Jane.' He closed his eyes as another

342

jolt of pain went through him.

Ulfred sighed. 'The Vulpecula?'

Luca found himself shaking now, so much so that he could hardly respond; he simply nodded.

Ulfred seemed to be considering, watching Luca carefully, as though weighing something up in his mind. He pushed the boy's hair back off his face in a tender gesture; seeing the pain in Luca's eyes perhaps, he cleared his throat.

'There is . . . there is a way you can finish this,' he said.

'Father, I can't stay here while Jane is vulnerable.' Luca looked up at Ulfred. 'I love her. She is everything to me.'

'I can see that,' Ulfred said gently. 'And there is another way . . .'

'Another way?' Luca grasped his father's hand. 'Tell me.'

Ulfred glanced back at the house, where inside Henora was preparing the evening meal. He had such a troubled look on his face that Luca feared he would change his mind. But Ulfred knew he had already said too much to go back now.

'You must listen very carefully, because this solution poses great danger, for you, for Jane – and for us, here on Nissilum.'

'I'm listening.' Luca got to his feet, gaining strength at

343

this glimmer of hope. 'I have no choice. I have to do anything in my power. You see that?'

'I do.' Ulfred held out his arm and drew his son to him. 'And I am proud of you, boy. You're going to need every ounce of bravery and strength you have if you do this. If it doesn't work, the consequences are dire. If it does, then we have freedom from the Vulpecula for all eternity.'

# CHAPTER FORTY-SEVEN

She was lost. She didn't know this place. She had only a vague memory of where Lydia lived. Olivia looked back at the empty, dark road and froze. She wasn't used to the country, she was used to city streets.

A single light in the distance made her step back automatically, but it was a bicycle, slowly approaching.

The rider stopped some way from her and dismounted, removing her helmet; a lot of hair fell out. Olivia saw the girl only wore a dark T-shirt, her skin paler than anything Olivia had seen.

Olivia raised a hand in nervous greeting and the girl led her bike over.

At the sight of the girl closer up, Olivia shrank back. It was her. The sister. Polly. Olivia shook her head, but it was too late.

'You?' Polly's face was hostile. 'What are you doing here?'

Something careered into Olivia's mind: Polly's hand pinching her wrist, her dark-red hair brushing against her sharp intent face. And her eyes, reddish-brown, fierce.

'Please, leave me alone.' Olivia moved to walk past her.

'Wait.' Polly reached out and grabbed her arm. 'I can't just let you go.' She stared suspiciously at Olivia, who knew somehow that she couldn't tell. She couldn't reveal recognition.

Polly's face was so close to her. 'You should never have come back,' she whispered gutturally. 'You were never meant to come back.'

Olivia said nothing, but the tremor in her heart was taking over her whole body now.

'We don't want you in our family,' Polly continued. 'Nobody wants you – not even your own mother. Certainly not mine.'

Olivia whimpered as the image of a woman's face flashed into her head. A face she had only seen once.

'She didn't want you. And you come back here, asking to be loved,' Polly sneered. 'And you start to tell tales about us. We don't like that, my brother and I. We don't take kindly to that.'

Olivia managed to nod, though suddenly memories were tumbling fast. As though they had been loaded, stored, and on release couldn't get out fast enough. She had come back here to find her birth mother, come to Polly's house and asked. Only Polly and her brother were home and she had never got further than the doorstep.

The next thing she knew she had come to in that stinking cave.

Polly and Ade had tried to kill her – they had tried to bury her alive.

'You tried to kill me!' Olivia stated, clarity hitting her. 'You and your brother.' She felt calm all of a sudden, from the relief of her memories returning – and her sanity. She was surprised to realize she wasn't scared. Not any more.

Polly's nose quivered. Her eyes were like ice. Emotionless.

'And we didn't succeed,' she said then, in a bored tone. 'Because here you are, kicking up a fuss. Again.'

'I came here to find my family – to find my mother,' Olivia went on, as much to prompt herself as anything. 'Because that woman you live with – she's my aunt. My mother's sister. But you—'

'We didn't want you in our family,' Polly said matter-of-factly. 'We didn't want someone else ruining things. Ade and I have managed very well over the years making sure that your Auntie Lydia never quite catches on to who we are. What kind of "monsters" she adopted. And then you come along – little homeless waif, Olivia. We couldn't

347

take the risk that mortal blood would prove to be thicker than ours.'

'Mortal blood?' The calm that Olivia had been feeling was pricked. 'What are you talking about?'

'Never mind.' Polly shook her head. 'We had to get rid of you. We had something important we needed to do – and you would have been a serious distraction.'

'Well, do it,' Olivia said quickly. 'I'm not here to bother you. I'm here to try and find out where my mother is. Lydia would know – she must know.'

'Forget it,' Polly snapped. 'Lydia is insane, or near enough. More so now that her father is dead. And that's the way we want her to stay – sedated, living in her own little world. Oblivious.'

'My grandfather died?' Olivia said sadly. 'I didn't know I had one.'

'Oh boo hoo.' Polly puffed out her cheeks. 'What you never knew you can't miss.'

'What's wrong with you?' Olivia gaped at her. 'You're inhuman.'

Polly stared at her, a look of mild amusement on her face. 'Sharp as a tack, aren't you, Olivia?'

'I am not going to let you treat my aunt like that,' said Olivia, not picking up on this. 'And what have you done to her – are you drugging her or something?'

'In a way . . .' Polly said cryptically. 'But that doesn't matter. What matters is that you are in our way.'

'I don't care,' Olivia said, using every bit of courage she still had. 'She's my family. Not yours. Not really. And she can tell me how I can find my mum.'

At that Polly let out a kind of sneering laugh. 'I doubt that,' she said.

'Because you've totally brainwashed her?' Olivia was disgusted.

'No,' Polly said, looking directly into Olivia's eyes. 'Because she is clueless. She doesn't know that your mother is dead.'

Olivia took a second to digest this, realization slowly dawning. 'You killed her,' she said slowly. 'You killed my mother?'

'So you see,' Polly said, 'we simply can't have you hanging round like a stray. It's far too messy.'

Olivia stepped back. But there was nowhere to run, nowhere to hide. Not in this bleak, empty countryside, for sure.

'I just wanted to find my mother,' she gasped. 'I never meant to get in the way.'

'Well, you did,' said Polly nastily. 'And you're going to regret that, Olivia. You're going to wish you'd never been born.'

# CHAPTER FORTY-EIGHT

Ade was driving again, out of Bale. I sat helpless in the back seat.

'Ade,' I said quietly, 'please. Can't we talk about this?'

'I offered you that opportunity,' he told me, picking up speed. The sign for Bale flashed past us as he drove out of town. 'But you haven't exactly been cooperative.'

'I told you. Luca left of his own volition.' I kept my voice steady. 'There was nothing I could do.'

'Because he isn't safe here.' Ade half turned to me. 'Yes, I get that. But he would never leave you with us – he will come and get you.'

'No, he won't. He doesn't know—'

'Whatever. One way or another we will have him,' Ade said acidly. 'You see, Luca is our only hope of righting a great injustice done to our family. Once upon a time, a member of his breed behaved very badly. Very ungratefully. And it was nearly too late. Polly and I are the only remaining members of that family. We have a quest passed down to us over centuries. We will not fail in that quest.'

'But Luca is innocent. It isn't his fault!'

Ade laughed, low and dark. 'You have no idea, do you, Jane, of what you've got yourself mixed up in?' He picked up speed, as though to reinforce the danger.

'Slow down!' I leaned forward. 'You'll get us killed.'

'Not me!' Ade laughed. 'I don't die – didn't you know that?'

My lip curled at his recklessness. 'Where are you taking me?' I was amazed at how calm I sounded, because my heart was beating double time.

'In time. We need to do a pit-stop first.'

Ade slowed as he approached a crossroads. As he turned left it took a minute for me to figure it out. This road was horribly familiar to me. All because of one fated night. We were heading for the training ground.

'My family will worry,' I told him, pointlessly, 'if I'm not home soon.'

He shrugged. 'They'll be doing more than that come tomorrow morning.'

My mother's face flashed into my head, then Dad's, and finally Dot's. I blinked away frightened tears. I couldn't cry, not now. If there was any way out of this situation, I needed to stay strong. I leaned back in the seat, my heart still pounding, and stuck my hands in the pockets of my jacket. Looking down at it, I felt a crashing sadness as I remembered I was wearing Luca's old leather jacket. I told myself that if I was going to die, then I'd die wearing something of his. It was a tiny comfort.

In my left pocket, my hand encountered what felt like a box. I drew it out and stared at it. Just a box of matches Luca must have picked up from Pete's yard. I was about to stuff them back in when a light went on in my head.

A box of matches.

I quickly pushed them back into the pocket, wincing at the rattling of the matchsticks inside. But Ade hadn't heard, he was intent on driving, his face in profile looking less human by the minute. Distinctly bestial, in fact.

The sky was pitch-black, not a star to be seen. I craned out of the window to find the moon, finally seeing it, a sliver slicing through the darkness. I thought of Luca. I would never see him again.

*Don't think about it*, I told myself, *just don't think about it*.

Ade slowed the car down and ahead of us I saw two

figures at the side of the road. Hopefully I thought about winding down the window and yelling for help, but as the car drew closer, I could see that familiar long, Titian hair and pale gamine face.

Polly had her bike with her, leaning up against her as she stood with another girl I didn't recognize. I looked back at Ade.

'What's happening?' I asked.

Ade raised a hand in greeting at Polly, who nodded back, before giving me a supercilious look.

'My sister's coming along for the ride,' he said. 'If that's all right with you?'

'Who's that with her?' I craned out. The girl with Polly looked terrified. Her short blonde hair revealed a pretty, open face – at this moment a pretty, scared face. She was woefully underdressed, wearing only a thin dress and a denim jacket. She was shaking, I could see that even from a distance.

'Ah. Our local celebrity,' replied Ade, leaning over the passenger seat and opening the door. 'That's very convenient.'

Polly climbed into the front seat, glancing cursorily at me in the back seat. She flicked her hair back.

'I found her,' she told her brother. 'In the nick of time it looks like. The idiot was on her way to see Lydia.'

The door next to me opened and the girl bent to get in. She looked at me as though I were the enemy. As I shuffled along to make room for her, she clutched her bag tightly to her and looked as though she were doing breathing exercises, slowly in and out. I recognized those; I used to do them when I was being terrorized at school. I stared at the side of her face. I wanted to tell her that everything was going to be all right. But I couldn't.

'Jane, meet Olivia. Olivia, Jane,' Polly introduced us crisply. Olivia and I exchanged a look and I smiled faintly at her. She looked so thin and wretched I wanted to hug her. Her eyes met mine in understanding for a second, before she twitched away, studiedly staring out of the window as the car pulled off again.

'Isn't this nice?' Polly turned back, fixing her eyes on me. 'Going on a little road trip, the four of us.'

Beside me, I was aware of Olivia's body shuddering and when I looked she was crying softly, tears rolling down her cheeks. Deciding it didn't matter any more, I spoke up.

'What the hell is going on?' I glared at Polly. 'What has this girl done to you?'

'I'd better fill you in,' Polly said chummily. 'Olivia came looking for her mother at our house, because Lydia Ellis is her aunt. But Ade and I weren't happy about that.

Not least because we got rid of Olivia's mother a while ago. And we didn't want any awkward questions. Not to mention some freeloading little hobo girl wheedling her way into our family.' She glanced at Olivia, who was still crying quietly. 'Anyway, we kind of botched up killing Olivia – ' Polly paused to frown at Ade ' – and she kind of escaped, went to the police, and . . . well, the rest you know from the news. She's still hanging around like a bad smell. And that has to stop. You understand?'

Olivia and I locked eyes. In hers I saw fear and pain combined. I felt overwhelmed by helplessness. In my pocket I gripped the matchbox – our only salvation.

But then something else happened. Something so gloriously simple occurred to me that it was all I could do not to laugh in relief.

'You're actually going to kill us?' I said. 'What good will that do?'

Polly sighed melodramatically. 'We're not going to do that – not yet.' She gestured at Olivia. 'Well, maybe her. But not you, Jane. We have something much more productive lined up for you.'

I bit my lip, waiting. Beside me Olivia shifted in her seat, her small thin hands gripping her knees. I sneaked out a hand and closed it over one of hers, trying to signal to her that it might be OK. It just might be OK.

A miracle could happen.

Ade started to drive off again, as Polly left me hanging.

'Well?' I prompted.

She laughed, a low, dark sound. 'You're going to take us to what we really want, Jane. You're going to take us back.'

'Oh,' I said, understanding. All hope fizzled out. 'I don't think I can do that,' I said lamely. 'It's not possible . . .'

'Of course it is,' she countered briskly. 'We know how it works.'

'Forget it,' I said blankly. 'Even if I could take you back to Nissilum, I wouldn't do it. My link isn't strong enough.' I paused. 'And why have you waited till now? You could have cornered Luca at any time.'

'We like the slow approach and to play with people,' she said lightly. 'It's much more fun. Though in this case possibly a bad idea.' She turned to Ade. 'We misjudged that rather.' She sighed. 'It would have been fairly straightforward, too. We would never have just killed him. That wouldn't have got us anywhere. Instead we worked our "mental magic" on the two of you – on Luca particularly. But it turns out he's a little brighter, a little more sensitive, than we thought.'

Ade was very quiet, but his profile seemed to be altering by the minute – the down on his face first, then, as I looked at his hands on the steering wheel, the coil of his fingers, like claws digging into the plastic.

'I can't do it,' I said. 'I won't.' I looked at Olivia. 'You can do what you like with me but Olivia has done nothing – except turn up when you didn't want her. She doesn't deserve to die.'

'Shut up!' Polly whirled round and I gasped at the sight of her face, narrowed down to a tip at the chin; her eyes were dark – no longer blue, but a greeny-brown colour, and her long red hair seemed to have merged with her body. She stared at me, opening her jaw just enough for me to see the sharp teeth inside her mouth.

I tried very hard to conceal the extent of my shock – my terror. I kept to the mantra playing inside my head. Stay calm. Whatever you do, stay calm.

'I have the necklace,' I said quietly.

Polly's eyes were looking more feral by the second. 'What are you talking about?'

I was still holding Olivia's hand and I squeezed it as I went on. 'Olivia's necklace. Remember? You tore it off her neck when you tried to bury her alive.'

'So what?' Polly said raspily.

'Let me clarify. My mother has the necklace. And she also knows of my . . . suspicions.'

'How did you get hold of it?' Ade suddenly came to

life, his voice now as gruff as his sister's. His claw-hands, I noticed, were strained. His ears were now different too. Sharper. He still looked human. Just.

'Luca found it. Weeks ago.' I waited.

Polly shrugged. 'So we just go back for your family,' she said with unconvincing nonchalance.

'Don't you see?' I half laughed. 'If I don't get home by midnight my mother will call the police.'

'I don't think so,' Ade said, and to my horror I saw we were at the entrance to the training ground. He flicked on the indicator, unnecessarily, as there were no other cars around. 'I called your mother earlier. I told her not to worry if you weren't back tonight. That I was probably taking you back to Ashley's for a sleepover.'

My heart fell. 'She'll never believe that.' I didn't add, 'Because I've never been to a sleepover in my life'; I left it at that. But despair was descending. She might just believe that. Hadn't I made a show of being more sociable from now on just before I left the house?

'We'll see, shall we?' He smiled darkly and brought the car to a stop. The eerie quiet of the training ground seemed to mock me. I almost wanted to die now. Give up. Just allow them to do what they wanted. But I would never take them to Luca. I was certain about that. I shivered and my hand closed even more tightly over the matches in my pocket.

I couldn't die. Not with all the rotting wood around this place. And some firestarters in my hand.

# CHAPTER FORTY-NINE

'What's going on?' Dalya appeared in the doorway of Luca's bedroom, her face a picture of anxiety.

'Nothing for you to worry about,' Luca told her breathlessly as he gathered a few possessions, stuffing what he could in the pockets of his coat. It was one of his father's. His leather jacket he had left with Jane. A tiny sliver of comfort came from thinking of her wearing it. He stopped, breathing out to calm himself down.

'You're going back,' said Dalya, 'to Jane.'

Luca stopped what he was doing and looked up at his sister. 'I have to,' he told her. 'She isn't safe.'

'Neither are you.' Dalya sighed. 'Luca, you will be careful, won't you? I mean, if it's you they want . . .'

'It's all right,' he said, putting both hands on her shoulders, looking into her anxious brown eyes. 'I will be careful. But I have no choice. The thought of anything happening to Jane . . .'

'I know,' she said with an air of finality. 'You have to go.'

Luca hugged her tight, hoping that this was not the last time he saw his sister.

'What did Ulfred tell you?' she asked, pulling away. 'I thought there was nothing you could do.' She looked up at him through large eyes. 'Is there something after all?'

Luca bit his lip. He had sworn to Ulfred that what has passed between them earlier must never be repeated. Particularly not to Henora or Dalya. Again, he felt glad that Lowe was not around. Lowe had a way of sniffing out trouble. And in this case, he would be eager for retribution.

'It will be all right,' Luca said eventually in answer. 'You need to believe that. Believe in me.'

She nodded, but protectively did up a button on his coat. 'And you need to believe in yourself, Luca,' she told him softly. She stepped away from him then, clasping her hands together. 'If you need me, I will come at once.'

'Thank you.' Once again he embraced her and then watched her walk away before looking down at his jacket and briefly shutting his eyes.

He was scared. More than he'd ever been. This felt

nothing like the danger posed by Nissilum's renegades. This was a whole new level of danger. The Vulpecula had no interest in goodness, or forgiveness, or salvation.

They simply wanted revenge.

# CHAPTER FIFTY

'Out.' Polly held the passenger door open and stared stonily at Olivia, who appeared to be frozen into her seat. Polly's slender physique was quivering slightly and, glancing at her hand on the door, I saw her long fingers curling and her nails sharp. I nudged Olivia.

'Better to do as she says,' I whispered, adding, 'Don't worry, it will be OK.' I had no idea if that was true, but Olivia looked frightened out of her wits. Probably reliving the last time she had been here.

Olivia stepped shakily out of the car, but her expression had turned a little tougher. She lifted her chin at Polly.

'How can you think you'll get away with this?' she asked steadily. 'It won't take the police very long to work it out.'

Polly smiled nastily. 'The police? Do you really think we're worried about the police?' Her teeth were feral and pointed, I saw, and her eyes were practically narrowed to strips. She leaned forward, putting her face closer to Olivia's. 'We've already informed them of your drug habit. Living all this time on the streets, who could blame you for falling into addiction?' She stepped back. 'And you know what drugs do to people, Olivia?' She waggled her finger against her head in the global sign of lunacy. 'Send them a little paranoid.'

'But you've already tried to kill me once. The police are on the lookout—'

'Oh, didn't I tell you? That was a natural disaster. You fell into that cave – easy to do when you're high.' Polly eye's flickered over to me. 'Ade has explained it all to that nice policeman. He thought it seemed the most likely explanation.'

'No.' Olivia shook her head. 'He believed me . . .'

Polly sighed, raking her hand through her long red hair. 'He did – and then he didn't. My brother can be very persuasive and charming when he wants to be.' Again, she glanced at me. 'Jane seems to be the only girl so far who hasn't fallen under his spell.'

I shuddered. The thought of Ade repulsed me now. But deep down, there had been a glimmer of attraction, if I was being totally honest. But it was that kind of involuntary attraction that isn't real.

'Olivia . . .' I spoke at last. 'Don't listen to Polly, shut her out. Don't engage – this is how they get to you.'

Olivia looked uncertain, while Polly merely looked amused. 'A bit late for that now,' she rasped.

Ade, who had been pacing the ground, restlessly marched over to the three of us. Olivia and I waited for something awful to happen as he put his hand on Polly's shoulder.

'I don't want to waste any more time,' he told her. 'I'm already bored with this.'

I stared at him. 'What about Ashley?' I asked. 'How are you going to explain my disappearance to her?'

Ade raised an eyebrow at me. 'You don't have to worry about that.' Then he tilted his head upwards, looking up at the night sky, his dark-red curls smoothing against his scalp. Before our eyes, the shape of his face changed from human to something distinctly animal-like. His body stretched for a moment, with an almost visible snap, before his spine curled and his hands hit the ground. Moving his head slowly from side to side he finally turned it to face Olivia and me as we stood, watching, both mesmerized and horrified at once.

As my heart pounded, I put an arm out in a futile attempt to protect Olivia, whose shaking had upped to a whole new level.

'It's all right,' I whispered, against mounting odds to the contrary. 'It will be all right.' I dragged my eyes away from the creature in front of us, with its eyes like granite, only to be met by an identical creature to my left.

Polly, too.

I had no time in which to think, I just focused my thoughts on one image, though it felt like every drop of blood within me was swirling, pounding. I thought of gentle green eyes, a mop of messy brown hair.

*Luca!* I made my brain chant, calling. It had worked before. Perhaps it would work again.

But there was no other sound now but the snarling of the fox-humans to the front and the side of us.

The Vulpecula. Their jaws dripping with saliva, their clawed paws digging in to the earth beneath them.

Ade growled a low, contemptuous noise, the kind a wild dog might make. I swallowed, keeping the image of Luca in my mind, and took a step back, my eyes flickering to Olivia, who was rooted, terrified, to the spot.

'When I take your hand,' I said as quietly as I could, 'run with me. Run faster than you've ever done in your life.'

Only a bewildered blink gave me a signal that she understood. I turned back to Polly and Ade.

'What are you going to do?' I asked them, desperately

trying to keep the wobble out of my voice. 'Eat us?'

The growling increased in volume and I jerked as the two foxes – a good deal bigger than their earthly counterparts – started to move closer to us. Instinctively I reached out and grasped Olivia's hand and hissed, 'Run! Just run!' And dragging her behind me, I began to sprint, across the damp grass, as fast as my legs could carry me.

While behind us the Vulpecula were in pursuit.

# CHAPTER FIFTY-ONE

Luca came to, wedged between a couple of birch trees on the hill leading up from Jane's house. He squeezed himself through them, pulling his jacket lapels closer together and brushing flakes of wood from his sleeves. Only the sound of a gentle night-owl hooting could be heard – that and the chiming pain inside his head.

He closed and then opened his eyes, trying to keep alert. The sense of danger, like an alarm, was almost blinding. He started to run down the hill, dodging the trees, snagging himself and barely feeling it. Glancing at Jane's house, he knew she wasn't there. She had made contact with him – he had felt it as clearly as though she were standing in front of him. Her frightened grey eyes had swum in front of his and then disappeared.

Luca kept running, beyond the house, feeling his body straining against his clothes. A different kind of pain hit him now. The pain of turning. Always more acute when it was done out of sight of a full moon. His neck snapped almost agonizingly as his speed picked up an altogether less human pace and he was bounding urgently in the direction of the town and beyond.

*I'm coming*, he told her, inside his mind. *I won't let anything happen to you.*

# CHAPTER FIFTY-TWO

My breath was coming so thickly I thought my heart would explode. Just a little behind me, Olivia was moving with the kind of agility that comes from sheer adrenalin pushing you on. I glimpsed the fence, covered in foliage, with no discernable escape route.

The Vulpecula were so close behind us they were practically snapping at our heels. I scanned all that I could see ahead of us and, to my relief, saw a stretch of broken fence, mercifully free of ragged hedgerow. Grasping Olivia's hand tighter I pulled her, with strength I never realized I had, in the right direction. As we ran through the gap I used my free hand to wrench a hefty piece of broken wood free, darting behind the hedgerow and virtually throwing Olivia into the ditch.

'Stay there,' I panted, nudging her deeper into the ditch with my foot, before turning to meet the enemy. It was just in time, as one of the Vulpecula – I couldn't tell which – had reared up on its back legs, its vicious jaws open to reveal deadly teeth.

Shutting my eyes, I forced the thick piece of wood up in front of me, just as the fox's head hit it.

I winced at the impact and the sound of bone against wood. The fox dropped limply to the ground. Astonished at what I had done, I lowered the heavy wood, only now registering my aching arms, and stared breathlessly down at the fox's body. It was alive for sure, but stunned. It was only a matter of time before the animal regained its strength.

Lifting my head I saw the other one – at this distance, the smaller of the two, and clearly Polly – sniffing anxiously at her brother's injured form. I swallowed, knowing I had very little time in which to exploit this diversion.

Dropping the wood, I moved back quickly, urgently feeling in my pocket and taking out the thankfully dry matchbox. Keeping one eye on Polly, still pawing Ade, I silently used my foot to draw the wood towards me on the ground. As a mountain girl, I knew how unlikely it was that one flame would set a thick damp piece of wood on fire. But setting fire to the plank was not my first thought.

I bent to check on Olivia, seeing only frightened, confused eyes. I put my finger to my lips, while nearby, Polly had sent up an excruciating screeching sound.

I took out two of the matches and looked up above me at the mass of tangled sticky branches and hedgeleaf. I stood shakily upright, striking the matches and tossing them into the hedge.

I saw the bright glow flare, catch a leaf alight, only then to fizzle out. I drew out a clutch more matches and struck them hurriedly, again tossing them into the mass of green and brown.

Screwing up my face tightly, I willed the hedge to respond this time. But the heavy rustling next to me drew my attention away. To my horror, I saw Ade getting up on to his feet. He appeared to be sniffing aggressively.

Ignoring the fact that I was shaking like my mother's washing machine on full spin, I looked back. Relief flooded through me as I heard the crackle of wood catching fire and then saw the glow of the spreading flames.

It wasn't much, but it was a start. I stepped back and then lowered myself, grabbing hold of Olivia's hands and wrenching her forcefully out of the ditch, pushing her behind me.

The foxes had stopped moving, transfixed by the

growing licks of fire. I could see something in their eyes that I had never seen before.

Fear.

Polly stood on her hind legs, quivering. In front of her, Ade tried but failed not to react. He backed into his sister, pushing her away from the flames.

'Scared?' I asked breathlessly, swallowing my own fear back. 'How does that feel?'

Ade simply growled, a string of spit hanging from his jaw. Polly whimpered, her pointed auburn ears twitching.

'You don't like fire?' I waved my hand at the hedge, now burning for all it was worth. 'What's the matter? Worried your souls will burn in hell?'

And then, above us, the skies rumbled and a mass of dark clouds swirled uneasily. It took a minute for me to realize what that meant.

Rain. Now, of all times. It was going to rain.

A dog barked from somewhere and for a second I dismissed it, before a new glimmer of hope sparked inside me. I concentrated on keeping my breath even and steady. Not easy. I felt Olivia pressed against me, her head buried in my back.

As I listened out, another bark came. Not the bark of a dog after all.

It was the sound of a wolf.

And there, sprinting towards us at the speed of light, was the longed-for wolf-boy I thought I might never lay eyes on again.

Luca had come.

# CHAPTER FIFTY-THREE

Luca saw them, his heart sinking as he approached. The Vulpecula and Jane with somebody hiding behind her, both backed into a corner.

But there was something else. The orange glow, illuminating all four of them.

Luca stopped. He felt his heartbeat slowing as realization crept over him.

He couldn't feel thankful yet. The danger of this situation was stark. He knew that the Vulpecula would not disappear without a fight, though he knew now that their fear of fire was debilitating. And even from this distance he saw the demeanour of the two creatures: cowed, impotent.

But with rain threatening overhead, there was no time to lose.

Luca began to move, picking up speed again. At his

approach the bigger of the foxes turned and, for a second, the animal's face twisted into a snarl.

As Luca faced him, Ade bared his teeth, and that was all Luca needed to summon every bit of the wolf within in him.

With a ferocious roar he snapped his jaw at his enemy and the fox jerked away, its red-gold fur shimmering in the light from the fire that was still burning behind it.

The smaller fox moved to protect her brother, trying to form a unified shield, but there was a lack of confidence in her gesture. These creatures were doing what all wild animals know lays them vulnerable: showing fear.

'Luca!' He heard Jane call and lifted his head momentarily to see the anxiety in her eyes. He saw her struggling with something in her hands. She was lighting more matches, desperately throwing them on to the dying fire in the hedge.

Exploiting the distraction, Ade leaped, his clawed front paws tearing at Luca's face. The fox's face was so close that Luca could smell its acrid breath. He used his strength to swipe at the creature's nose, leaving a bloodied gash.

Luca barely felt the pain when Ade tore through the flesh on his arms; he was too intent on closing his sharp incisors over the fox's ears. At the sound of something ripping he pulled away for a second and saw the fox's ear hanging, dislocated. Yet Ade looked as though he had hardly felt it.

These creatures had formidably blunted nerve endings. Or lead-like skin. Luca kept Ade at bay with regular nips at any visible part of the animal's body, but inwardly he knew this method of action would leave no more than a dent.

Out of the corner of his eye he saw the lick of flames climbing. He thanked the Celestials for Jane's quick-thinking. But as he backed off from the fox in front of him to recoup a little strength, he saw that Polly had cornered Jane and her terrified-looking companion, forcing them closer and closer to the fire.

Seizing a chance, he leaped out of Ade's way, charging towards Polly's intimidating shape as she stood on all-fours with her back to him, yapping. Bundling into the back of her, he forced her forwards, willing Jane to leap out of the way – which at the very last minute she did.

Polly tumbled forward into the ditch, unbalanced and trapped, while the fire helpfully lashed out at her, catching her fur.

She let out an excruciating screech of pain, finally. Luca felt a rush of euphoria – and a moment's instinctive horror at the smell of burning flesh and his part to play in that. He twitched, refusing to let that get in the way of what he had to do next.

Jane had her hand over mouth, but one arm still around the other girl. She looked over at him, her eyes almost opaque with shock.

She took her hand away from her lips, her mouth widening, then shouting, 'Luca!'

But before he could react he roared in agony as Ade's sharp teeth bit into his shoulder. With miraculous speed he shot forward and turned, ready to face the apoplectic animal before him.

# CHAPTER FIFTY-FOUR

I could barely take in what was happening in front of my eyes. All I knew was that Ade's sense of retribution would be tenfold now that Polly lay burning to death in the ditch.

Luca was growling, sidestepping the great fox, but even as a werewolf, he had his work cut out. The fox's face was covered in blood, his mouth red and dripping, giving him a mad, ravaged appearance. I swallowed, willing something to intervene to stop this.

But it had to reach its final conclusion. If Luca was ever to be free, he had to fight this out.

Behind me the fire had properly taken hold and, glancing to the side, I saw it ripple further along the hedgerow.

Below me, Polly's body was inert. I dropped my arm from around Olivia, hoping that Ade had not yet seen the full extent of the damage.

But the fox and the wolf were deep in fighting, like a macabre animal fable. Was this really happening?

Suddenly behind me the fence collapsed, scattering fire perilously closer to Luca and, in front of him, Ade. Luca was too busy fending off the insane creature to take advantage of this piece of fortune.

But I wasn't. My eyes darted around me, alighting on a hefty piece of kindling nearby. Moving quickly I picked up the wood, poking it at arm's length into the expanding fire. The heat nearly made me drop the thing, but I held steady, gritting my teeth and praying to whomever might be on my side that the kindling would catch light.

For an awful moment it looked like it would remain unresponsive, but then the sliver of ember at the tip glowed fiercely before bursting into life.

Though the heat was nearly unbearable and the danger increasing by the second, I held on, waiting until the flames crept far enough along it, and then I launched it, with untested precision, at Ade's moving body.

It missed the fox's chest but struck his face, then snagged, hanging from his fur. It took a minute before the creature grasped what was happening. But when he did, the realization was visible in his eyes.

Ade howled, letting go of Luca, and staggered back,

trying to use its mouth to wrench the wood free. But it was stubborn. It wouldn't budge. Ade's fur was blackening and a potent smell drifted over us all.

Inside I felt like fireworks of my own were going off, but it wasn't the time for celebration. And when I saw Ade attempt one final attack, launching his burning body at Luca's, I yelled and ran forward.

'Luca!' I screamed again, grabbing his wolf-leg, which felt thick and strong, rigid with muscle. But he threw me off.

And then I almost passed out at the sight of his body on fire. I vaguely heard Olivia next to me softly, before I screamed again – a scream of pure, frustrated despair.

Luca finally fell on to his back, while Ade had already collapsed, the whole of him up in flames. I registered that this was a good thing. Mission accomplished. But I couldn't revel in the victory, not while Luca was fighting off death himself.

I tore off my jacket – Luca's leather jacket – and knelt beside him, covering his smoking torso with it, desperately trying to dampen the flames. I pounded the leather down, eventually realizing that it had done its work.

The fire was finally out.

I sat back breathlessly, so overjoyed that I had succeeded, that it took a few seconds before I realized that

Luca had turned back into a human and that his body was motionless.

I reeled forwards, swallowing back tears.

'No. No . . . Luca, no!' I wailed, bringing my head forward on to his chest.

All at once the whole training ground was silent, but for the noise of the fire all around us, picking up momentum. Slumped over Luca's unmoving body, I was now aware of the heat. My own face was burning from it.

Olivia stepped forward timidly, kneeling down next to me. She stared in shock at Luca and then up at me.

'Is he . . . dead?' she said in a hoarse whisper.

I touched his face. It was hot from the fire, so it was impossible to tell. Vaguely remembering some first aid learned at college in my first week there, I lifted his wrist, feeling for a pulse.

There was one. Faint, but there.

I started to stand, shaking so badly that it took some effort.

Olivia waited, expectantly. Poor kid was confused – and I didn't blame her. This was one weird set of events she had got herself embroiled in.

'We need to get help,' I said. 'Luca needs to get to hospital.' But as I spoke it occurred to me that too many awkward questions would be asked. Luca was only half human. Once he was in hospital, his true nature would be exposed.

If Luca was only half human then his ability to heal was greater than a mortal's, wasn't it? He was immortal, after all. He would never die. Reminding myself of this brought such relief I nearly gasped out loud.

'Change of plan,' I said, almost cheerfully, to Olivia. 'But we need to move him away from the fire . . .'

We sat by Luca for what seemed like hours, but he didn't move. I could see him breathing though; I knew he was just unconscious. Perhaps it was only a question of waiting. Olivia and I had dragged him laboriously over to one of the creepy Nissen huts, as far from the fire as possible. Just as we had got there it had started to rain, quenching the raging flames. Now all that could be seen was a long length of smoky, charred hedgerow and, just visible, the lifeless bodies of Ade and Polly.

I stared up at the sky, willing for something to intervene and put this right. For someone to just appear and make it all right. It seemed impossible. Who on earth would understand?

'Jane.' A deep, familiar voice came from behind us. Turning, I saw the tall, bearded figure of Ulfred. And next to him, a beautiful young woman, her black-brown hair in a single braid, her large brown eyes glistening with emotion.

'Ulfred,' I croaked, getting to my feet. 'Dalya . . .' I stumbled as I stood and both Luca's father and his sister reached out instinctively to catch me. As soon as they touched me, something happened to release all the fear and the trauma of what had happened that night.

And I collapsed, sobbing, into Ulfred's chest.

He stroked my hair, keeping me safe in his arms.

'We're here now,' he said softly, soothingly. 'The boy will be fine. He is recovering from the stress.' He released me and went over to Luca. With one seemingly effortless movement he lifted his son into his arms.

Dalya linked her arm through mine. She had no idea the comfort she gave me. How much she and her father were the only people I wanted to be with just then.

'Thank you,' I said. 'If you hadn't come . . .'

'Ssh.' Dalya squeezed my arm. 'It's over now.'

And as Ulfred walked towards us, I saw Luca finally open his eyes. He blinked at me, then smiled weakly.

'I love you,' I told him. 'I'm so sorry . . .'

'No need.' Both Luca and Ulfred spoke together and I realized how startlingly similar they looked and behaved. Both gentle, yet strong at the same time.

'We're family now,' said Dalya warmly. 'And you have rid us, finally, of the Vulepcula's curse.' She looked me full in the face. 'For that we will be for ever in your debt. And you will always be one of us.'

# CHAPTER FIFTY-FIVE

Lydia stepped forward. Clothed entirely in black, she looked even more of a shadowy, defeated character. Behind her, the vicar was shaking hands and nodding at the trail of people coming out from the church.

She held out both hands, a little shakily, and grasped one each of mine and Luca's.

'Thank you,' she said quietly. 'I know you tried to save them.' She looked pained as she went on. 'They were always so wilful. I think that I always knew they would take their need for excitement too far.'

Luca didn't look at me as he replied. 'It was an accident. Someone lit a match and that place just erupted in flames. They couldn't have known the danger they were in.'

Lydia nodded and suddenly her eyes filled with tears. 'I'm so glad my father didn't know – it would have broken his heart. But at least . . . at least there is comfort in them all being buried together. The family together.'

'Yes,' I said lamely. The truth was beating against the sides of my brain. That terrible night, with Luca barely conscious. But just conscious enough to tell us what to do.

We had waited until the rain stopped. Thankfully it didn't last long. It took Dalya and me to carry Luca to a safe distance, with Olivia sobbing behind us, and Ulfred running back with the last of the matches. He found a large plastic petrol container in the back of one of those horrible dank huts – just as Luca had said he would. And then . . . well, he made sure that the Vulpecula and the ghost-filled old grounds died together.

Strangely, tests revealed human DNA.

It had turned out easier than I thought to convince the police of our story. That it had all been just a harmless prank, but it went horribly wrong.

'I'm so sorry,' I whispered, as bearers carried three coffins past us, on their way to their burial plots. 'You have lost so much.'

And she had. Olivia had yet to tell her aunt that Lydia's beloved little sister, Eva, was dead. We all figured she wouldn't be able to handle that. Not now. And Olivia needed time to grieve herself. For the mother she never knew – and never found.

We would have to wait until Eva's body was discovered, if it ever was. Olivia knew everything now. Though she was freaked out, she understood that we would have to keep silent.

Olivia was the last to come out of the church – a slight girl with huge eyes; pretty, a strange combination of innocence and worldliness. She had been through so much in her life. No wonder nothing really surprised her any more.

She approached us, nodding shyly at Lydia's husband. She stopped next to Lydia, whose face lit up at the sight of her.

'Olivia,' Lydia said softly, taking her in her arms and holding her tight, 'I'm so glad we have you back – at last.'

Olivia hugged her back, trembling a little. She had finally found her family. At least something good had come out of this.

I turned to Luca, gesturing with my eyes for us to leave Lydia and her niece to grieve together. Smiling sadly at me, he put his arm around my waist and we walked slowly out of the church grounds, leaving that grisly funeral behind.

'Want to sit down?' He nodded at the ancient old bench by the gates.

As we sat, I nestled my head into his neck, holding tightly on to his hand.

'You're gripping my hand as though you never want to let go,' he whispered into my hair, and I knew he was smiling.

'I don't,' I said seriously, squeezing it even tighter. 'And I'm never going to.' I sat up, moving subtly away from him. 'I'm going to become one of those intense stalker girlfriends who keeps tabs on your every move.' I grinned sheepishly, feeling all over again that the two of us had only just met. The air around us seemed to crackle with tension. But good tension.

'You know what, Jane Jonas?' He looked straight into my eyes. 'I'm never letting you go either. And as long as time allows us to I will spend the rest of my life with you making you happy. And safe. And loved.'

It must have been sheer relief that our ordeal was over, along with Luca's words, but it was my turn to cry now. And once I started, I felt I couldn't stop.

'I would go through all that again, in a heartbeat,' I said. 'Everything. Anything.' I kissed his hand through my tears.

In that moment I knew – call it an instinct – that Luca and I were simply fated to be together. From the moment he had appeared in my dreams, it had been written into our destinies.

That our hearts were entwined through darkness and light.

# DARK HEART

# LEE MONROE

## ANSWERS OUR QUESTIONS ...

WHO WOULD BE YOUR DREAM CAST IF THE DARK HEART
BOOKS WERE MADE INTO A FILM?
Eddie Redmayne as Luca and Jessica Brown Findlay as Jane.

WHICH SONGS WOULD BE ON *THE DARK HEART
SURRENDER* SOUNDTRACK?
A mix of melancholia and pop: *Last Night I Dreamt Somebody
Loved Me* (The Smiths); a bit of The Donnas; some classical piano
from Satie; *Who Knew* by Pink; *English Rose* (The Jam); *A Nice
Day for a White Wedding* (Billy idol) amongst others...

IS JANE BASED ON ANYONE IN PARTICULAR?
Jane is every girl. Confident but a little uncertain too. Beautiful
but oblivious to it ... passionate but practical ... I don't know
anyone exactly like Jane. I wanted her to be a blank canvas, but a
girl the readers would warm to, and want to be perhaps ...

## IF YOU COULD BE FROM NISSILUM, WHICH SUPERNATURAL CREATURE WOULD YOU BE?

Easy, I would be Vanya! Glamorous and deadly ...

## IF YOU COULD INVITE FIVE PEOPLE TO DINNER WHO WOULD YOU INVITE?

Mary Portas, Lily Allen, Woody Allen, Jon Slattery and James Gandolfini.

## WHO IS YOUR FAVOURITE AUTHOR AND WHY?

I don't have one favourite, but an author I absolutely love is Elizabeth Taylor, who wrote most of her novels in the period from 1950 to 1970. She was so insightful about the human condition – razor sharp in her wit but empathetic and kind. She wrote a book called *Angel* all about a somewhat delusional teenage author ... Very funny and poignant too.

## WHAT BOOK DO YOU WISH YOU HAD WRITTEN?

Well, *Angel* ... obviously. But also *She's Come Undone* by Wally Lamb.

## TELL US ONE THING YOUR READERS WON'T ALREADY KNOW ABOUT YOU.

When I was thirteen my father moved our family to live on a Thames Barge in Essex where I lived until I was eighteen. It had its ups and downs but most surreal was when my bedroom travelled with me on holiday.

## WHAT ARE YOU WORKING ON NEXT?

It's a bit of a departure – my next novel will be very much rooted in reality, though it will most definitely be a 'fated love' story.

If you've got a thirst for
fiction, join up now

## bookswithbite.co.uk

Packed with sneak peeks, book trailers, exclusive
competitions and downloads, **bookswithbite.co.uk**
is the new place on the web to get your fix of
great fiction.

Sign up to the newsletter at
**www.bookswithbite.co.uk**
for the latest news on your favourite authors,
to receive exclusive extra content and the
opportunity to enter special
members-only competitions.